WAR RELIC

WAR RELIC

A WESTERN STORY

MACKEY MURDOCK

**BLACK
STONE**
PUBLISHING

Printed in the United States of America

ISBN 978-1-9825-6309-7
Fiction / Westerns

1 3 5 7 9 10 8 6 4 2

CIP data for this book is available
from the Library of Congress

Blackstone Publishing
31 Mistletoe Rd.
Ashland, OR 97520

www.BlackstonePublishing.com

CHAPTER ONE

Wilbur "Bones" Malone pawned youthful vigor in search of honor during the earlier War Between the States. Today only a cool flicker shone from the charred wick of his once bright flame. Churning post-war dregs of shame and guilt had levied a toll. He slumped on the seat of his wagon, his thoughts the color of ash.

The wagon was loaded with bleached buffalo bones. Three years after the great slaughter, they were in demand as fertilizer. The guilt weighing on his shoulders stemmed from a feeling of having robbed Robert E. Lee of the Confederacy's best chance for victory.

The war had taught him that arms and munitions trumped cotton and noble causes. In the years since, onerous longhorns, bad horses, and scandalous women clouded its memory. Cheap whiskey helped. The bones paid the bills.

He entertained little curiosity about what lay down the road and less inclination to get there. Still, he brought the team to a stop for their sake, not his own. Pulling the sand of the incline earned them a blow. He packed his pipe, lazily allowing his gaze to range.

The Colorado River lay to his right. To the left a herd of milling cows stirred dust near gleaming new rails. In the valley close to the river, he could see the upstart town of Sundown City, Texas.

The prior year had brought the Texas and Pacific Railroad to the town—a forty-seventh birthday to Bones. The town thrived, enjoying its best days. Bones agonized through his worst. Rails end turned the dugout shanties on the riverbank into a bustling town.

He fired the pipe and clucked the team into their traces. The Studebaker moved dutifully down the rutted road parallel to the tracks. The favorable grade offset the wagon's load of bones. The mules took the opportunity to direct wide-eyed attention at the cattle across the tracks.

One of the herd's drovers, a withered little man in his fifties, raised his hat to shade his eyes. He turned his lathered horse toward Bones.

"Wil Malone, you Mississippi-looking son-of-a-gun, is that you? What you doing out in this old short-grass country sitting on a pile of bones? Hey, boys, look who's here." The drover waved to the nearest riders.

Bones pulled up the mules and took the proffered hand of the drover. "Ee-God, Peaches, you gaining weight. Wouldn't've known you. Lost again, I bet. Don't you know y'all got that bunch four days west of the trail?" He stuck his hand out to the two younger riders following Peaches. "Juan, Jesse, good to see you. Peaches ain't turned you boys to rustlers, has he? Everybody around here knows they ain't no legal cows west of Buffalo Gap."

Peaches bit one string attached to his makings sack and pulled the other end tight with his right hand. With the bag shut, he shook it at Bones. "Don't worry none about them cows. They're legal as a Sunday preacher in a pulpit. Problem is, the whole damn herd's ornery as sin. Run four times since leaving Goliad, and now they balked fast at them damn tracks. There's a story goes with them you're gonna find interesting."

"Be the first of yours I ever found interesting. Want a drink?" Bones pulled a bottle from the bags of an old double-rigged saddle riding the sideboard.

Peaches shook off the drink, then scratched his head, eyeing the stubborn cows. The two cowboys followed his lead and waved away the offer of a drink.

Bones took a long swig. The whiskey brought a sigh.

"Wil, you was always part cow. What you think? How's best to get this bunch across them tracks? We've tried crowding them, and they jest double back on us. Ain't got feed, and they're too dumb to follow it, nohow. Guess we could just cover the whole damn roadbed with dirt, and let them mill around till they're used to it. Juan and Jesse roped two and drug them across. Darned if the brutes didn't beat the boys back to this side. Guess I'm gonna have to take down my flag as a drover and get me a job swamping saloons. Maybe I could give you a hand fighting scorpions off them old buffalo remains."

"Well, everybody's gotta move up sometime, but 'fore you do, why don't you try letting Jesse and Juan rope a couple of them babies. If they'll heel them and drag them across where they're making lots of noise, that whole bunch will most likely chouse right along."

A sheepish expression appeared on Peaches' face as the practicality of the suggestion soaked in. The ramrod nodded at the two cowpunchers, and, in less than a minute both had a calf roped by its hind legs and dragging, tail-first, at the end of their ropes. At the first bawl of panic every cow in hearing responded and moved toward them. Peaches' small frame seemed to shrink as he ducked his chin and wagged his head.

For once compassion outweighed Bone's devilment. "Come on, Peaches, you buy me a drink every time you see me, I ain't gonna tell a soul about this. Me an' old Sam Reed spent two days trying to get a herd to take to the Cimarron back in 1876 'fore we thought of that little trick. What's supposed to interest me about that bunch?"

"Fellow that owns them said he's a cousin of yours. Said his name's Wade Malone, and he's from Mississippi. See the dollar sign branded high on that left hip. That stands for the Crooked Letter I Ranch." Passing on the range gossip appeared to aid Peaches' spirits.

"I mentioned your name, saying we rode with Hood together, and he says he's your cousin. He must have asked me a hundert questions 'bout you, but his missus asked more. I couldn't help them much. Told them last I saw of you was six year ago, in 1875, when you left Doan's Crossing with Sam Bass and that herd heading toward Dodge."

Bones turned his face from Peaches and looked in the direction of the last of the herd crossing the rails. He didn't see the cattle, but instead, from the reaches of his memory, a beautiful girl beckoned, held her arms open, and her laughter rang in his ears. It didn't surprise him that after over twenty years a tingle of anticipation accompanied the mere thought of her. Squinting at the new brand, a faint smile battled the scowl on his face. The burn had Wade Malone's flair written all over it. He turned back to Peaches.

"How'd Irene look?"

"Irene? Is that Missus Malone? He called her Sassy."

"That's her."

"She looked fit. Yeah, I'd say more'n fit. After me and Wade made our deal, she took me aside, took this old hand in hers, and tells me how great it were for her to meet up with someone who rid with you. Called you her cavalier." Peaches' eyes twinkled with amusement.

Bones refused Peaches' bait and gestured toward the herd. "Is Wade trading with this bunch or is he stocking a place?"

"He's building up a ranch five days north of here, on the Double Mountain Fork of the Brazos. We're taking this bunch to him. Said he'd hire us on regular if we got there without losing more'n seven out of a hundert. He may not want us, though, 'cause we lost a passel that last run, over by deep creek. If he wants us, reckon I'll stay. Want I should tell him anything for you?"

"Yeah, tell him I'm freighting down here, an' I'll be up that way in a few weeks."

Peaches leaned down with crossed arms resting on his saddle horn and looked steadily at him. "Wil, you still get them old bad nightmares?"

"Not often," Bones lied. "It's been good seeing you."

The drover reined his horse away. "Same here, and, Wil, another thing. Them kin of yours got a grown boy they call Ruben ... and Wade's talking barbed wire."

Bones watched as the herd moved away. They were mostly good young cows with calves at their side. A few yearlings were mixed making up a herd of what looked to be about 900. They seemed anxious to leave the tracks behind.

Thought of barbed wire brought a frown, then Bones wondered about the age of the boy named Ruben. He clucked the two mules into movement. A long-legged bird, mottled gray and black, swooped up and perched on the wagon's tailgate. The bird had joined the man on his second trip, months earlier. Collecting the bleached buffalo bones from the recent slaughter served their common interest. Demand back East for fertilizer drove a healthy price for the bones. The roadrunner's interest centered on unearthed insects during their gathering. A wagon free of scorpions and other crawly things made it a welcome guest. The freighter didn't bother it, and since, unlike the mules Pete and Barney, it didn't sing or bray, its company was tolerated.

The chaparral sat erect, alert, and apparently immune to heat or dust. Contrarily Bones slumped and dozed. Sweat darkened his shirt beneath each armpit. His appearance reflected the features of the land, wrinkled and lonely. A V-shaped notch from a Yankee saber decorated his right ear. His forehead wore wrinkles beneath a high-crowned, tattered hat that shaded a hawklike nose. Loose-fitting clothes covered his six-foot, angular frame. Calm on the surface, only the grimness around his mouth hinted at the volcanic turmoil he bore inside.

Bones stirred. Entering town, the wagon rolled down a steep incline and sand rode upward on the wheel's rim. The bird took flight from the end gate and hit the ground running. The team followed their shadows past unpainted storefronts, driving small puffs of dust from beneath each hoof. A shaded image of Bones, high atop the load, snaked above them.

The roadbed pointed toward a new two-story hotel and the rolling hills beyond rail's end. To the left, along the tracks, a huge pile of bones awaited loading onto freight cars. Men milled about a loaded wagon. A red sow, with four trailing piglets, trotted across the road.

Bones raised his gaze from street to the buildings, then lifted a finger in greeting to Old Man Quinley. The banker stood in front of his business, his thumbs hooked in his vest and sunlight glinting off a watch chain looped across his generous girth. Like everyone within 100 miles, Bones owed the banker money, so it was Mr. Quinley across the banker's desk and Old Man Quinley to his back.

He traveled another block and pulled the wagon to a halt at the bone pile. He walked the spokes of the left wheel down, then stepped to the dirt.

The biggest thing about the man coming toward him was the smile on his face. "Hey, Bones, what is this? Three loads in ten days?"

Bones wiped his forehead with an arm sleeve. "Guess so, A. J. Gonna be another hot one, huh?"

A. J. walked around the wagon and felt of the bones. "Damnations! Where'd you get them things ... bottom of the Colorado? I know you boys wet them down, but this is too damn much. Gonna have to dock you about four-bits."

"What does that leave?"

"Twelve dollars a ton, same as last. How's the pickings out there?"

Bones rolled the numbers in his head and figured twelve dollars a ton rounded to about ten dollars for the load. "Getting scarce as hen's teeth."

"Times are changing, getting plumb civilized. Buffalo all gone, railroad in town, and I heard yesterday they killed that runt, Billy Bonney, over in New Mexico. Just weigh her out and push them

off, Bones. Maybe I'll see you over at Charley's later for a drink."
A. J. patted the dun mule, then kicked at two dogs squared off and
snarling at each other.

Later, Bones left his rig in the wagon yard and released the team
in the livery stomp lot. He threw them some hay, and the liveryman
promised to grain them later in the day. He headed for the Sally
Good 'Un Café. Far as he could tell, West Texas lacked most of the
civilized world's comforts, but Bones took luxury where he found
it. Next to corn whiskey, store-bought victuals best suited his taste.

Rumor said Sally had worked the dance halls before extra weight
and bad feet had forced her to respectability. He never knew her in
the dance halls, but he was in love with her cooking. He made short
work of the meal, mentioned his belt was growing shorter with her
cooking, and headed for the Sea Breeze Saloon. They said every fool
had his day, and he figured the rest of this one was his.

He crossed the street and stepped carefully around horse droppings that indicated a good crowd had been at the Sea Breeze last
night. It seemed to Bones only Charley Lonzo could get by putting
such a moniker on a place 600 miles from the nearest puddle of
water. The barkeeper had spent eight years on a cattle boat between
New Orleans and Galveston.

Although opposites, Bones accepted his friendship. The ex-sailor
leaned to outgoing and friendly when sober, surly and mean when
drunk. Since Charley didn't drink often on his side of the bar, they
mostly caught each other in friendly moods.

Inside the batwing doors, he stopped a moment, blinking the
sunlight from his eyes. "How you expect a gentleman to keep his
boots clean with all that stuff piling up out there?" he asked.

From behind the bar, Charley studied the end of a wooden
match he had whittled to a fine point, then went to work with it on
his left molars. He looked at Bones' boots as they closed from across
the room. "Don't guess I know any genteel men, and any Injun will
tell you them horse apples soften leather. How you been?"

"Somewhere between tolerable and turrible. Speaking of gentlemen, I saw Old Man Quinley standing on the walk checking his collateral when we came down the street. Anything behind the mahogany that ain't on sale?"

Charley hoisted a bottle from behind the bar. "We ... who was with you?" He filled two shot glasses.

"Me and the mules." Uneasiness crept into Bones' voice. "You ain't gonna be drinking today?"

"Just a morning toddy to get me past your peevish ways."

They tossed off their drinks in silence. Charley poured Bones another and went back to his picking. Bones studied the flimsy material draped around the shoulders of the painted lady in the picture behind the bar. He could never understand why the artist had done that. He threw down the second drink and grimaced. "Stuff's shore got a rank taste, don't it?" He looked back at the picture. "Must have been a Methodist."

"Who?"

"The fool that draped that cloth across her front." Bones struck a match with his thumbnail and puffed his pipe to life. "You always so lonesome here this time of morning?" He studied his companion fencing with the tooth and poured another drink. "Almost got et by a mad wolf yesterday, and it on my birthday, too."

"Probably would've only et one bite. What happened?"

"Tried to jump out and bushwhack me from a bone pile. Fell, or he'd've got me shore."

"It's bad this year. Everything around is going rabid. Fellow from Champion Creek said he killed two polecats had it. Say they get scared of water."

"That's another Methodist thing."

CHAPTER TWO

Bones sat with glass and bottle at one of Charley's rear tables. He shifted the Remington .36-caliber revolver, resting in a cross-draw position on his left hip, out of the way and leaned with his back to the wall. A grease-smeared deck of cards had tempted him into a game of solitaire. Sounds of Charley rummaging around in the lean-to behind the saloon joined those of the cards slapping the table.

Three men entered, stopped just inside the door, and inspected the room carefully before sauntering to the bar. The youngest of the trio wore clinking, jinglebob spurs. Bones noticed one toted a carbine, another a shotgun, then returned again to his card game. Long guns indoors, even in Charley's, seemed out of place. He looked again and saw no law badges. Six-shooters swung at the side of each. Jingle Bob appeared to be in his late twenties. The other two pushed forty.

"Where's the bar dog, old-timer," the youngest asked.

"Around back ... he'll catch you directly," Bones replied.

The younger man snorted and started around the bar. He was stopped by his companion's arm. "Hang on, Allen, we ain't in no hurry. We don't need much of this rotgut today, no way."

Charley entered and interrupted his whistling to ask: "What'll it be, boys?"

"Whiskey, if it don't wiggle too much," said the tallest of the three, holding up three fingers. "You got a train coming in today?"

"Supposed to have one about three this afternoon. Meeting somebody?" Charley asked.

"Yeah. A hoss busted up one of the boys over Baird way. Doc said he ought to be able to load him on the westbound by today. We got a buggy for him, outside. Our pack train's a hard day north of here, heading to Santa Fe. I'm Lathum Ferrell … this here's Allen, and that's Raymond."

Charley nodded. "Charley Lonzo. Old baggy britches over there is Bones Malone."

The youngest of the men, the one called Allen, looked at Bones. "How about it, old-timer? Looks like we got some time to kill. How about you an me getting up a little game of five-card draw?"

Bones waved him to the empty seat. "Only to pass the time, son. It's a two-bit limit." Out of sight, under the table, he loosened the Remington in its holster. He still didn't have this bunch figured, but they seemed overly loose-mouthed about their business. If they were muleskinners, he was a goat's uncle. "How about it, gents, want in?" He looked at Ferrell and Raymond.

Charley sent him a look of wariness. The ex-sailor had a cautious side.

Allen swung his leg over the back of a chair and seated himself. "Ain't your son, old man," he said coldly.

The other two seated themselves. Charley brought chips, and they all bought in for five dollars. The game continued through the next couple of hours. A light breeze drifted through the windows, warming the interior while outside flies migrated to the growing shade.

Earlier, Charley had given up his toothpick for a rag, and now surrendered that for a fly swatter. Seemed to Bones, his friend enjoyed the killing more than the wiping. The three strangers were down to the last of their bottle when the sound of the train whistle prompted them to cash in. Bones was a dollar ahead.

Allen exchanged his last two chips, stuffed the coin in his pocket, picked up the shotgun, and walked past Bones with the end of the barrel pointed in his direction. "Don't get too friendly with that dollar, old man. I'll want it back 'fore long."

"You go to hell, sonny," Bones whispered loud enough for all to hear.

Allen grinned crookedly as he followed the other two out.

Bones placed the pistol on his lap, while watching both the door and front window. In a moment, Raymond and Allen rode toward the depot. Ferrell followed in the buggy. Bones let out a long sigh, and heard a scrape of heavy metal beneath the bar. Looking at Charley, he knew the twelve-gauge had been put back to bed. He returned the pistol to its holster and noticed a slight twitch of the muscle above his right elbow.

"Ever see them before, Charley?"

"No, but I've got a bad feeling we'll see them again. Damn you, Malone! You gone weak north of the ears, or what?"

"Aw, shit, you know you can't ride around trouble. Thing to do is, bust it right through the middle." Bones waved his right hand toward the door. "Besides, I make allowances for bronc's, bad trails, and most other things I used to think pleasurable. No two-bit pup's gonna call me old!"

Charley shook his head and poured himself a stiff drink. "Let's go out front. Ought to be a shade by now."

The hot desert air blew coolly on Malone's damp skin in the shade of the saloon. He leaned against the wall and watched the train ease to a halt 100 yards away. A small crowd of horse-drawn vehicles and mounted men had gathered. The people appeared to be as excited by the sight and sound of the locomotive as the shying animals. Bones watched Ferrell hold the horses while Allen and

Raymond assisted a man on crutches down the steps of the train. The man moved easily on the crutches after reaching the ground and showed no difficulty climbing into the buggy.

Bones let his gaze drift to the cattle and freight cars. A colored man swung to the ground from the open door of an empty cattle car. He was too far away for Bones to make out his features, but something about the tall broad shoulders looked familiar.

Charley touched Bones lightly on the arm, and he looked back toward the crowd. The three men and their new companion rode toward them with the buggy in the lead. Between them and the strangers, a stooped old man wearing sandals and a straw hat pushed a wheelbarrow loaded with horse manure.

Maurice Rojas lived near the river in a brush arbor lean-to. The merchants paid him a penny a load to clean the streets, and he did it with dedication and dignity, in spite of his age. He looked down, straining with the load, unaware of anything except balancing the wheelbarrow. His path carried him directly into that of the four strangers.

Ferrell stopped the buggy and let Maurice pass. He turned to his passenger and spoke. Both men laughed. Behind them, Allen formed a loop with his quirt and flipped it under a handle of the wheelbarrow as he passed Maurice. In a single motion, he dumped both man and load in the middle of the street.

"Oops, sorry about that, amigo," he mocked. A couple of more steps brought him even with Bones and Charley. He looked hard at Bones. "What you so down in the mouth about, grandpa?" His right hand rested on his six-shooter, and a sneer covered his face. "You been drawing to inside straights all day. Why don't you draw for that old hogleg?"

Bones leaned forward. "Sonny boy, you got poor manners. Take your hand off of that gun butt and apologize to my friend there, or die where you sit. Talking is over."

"Hold it!" The injured stranger's eyes flashed authority, and his handsome face twisted with anger. He looked back from the front seat of the buggy. "Allen, I told you no trouble. You cause a ruckus an' you're on your own. Come on here!"

Allen turned to ride off, and Bones jerked out his gun with surprising speed. It was cocked and coming to bear on Allen's back when Charley grabbed his wrist.

"Let them go, Bones. It gets too complicated."

"You hang around, old man. I'll be back," Allen promised over his shoulder.

Bones put the gun away, turned in a tight circle, and kicked a warped plank lying on the ground. He thought the wood would give, but one end had become deeply embedded during the last rain. Sharp pain racked his toe. He tilted his face skyward, brought both hands up, then dropped them in disgust. He hobbled to the overturned wheelbarrow. Maurice met him, hat in hand, squinting to peer at the four strangers. Together, they righted the wheelbarrow.

"Your name's Maurice, ain't it?" Bones asked as the man turned to fetch his shovel.

"*Sí, señor, gracias.*"

"That was my daddy's name. French, ain't it?" Bones asked.

"Don't know. Your *padre*, he live here?"

"Never knew him. You want some tequila?"

"No, amigo. Watch out for yourself." The old man shuffled away.

"What kind of deal you suppose Lathum Ferrell and them others got cooking?" Bones asked as he and Charley headed back into the saloon.

"No good," Charley said.

"Should've let me finish him. It'll be to do later, if we meet up." Bones stuck the fingers of both hands inside his waistband so Charley wouldn't notice the trembling. "What did you mean by complicated?"

"They elected a constable the other day. Circuit judge comes from Abilene once a month. I tell you … times is changing, and you and me gotta change with them."

Thinking of his trembling hands, Bones said: "Hell, I'm changing faster than any of it." He frowned and shook his head sadly. "That boy, what was his name, Allen? He'll be lucky to get much older, turning his back like that after calling a man out."

Charley went back to his station behind the bar. His normally cheerful face seemed to sag, and the two-day growth of stubble added to his hangdog appearance.

"Tell me, Bones, would you have gunned him, if I hadn't stepped in?"

Bones took time loading his pipe, then thriftily burned a match end to fire it. A soft, easy draw rewarded his effort with a cool burn. "Was a time, maybe not. Now I come across a snake, just squash him whichever way he's heading."

Suddenly he felt tired. He eased himself into a chair and, with his feet resting in another, pulled his hat over his face. He sighed. "Wake me for supper."

CHAPTER THREE

Pain slashed through Bones' foggy world of drowsiness. Ants seemed to be feasting on his one living leg. He shifted his weight to the other hip and the numbness waned to pain in both buttocks.

Rousing, fear drained and consciousness returned. The frightening vision of being trampled, of hair forming a horse-belly bull's-eye, of dying men and thrashing animals disappeared. The awareness that he fought sleep in Texas, not Yanks at Second Manassas came with comfort. The voices were from the street outside the bar. He tilted his hat and opened his eyes. His hand rubbed away the last vestige of the horse.

A woman sat across from him. A look of amusement glittered in her eyes and the sound of laughter in her voice soothed him. "There's better places to sleep in this town than propped in a straight-backed chair."

Bones placed a hand to the back of his neck and gently cradled his head while shifting upright. "Sleeping ain't bad … it's the waking up plagues a man. Where would these places be you're talking about?"

"Maybe we'll get to that later. I'm Estella."

"Wil Malone. New, ain't you?" His eyes balked and would not leave the woman's strong face, her laughing eyes, or her brown hair.

The word pretty came to mind. He forgot the stinging.

"Not plum new, but a little newer than you, I'd say. Charley said you wanted to be waked for supper."

"Charley 'members some things better'n others." He thought he detected an undertone of pain in her comments, and realized she thought he'd classed her as merchandise with that word new.

"Things like what?" Estella asked.

Yes, her voice had tightened. "Like he forgot to tell me about you. How long you been watching me sleep?"

"Not long. Does it bother you?"

Bones looked at the windows and saw that the sun had gone down. "Well, naw, but my natural beauty's best when my mouth's shut. I'd've probably hid out if I'd known you was around." They both laughed.

Estella stood and he sensed a whiff of her bath oil, and it didn't smell dance hall. It had the aroma of Southern ladies before the war, when the European trade still thrived and cotton and slaves built mansions throughout the South. For a moment he thought of Sassy.

Estella turned to go.

Bones pushed himself erect. "Miss Estella, if you're a mind to, I'm going over to Sally's for dinner. I'd be pleased if you'd join me."

Estella looked at Bones a long moment. "Yes, I'd like that."

He turned his hat brim and looked out the window at the light shining from the barbershop. He sidled toward the door. "I'm going over and get a shave and spoof up a bit. Be back and get you later." He noticed a soft sadness behind the smile on her face as he looked over his shoulder.

A shave cost him two bits. Hot water for the tub another. A sign over the bathtub told him the proprietor guaranteed the water to be wet, and fourteen happy customers had used it without complaint. Climbing out, he noticed a small mirror hanging below the sign. Near it sat a long-necked bottle filled with red liquid. The label read: TOILET WATER. Bones removed the cork, then took a drink and gargled. His aim at the spittoon met with limited success. He splashed a good part of the contents on all fur-bearing parts of his body and winked at his reflection in the mirror.

An old trunk strapped to his wagon surrendered a clean shirt. He tucked it in on his way to Charley's. Things had picked up at the Sea Breeze. A harmonica player livened up the place. Estella danced with a bone buyer from Fort Worth. Another girl, Alice Marie, fought off the hands of a reeling cowboy while moving with the rhythm of the music. Estella smiled as she twirled past. A poker game occupied one of the tables.

He walked to the bar and ordered whiskey. A large man's elbow rubbed his. He held a drink in one hand and the attention of those around him. High Pockets Pinella took up four feet of bar space. Built close to the ground, his barrel-shaped body tended to grow from side to side—not up. He owned the blacksmith shop. As the Texas and Pacific had built west, High Pockets had followed, plying his trade until they reached Sundown City. When the tracks stopped at the river, High Pockets set up a permanent forge and said he was home. Stout, happy, and honest, he loved his wife and a good time. Sometimes the two conflicted, but it was always a short war. Those keeping score said it was Erma Lou forty-seven, good times zero. High Pockets slapped Bones on the back and continued his story about a snaky roan and a one-eyed man.

When the music stopped, the man Estella danced with walked to a card table. She came to Bones. She'd changed dresses while he had visited the barber. It clung about her curves in a way that stirred a man.

"Wow! You smell good," she greeted with a big grin.

High Pockets turned and fanned the air in front of Bones while winking at Estella. "Ma'am, you better watch this old goat tonight. Ain't never seen him fragrance up like this before."

Bones touched his hat brim. "Don't pay no attention to him, he's been kicked so often his brain rattles. You hungry?"

"Starved," she said, taking his arm.

They walked briskly to the door. Bones measured her at about fourteen hands. He could level a rifle over the top of her head. Slender, but not frail, each time he glanced at her, she held steady. It occurred to him that he was being teased. It was OK. For her, he would happily play the fool.

Bones removed his hat inside the door of the café, and finger-combed his hair. He carelessly draped the Stetson on a corner rack. Holding the chair for Estella brought memories of socials at his grandfather's plantation before the war. Across the room, Old Man Quinley stared at Estella. The lady seated with the banker was thinner than a bird, but sat rigidly straight in her chair.

He had never met the banker's wife but, from town gossip, knew her to be limited in ability to get about. The walking cane on the arm of her chair verified the story.

"Howdy, Mister Quinley, Missus Quinley," Bones said. "I'd like you folks to meet one of our newest residents. This is Estella … Estella …"

"Estella Emory. Mister Malone and I only met recently." Her bearing was regal, and she smiled sincerely at Mrs. Quinley.

"Mister Malone, Miss Emory, I'd like you to meet my wife, Missus Abigail Quinley. Just call me Milton." The old rogue appeared the spitting image of gallantry. He made a brave attempt at holding in his stomach as he partially rose and bowed slightly. Mrs. Quinley nodded at Bones and smiled warmly at Estella.

The banker settled back. "Bones, come by when you get a chance. Rosco's selling a new wagon for me over at the yard. You might want to look at it."

"I'll do that, Milton," Bones said. He whispered loud enough for only Estella's ears. "Milton comes from a long line of penny-pinching Quinleys. He's nice as pie on the loaning and hard as nails on the collecting. Most attention he's ever paid me. You shore are raising my social standing."

"Why, Wil, Charley tells me they sometime hang flags in the street when they hear you're coming to town. Said your celebrations are talked about all over."

Looking at her, Bones understood how a mouse felt in the paws of a cat. She was playing with him.

Sally interrupted his thoughts. "Here's coffee … food's on its way." She winked at Estella.

"Missus Quinley looks ill," Estella said.

"I hear they got a maid that looks after the house and helps take care of her. They say she can hardly get up and down stairs without help. You likely saw their house on the hill when you came in to town." Bones started to pour his coffee into the saucer, but thought better of it. Too late, he realized Estella noticed the awkward move.

She reached over and put a hand on his arm. "Wil, relax. I haven't enjoyed myself so in a long time. Here comes the food. Tell you what … I'll let you blow that coffee if you'll let me sop cornbread in my gravy."

No question, he was in over his head and sinking fast. Hell, he'd probably lose the wagon. Even the roadrunner would be lucky if he didn't end up in a damned chicken coop scratching for shelled corn. This was quite a gal. His last drink seemed distant and his old noggin too slow for this filly. He poured his coffee in the saucer.

"Missus Quinley's daddy made whiskey in Kentucky before the war. Old Man Quinley married her and got his hands on the family fortune. Now they're both teetotalers. He makes money and climbs to the maid's upstairs room on a ladder he keeps leaning against the side of the house. Missus Quinley told High Pockets' wife, he was getting ready to paint." He nodded knowingly. "Guess she saw the ladder."

Estella's laughter appeared genuine. She almost choked, then put her hand to her mouth and chuckled. "Wil, I declare, you're a gossip." She smiled while Sally refilled their coffee cups.

"Naw, t'ain't that … I'm just a good listener. People like to tell me stuff. The important things stay with me, the other I just keep a-moving."

Estella worked her plate, looked at Bones with amusement, and chewed, ladylike, on a bite of steak. The food was good, and they ate a few minutes in silence. Maybe he wasn't so slow after all. He relaxed. It felt good to be across from this woman whose age remained a mystery. She could be twenty-six or forty. Certainly she failed to fit the mold of most dance-hall women he'd known—no hard lines around the mouth or cold eyes here. Still, he suspected her interest in him was about the same he'd have looking over a new team.

He poured steaming coffee in the saucer, then grasped it with his thumbs and the fingertips of both hands. It was almost to his pursed lips when it exploded. Wet fire covered his face. Hot coffee dripped inside his shirtfront, and the pain spread.

The *crash* of a gunshot filled the small room, and the walls seemed to sway from the force of the sound. Mrs. Quinley screamed, and he heard a soft grunt that he believed came from Sally. Bones threw himself from his chair. He wiped at his face with his left hand, grabbing for the Remington with his right. As his shoulder hit the floor, he rolled. He looked up to see High Pockets rush in the café and his huge fist slam into the face of the man, Allen, who had tripped Maurice earlier. Allen's head flopped, and he stumbled backward, almost falling over a table before righting himself against the wall.

Bones raised his pistol. He was too late. High Pockets' bull-like body was lunging for the smoking revolver in Allen's hand. An expression of relief and cruelty crossed Allen's face as he pulled the trigger again. And the six-gun fired just in time to beat the rush of the blacksmith. A hunk of bloody meat ripped from the back of High Pockets' neck.

Bones' own gun bucked in his hand. A bloody hole appeared in the gunman's cheek. Bones' ears registered no sound, and he stupidly watched High Pockets' body drape over that of the smaller man. Then both lay still.

He looked for Estella, but saw only Sally, standing with her back to the food counter. Her arms were extended, her hands gripping the edge. She was facing him, a puzzled look on her face. A soft, strange sound escaped from her colorless lips. Her legs sagged, and she wilted slowly to the floor, eyes unseeing. He noticed a small drop of blood in the modest cleavage exposed just above her apron.

Estella appeared from behind the counter, and somehow she was in his arms. They held tightly to each other for a few moments. She quivered, and he wanted to reassure her, tell her he would protect her. He wanted to continue holding her, but the battle raging inside him would not allow it.

He turned away and began to shake. Alternate waves of ringing and silence raced through his head. Estella helped him toward a chair, then followed when he jerked free and lurched out the door. A figure ran toward him from the shadows, and he struggled to raise the pistol before recognizing the Quinleys' colored maid. Holstering the gun took three attempts.

"Is Sally dead?" he asked, looking at Estella, fearing he would have to read her lips.

She nodded.

He reached for the hitch rack, bent over it, and lost Sally's last meal. He straightened to sounds of a crowd gathering around them.

"You all right, Bones?" Charley's voice seemed to come from a cave.

"Just a little ringing in my ears. Be better directly." Bones went back inside the café, found water and a dishtowel in the kitchen, and cleaned his face. Reentering the dining room, he saw Arnold, the barber, straightening from examining both High Pockets and Allen.

Arnold looked at him and nodded. "They're dead as yesterday. All three."

The Quinleys' maid helped Abigail toward the door, and the banker followed. Mrs. Quinley held a lace handkerchief to her face.

Her voice rang clearly through the small room. "Land's sakes … I never … poor, poor Mister Pinella."

Singletree Sadler stood outside the doorway, pointing a big Colt straight at Bones' face. The badge on his old friend's shirt told Bones he looked at the new law in Sundown City. Two weeks ago, he had carried the big man home after a few hours' drinking at the Sea Breeze. Singletree had passed out, and it was all he and Charley could do to hoist him into the wagon. The next morning they had speculated about their ignorance in risking rupture by not letting the man sleep it off on the saloon floor. At the time, they'd felt noble. Singletree had flopped loudly upon hitting the ground in front of his one-room shack. Last he'd seen him, a little yellow dog had been licking at the constable's face.

"Take it easy, Singletree. I'm peaceable," Bones said, holding up both hands and stepping outside.

The lawman walked around him and lifted the Remington from its holster. "What happened here?"

"This fellow come gunning for me," Bones said.

"He's right, Jerry," Quinley said, using Singletree's real name. "I saw it all, but it happened too quick to stop. That dead man in there stepped in the door and pointed his gun at Bones. High Pockets was passing by and saw it. He whirled and hit the man's arm as he shot. Must have been the Lord's will that bullet hit poor Sally. Then the man killed High Pockets, and Bones killed him. Your job's finished for the night, Constable. 'Scuse us, we're going home."

Singletree stuck Bones' gun back in its holster and put his own away. "OK, Bones, just doing my job. We're through, but did you boys know each other from somewhere else, or what?"

"Not 'fore today. Don't think he liked my table manners. Can we get out of here?"

Estella stepped near him. He reached and took her hand and found it even colder than his own. As he was leading her through the people, he saw Erma Lou Pinella racing down the street, holding her skirt knee-high, heading for the café. The light from Arnold's barbershop window showed fear on her face.

"It's Missus Pinella," Bones said. He knew her from visits when she had brought a snack to her husband at the blacksmith shop. He stopped her by grabbing her by both arms.

"Erma Lou, no. Don't go in. He's gone."

She looked at him with no sign of recognition. Her eyes glazed. She appeared almost to collapse, then straightened and wrenched herself free. Through the window, they saw her kneel beside her husband's body.

"I'm going to her. I'll see you later, at Charley's," Estella said. She walked inside, and Bones watched her put her hand on Erma Lou's shoulder. She helped the woman to her feet as Arnold placed a barber's apron over the corpse. Sobs from inside knifed painfully through the darkness.

Bones closed his eyes and leaned against the wall of the café. A scene from his most stubborn nightmare drifted inside his closed lids. *A rickety wagon jolted down a rutted road. Drab forms of leafless trees silhouetted against a gray sky bordered the right of way. The rig was filled with red-smeared, cheese-colored objects and dripped blood from every opening. A piece of the load fell to the ground. He reached for it, then dropped the severed arm in horror.*

A strong hand gripped his shoulder. "C'mon, I'll buy you a drink," Charley said.

Bones shook his head and started walking. "Better make it a bottle."

"You was right, Bones. If I'd stayed out of it, High Pockets and Sally would both be alive now. Should have let you finish it clean earlier. Damn, I'm gonna miss old Pockets."

"No, it's my doings. Like you said … I weren't thinking smart. I could've let that boy's lip drag without calling his hand. Seems I ought to be old enough not to go around with the bit in my teeth. He was riding me pretty heavy, though."

CHAPTER FOUR

Seated alone in Charley's, Bones found a bottle a poor substitute for Estella. She had yet to return from seeing Mrs. Pinella home. Several men had tried to start a conversation or buy Bones a drink, but a nod of his head had turned them away. His chair leaned against the wall, facing the door. He figured stupid once a day was enough. Allen's friends could still be in town.

Three-quarters of a bottle later, Estella returned. She came straight to his table and sat. Without asking, she picked up his glass and downed the shot. She gasped and made a face.

"How is she?" Bones asked.

"Did you know they got three kids?" Her eyes were red, and her lips trembled.

He nodded his head. "You want a glass?"

She didn't answer, but stood and walked to the piano. She sat and her fingers touched the keys. Sounds came from the instrument, and he watched her perk her head, listening to notes or chords or whatever people with music inside them listen to. Finally she appeared satisfied, and her body swayed to the rhythm of the sounds she made.

Bones had never heard music so beautiful. It washed over him, and, if he had heard the piece before, he didn't remember it. The dancers stopped and stood without talking, and, at the bar, most forgot about their glasses. Music drifted across the room for the next hour. One melody after another held him and the others. Some were familiar, others hauntingly mysterious, as though he had feasted on their beauty previously, but couldn't be sure. He blinked and wiped a tear a number of times. Others did the same.

Moved to action, he unsteadily walked to the piano and leaned there, watching Estella play. She looked at him and smiled. He grinned back. Suddenly she stopped, and silence ruled the room for a full two minutes. Then the crowd clapped, yelled, and whistled.

He put out his hands, and she stood and was close. He kissed her on the mouth. She didn't respond, and she didn't pull away. He drew back and read surprise in her eyes. His face smoldered. He couldn't find the right place for his hands. If she had hit him, it would have been OK. If she had responded, it would have been better—but nothing. He just didn't know how to handle that. He went back to his whiskey.

He finished the bottle, and she continued to play. The crowd thinned to a half dozen customers. The Fort Worth bone buyer went to Estella and whispered something in her ear. She shook her head.

Bones tried to stand. It was a chore. He struggled, then stood upright, but he was afraid to let go of the table. Seemed the floor pitched over to the left, or was it the right? He staggered to the center of the room.

"Charley, I believe I need a little drink," he said.

"You've had enough," the bartender said.

Since the shooting, Bones had noticed Charley uncharacteristically sampling his own wares, and now he looked like he had a sour stomach.

"I'll ... by Gawd ... decide when I've had enough. Give me a drink or uncork that damn old scatter-gun. I want a drink!" The mirror showed Estella turning on the piano bench with fear on her face.

"I don't know who the hell you think you are," Charley said, his eyes hidden behind narrow slits. "Don't try to push me. I say again, Bones, who the hell do you think you are?"

Bones stood, swaying like a willow in a breeze. "Who are I …?" He tried to turn, but his boots were nailed to the floor. "I'm a soljer … that hates war. I'm a bronc peeler … scared of hosses. I'm a cowman that don't like cows. I'm a lady's man … a-feared of women." He tilted, face forward and stiff. His momentum increased, and his words followed him down as he fell. "I'm Bones by-Gawd Malone." The floor *thudded* against his face.

*   *   *   *   *

He awoke in darkness, yet, outside, a rooster crowed. Its boasting suggested civilization. And he lay in an honest-to-goodness bed. A leg, draped partially over his body, shouted he'd hit pay dirt. He lay there, trying to remember last night's events. Thankfully he'd changed drawers at Arnold's. Things were a little fuzzy, but it all came back … all of it up to his big failure trying to kiss Estella. At that point, everything went blank.

The hairs on his legs touched cool sheets, telling him he had separated from his pants. If he knew where they were, he'd light a match and see who felt so good beside him. He thought he knew, but it wasn't something a fellow wanted to guess about. It was dark as a bat cave on a stormy night, but the cool breeze drifting across his face felt good.

He probed with his right hand above his head, trying not to move his body. It touched the iron railing of a headboard, and his pants hung on the post. A pocket yielded a broken match, and he struck it with a thumbnail. Cupped in his hand, its light revealed Estella's face on the pillow beside him. Her eyes fluttered, and he shook out the match. Even breathing told him she slept.

Bones took inventory. His head throbbed. His nose and

right cheek were sore. A rank taste, like he'd grazed with coyotes, coated his mouth, and his tongue felt moldy. He needed to move, needed to get his thoughts straight, but he didn't want to wake Estella. The frame of the window began to take shape, the sky lightened, and his eyes continued to accustom to the darkness. She stirred, and he took advantage of the movement to snuggle closer. Outside, the rooster got his second wind.

"Bones, are you alive?" she whispered.

"Partly."

She pulled him even closer, and their lips met. They kissed hard, passionately, each trying to engulf the other. She gave herself freely there in the darkness. When it was over, Bones was spent and she seemed as breathless in his arms.

Faint light touched the shadows in the room, and her face wore a smile. "I thought you were afraid of women?"

"Who told you that?" he asked, puzzled.

She giggled.

A few moments later, he sat on the side of the bed and pulled on his boots. "How about me getting us some coffee ... maybe, ham and eggs?" He stood and moved toward the hotel room's door.

"No, you go ahead. I'll see you later, and we'll talk. There'll probably be a funeral today."

He wondered if he should pull some money off his roll and leave it on the dresser. Her eyes were on him, and some of the joy washed off her face. When she spoke, he knew she read him like a line from a page of her music.

"I don't make money on my back, Wil. Charley pays me to play the piano, and dance if I want. I ain't supposed to make his customers mad, but if I make one happy, it's my idea."

He couldn't read any anger in her voice, maybe a little sadness, but no anger. He pulled on his boots and took his hat from the dresser. Two steps put him at her bedside. She let him kiss her. It was slow and gentle, and the feel of her, like a preheated and wrapped rock in a cold bed, warmed him. He felt like a kid.

* * * * *

He ate at Sally's, then walked to the livery stomp lot. It wasn't a large lot, but it was sandy enough to keep down chipped hoofs from constantly stomping at pesky flies. The mules stood facing opposite directions so the tail of each could switch flies from the other's face.

Rosco came toward him. "Bones, heard you had some trouble last night. Glad you're all right. I put grease on Pete's collar scald this morning. He don't like folks much, do he?"

"Naw, his daddy would be proud if he was to see him. I'll likely stay in town today. Just keep the wolf away from their door, and we'll settle up later."

At the Sea Breeze, Bones had a little hair of the dog. Charley seemed a mite standoffish, so he didn't hang around. Somewhere, he had a vague recollection of Charley taking a few drinks last night. He'd likely be out of sorts for a day or two.

The barbershop had a closed sign on the front door, indicating Arnold had changed hats. The barber cut hair, doctored, then acted as undertaker when his other skills failed. Except for Charley and Old Man Quinley, Arnold made more money than anyone else in town. Bones liked the man's industrious ways in spite of being puzzled by his choice of professions. It seemed awfully confining to him.

Maurice stopped his cleaning long enough to wave from in front of Sally's. Bones moved on to the horse trough across the street. He tilted the spout so water would run to the ground, then worked the handle a couple of strokes. He washed with soap he found hanging from the trough in a string net. After drying on a dirty cloth tied to the pump, he pulled his knife and worked on his fingernails.

He sat, leaning forward to keep his butt out of the trough water, and watched the red sow approach. Behind her, three pigs chased a fourth that carried the rear half of a lizard in its mouth. The sow circled the pump once, apparently watching to see if Bones was going to kick at her. Then she came to the trough, reared on her back legs, and ducked her whole head into the water. Coming up for air, she vigorously shook flopping ears, then sniffed at Bones' knee. She looked him in the eye as though she'd found a new friend.

Bones placed the point of his knife under his hat brim and pushed it up slightly. "Howdy," he said.

The sow didn't answer, but the pig with the lizard swallowed his prize, then all four siblings started rooting wet sand on his boot.

Arnold walked toward him. Halfway across the street he started talking. "Bones, we gonna bury High Pockets at three this afternoon. For the kids' sake, Erma Lou wants to get it done. Ain't no folks close enough to come. I told her Brother Rayfield's gone to Round Top for that revival, but she said to go ahead. Now here's what I need to talk to you about. She says to me, says … 'Ask Mister Malone to say some words over him.' Said High Pockets thought you hung the moon."

"Oh shit!" Bones said, holding his head with both hands. "I can't do that."

"I don't see no way out for you."

"Good Lord, can't you tell her I'm sick or something."

"Bones, I think you're stuck. Think you're it. Can we count on you?"

"Saved my life. Reckon I got to do it. Probably be a bunch there, won't they?"

"I expect. He's shore liked. See you at three. Oh, I was about to forget … here's some things wrote down about him you may need." He handed Bones a folded piece of paper.

Bones headed for the Sea Breeze, paper in hand. He walked in the door, gritted his teeth, and headed straight for the sour-looking Charley. Out of sorts, or not, he needed the man's advice. He felt the bartender's eyes all the way across the room.

"Charley, I know you're feeling poorly, but I need your help."

Charley stared. He reached under the bar and pulled out a bung starter. The *spat-spat* of the mallet in the palm of the big man's hand stopped Bones and brought him to stiff attention. "You don't even remember wanting a piece of me last night, do you?"

"What? What the hell you talking about?" Bones sputtered. "Charley, this is serious. Give me a drink. I gotta say words over High Pockets today." He waved the paper at Charley. "What am I gonna say?"

Charley handed him a glass and bottle, and took the paper.

Bones poured a drink and worked with his pipe. He fired it, took a drink, and looked at the painting behind the bar. His eyes were half up the lady's curves when he thought of Estella. He looked away.

"Says here his name's Richard, and he was born in New Orleans in 1842," Charley said.

"Let me see that," Bones demanded. He took the paper from Charley and busied himself in an effort to memorize it.

* * * * *

Estella and Alice Marie had agreed to ride to the graveyard with Charley. Bones retraced his steps to the livery and saddled Barney. He tied him outside the saloon and busied himself sitting in the shade and studying the note. It was a good three-quarter mile to the cemetery. Forking a saddle offered bad memories. Finally a crowd gathered for the stroll to the hill east of town. Still studying the note, Bones moved to the mule, tightened his cinch, and swung into the saddle.

Arnold drove a matched pair of blacks around the corner of the barbershop. He rode high on the seat of a new hearse of the same color. Behind him came Erma Lou and the kids, riding with the Quinleys in the nicest rig in town. Bones eased Barney into the procession behind Charley's rig.

The sun beat furiously against his shoulders, and his heart

raced—1,000 things to say, but none worthy of High Pockets. His mouth felt dry and his hand shook slightly when he tied Barney to a wagon, and stepped to the grave site.

Three colored men with shovels stood a distance from the crowd. Arnold called on Mrs. Lorene Watson to lead in the singing. Her strong voice boomed "Shall We Gather at the River." All joined in. The many and varied voices carried loudly on a strong breeze. Men stood with bared heads, mouthing soundless words, and the dry wind whipped the ladies' skirts about their ankles.

Bones looked at the toe of his boot and listened while Lorene sang "Amazing Grace" in solo, and then he heard Arnold say his name. He stepped closer to the grave and looked beyond the group, past the Colorado, across the empty spaces of the flood plain, then back to the reddish-brown earth of the freshly dug grave.

"Lord, it's Bones Malone here. We talked last on the Cimarron, two years ago, when I planted that poor cowboy and said some words. Now Azalea, from down in the quarters, told me ... when I was just a boy and didn't have no Mom or Daddy ... that you sometimes took good folks 'cause they is scarce. Said you need them worse than us down here.

"Well, I don't expect you need no introduction, but we're here today to bury High Pockets Pinella. His real name's Richard, and he's the best smithy I ever saw. Knowing you live in that sandy land with jackasses and camels, you likely don't need a blacksmith, so it must be the man, not the trade, that made you call him. And you're getting a good one. He's true all the way through. Died brave as all get-out a-trying to save an old sinner like me." Bones took a deep breath and looked at a cottony cloud pushing a shade across the slight rise of the cemetery.

"Well, Richard was born in 1842 in that tough old town down on the Mississippi called New Orleans. He probably can handle hisself up there, well as he did down here, so I expect the ones we need to talk about is these three little ones he left here with this good woman. They need your help, God, and this old bone-picker asks your mercy on them.

"I reckon that's it, except we're saying all this in your boy's good name … amen." He put on his hat, let out a sigh, and looked at Estella's reassuring smile.

People passed by Erma Lou and hugged her. Some patted the kids on the head, others kissed them. They shook Arnold's hand, then came and shook Bones'. The fingers of Lorene Watson's husband buried into his shoulder, and he barely avoided stumbling into the grave when Charley poked him in the stomach. Maurice nodded his respects. An old woman kissed his cheek, and a heavy lady gave him a damp hug. "Bless you," said more than one.

The last person walked away, and Estella squeezed his hand. "We may change your name to Brother Malone."

He turned, and there, before him, stood Catfish Jones with a smile bigger than life spread across his coffee-colored face. Bones felt Catfish's big hands grab his shoulders, then his teeth began to chatter from the shaking he received.

"Lord o' mercy! You done made a preaching man," Catfish said.

CHAPTER FIVE

Barney grazed nearby. The mule finished cropping the small circle allowed by his tether, then cautiously dragged his ground-hitched reins to more lush pickings.

Bones sat, cross-legged, watching the last wagon creak away from the cemetery. Catfish and two other men shoveled dirt into High Pockets' grave. Except for the loss of old Pockets, Bones didn't know when he'd felt so good. Maybe talking to God had done it. On the other hand, Estella might have had a hand in his good spirits. Anyway, here he was, having just buried one friend and sitting, looking at another he hadn't seen for years. Life did take queer turns.

He noticed time had sort of filled out the ex-slave, while it tended, more or less, just to gnaw on himself. When they got their growth, they had been about the same size. Now the dark man might outweigh him by twenty-five pounds, mostly in the shoulders. His friend's pistol belt, lying near the pile of dirt, looked like it would fit his own waist.

"Wil, don't yuh remember? My name ain't Catfish no more? Yuh know when your granddaddy sold me my freedom, I changed it to San Tone Jones." Each bite of the big man's shovel carried as much dirt as that of both his companions. "'Member that old Texas horse trader that crossed the river with them bad horses? Weren't a fence in Mississippi would slow them down. Yuh broke eight or ten, and I busted a passel. That Texas man bragged to your granddaddy, how good we was with hosses. Said them he brought came from San Tone. That name had spirit … a heck better than Catfish. Next year, when I was freed, I had them write it on the paper." San Tone straightened, one hand on his back, the other on the shovel. "Lan's sake, that was a good day." He raised his face skyward, and laughter rolled from his huge frame.

"I remember … San Tone … just been so long, some things get fuzzy in my mind. Besides, you was Catfish to me a lot longer than you was San Tone." Knowing how important it was to his friend, he added: "But I won't forget no more." Then Bones asked: "What you got to do, when you get this hole filled?"

San Tone talked without looking up. "Why, nothing. Just got here yesterday. Railroad fellow in Abilene told me they was gonna start on a bridge 'cross the river here. Found out this morning it won't start for a while. Have two more graves to dig with these boys in the morning. That's it."

"That was you I saw get off the train yesterday?" Bones said.

"Most likely, if you wuz looking."

"Guess who's a couple of days north of here?"

"Just tell me."

"Wade and Sassy. How long since you seen them?"

"'Most as long as since I seen yuh. Let's see they got married two months after yuh left. Then next year … before the baby came … Wade's daddy sent them to Vicksburg, to handle the cotton business. They never got back to High Manor. I was in Vicksburg later … there when the damn Yankees captured it, but they'd already gone. Ain't seen 'em since. Wonder what the baby were?"

"Saw a drover the other day knew them. Said it was a boy. Ain't that something? Sassy with a grown boy."

"Ain't half as much as Wade with one. Reckon he growed up, too?" San Tone said, grinning.

Bones tapped his pipe on a rock. "Listen, I got a wagon an' another good mule in town. Why don't we load up tomorrow and head over their way? We'll have a Mississippi reunion, here in West Texas."

San Tone stopped work and looked unblinkingly at him. "What yuh haul in that wagon?"

He was the only person Bones knew more cautious than Charley. "Buffalo bones mostly. What do you say?"

"Who wants a bunch of old dead buffalo bones?"

"Folks back East make them into fertilizer. What do you say?"

"I don' know. Bones is bones. Sounds to me like it would still be working with the near departed. We don't have to shovel or nuthin', do we?"

"I'm just talking old dried buffalo bones."

"Animals … beings … they all bones. Why don't they use chicken droppings? It'll make things grow." San Tone shook his head sadly.

Bones had forgotten how hard it was to change directions once his friend locked onto a path. It seemed he wore a blind bridle, nothing to the right—nothing to the left. "Don't know, maybe they ain't enough chickens. What do you say?"

"Seems to me they could hatch some more … easier than finding old dead buffalo bones. Can yuh wait till after the funerals?"

Bones nodded.

"Maybe, you could take that ole wagon to the crick and wash her off?"

"I'll do that."

San Tone turned back to his task. "Yeah, might as well. Yeah, why not? It's been a long time."

After filling the grave, San Tone made sure every clod was stacked properly on the mound. Bones borrowed a shovel and tamped the dirt evenly on all sides, smoothing the clods until the grave had the appearance of a sand dune. The other gravediggers gathered their tools and walked toward the river.

"Meet yuh here in the morning!" San Tone called out to them.

"Morning," one replied. The other lifted his hand without turning or speaking.

Bones and San Tone walked, side-by-side, on an unnamed street toward town. Barney's ears flopped behind them. Shadows lengthened, and the sun beat fully in their faces. Years spun away with each step, and Bones' pace quickened. Barney lagged behind, his rein tightening.

San Tone grinned like a toad in a swarm of gnats. Obviously he had picked up on the hastened step. Bones recalled the comfort of walking with his chum on a Mississippi cotton field turn row. He released Barney and broke into a run just in time to avoid San Tone's effort to trip him.

There were two days' difference in their ages, and the only physical contest Bones could ever best his pal in was running. San Tone had strength; Bones had the speed. He had proved it every day of their lives for years, and he would prove it today. Three quick steps were all he needed to move in front. Stiffness melted away, becoming no factor.

For several steps, he increased his lead, then it became harder to keep his feet in front of his leaning body. He slowed and heard San Tone closing. His side hurt, and he needed more air. A few more staggering steps and a blow on his left shoulder sent him sprawling to the ground. He rolled, and the big man tripped and fell over him.

Dethroned and exhausted, Bones lay on his back in the middle of the street, spread eagle, and gasping for breath. "You're gonna have to get the mule and tie me on, or leave me here," he laughed.

"I get the mule, yuh still walk," San Tone countered.

A couple of minutes later they rose and dusted off themselves. The Quinleys' colored maid stood in the front yard of a large two-story house. She had a sprinkler bucket in her hand and an amused expression on her face.

"Mister Malone, you spoke good on Mister Pinella's behalf today. His woman was pleased," she said. Her words were directed at him, her gaze at San Tone.

"Thank you, ma'am," Bones said.

She nodded without moving her eyes. San Tone returned her stare. Bones realized he'd lost all identity. Between these two, his importance challenged that of sagebrush.

San Tone walked toward the woman.

"I'll just go get my mule," Bones said.

He captured Barney without incident and rode him back to the Quinley place. He pulled to a stop in the middle of the road, several feet behind San Tone, and cleared his throat.

San Tone looked around, like at a dog returning from a skunk fight. "Wil, this here's Beula Ramsey. I'm gonna sit on the porch and have some lemonade. Yuh just go on. I'll find yuh later."

Bones turned Barney toward town. Hell of a thing—twenty years and he didn't rate a glass of lemonade. He laughed out loud and kicked the startled mule into a high lope.

While unsaddling at the livery, he thought of tomorrow's trip to visit Sassy. They would unhitch near the Double Mountain country at his last bone pile. The wagon would remain there and they would ride the mules to Wade's new spread. They would pick up the wagon load of bones on the return trip to the railhead. The idea of riding Pete clouded his spirits, but he'd out-fox old San Tone on that. Only thing missing was a second saddle.

Bones nodded a greeting at the stableman. "Rosco, that fellow I had to put away last night ... has his mount or rig shown up?"

"Yeah, Trina's oldest kid brought his hoss and saddle in this morning. Said someone left it standing at the River Cantina all night. Maurice picked it out as being the gunman's. Singletree came by later and told me how to handle it."

"How's that?" Bones' voice was cold.

Rosco looked uneasy. "Said sell all of it. Said Arnold kept the killer's gun and gun belt for funeral expenses, and we'd split the proceeds three ways on the horse and saddle." He pointed at the saddle as he finished talking.

"What three?"

"The city, him as constable, and me for my trouble."

Bones walked up and down alongside the lot fence. "Awful civic-minded, ain't he?" He looked at the ground, then circled his finger skyward. "That ain't the way it's gonna be. Your part's OK, you're entitled. You got expenses and a business to run, but the city had no hand in it, so they're out. The same is true with Singletree. The city's part goes to Erma Lou and them kids. Let Charley hold Singletree's part for anyone laying a claim on Sally's stuff. Tell Singletree, if he ain't happy, he can take it up with me. And here's eighteen dollars for that saddle. You see Erma Lou gets half. I'll give Charley nine to hold as Sally's part. I don't need the horse. You OK with this?"

"Seems right to me, but Singletree may think it's a little high-handed."

"'Tis high-handed … sometimes it takes that to beat low-handed."

At the bar, he handed Charley the nine dollars and told him of his conversation with Rosco. Charley agreed to look out for Sally's interest. Said he'd hold it six months, and, if nothing came of it, he'd see that Erma Lou got that part, also. He was back in an easy mood and didn't bring up the previous evening. Bones looked around for Estella.

"She'll be in directly, Bones," Charley said.

Bones nodded. He respected the seaman-turned-barkeep's disdain for gossip. Charley could know one's ancestors traced back to sea monsters and keep it to himself. The booze peddler, like Bones himself, kept his own council when it came to women. Since they were as scarce in this country as water and more refreshing, only a fool dared brand them.

"What did you think of my service?" Bones asked.

"Service!" Charley laughed. "You old hypocrite, I wouldn't've stood near you for all the steers in Chicago. More you talked, the louder that thunder got."

"Thunder! Naw, wasn't a cloud in the sky. Well, only one."

"Way you was going on, it don't take clouds for lightning." Charley chuckled his way to a customer at the end of the bar.

Estella entered and stopped at Bones' elbow. "You reckon we dare eat in public again?" he asked.

"If we're gonna eat, we dare. I've got a coffee pot, but it's been so long since I held a frying pan I wouldn't know what to do with it. Guess the hotel's it."

Leaving, he held the batwing door for her. "You know how to make biscuits?"

"If I put my mind to it. Where's your cemetery friend?"

"You know that pretty maid of Abigail's? Well, seems she and San Tone both got a sweet tooth for lemonade." He winked.

"Lemonade beats rotgut," she said, stepping into the hotel's dining room.

Waiting for their food, they drank their coffee in silence, then leaned, elbows on the table and both hands on their cups, staring at each other. Beauty again pushed pretty out of his mind, and he wondered what she thought of his notched right ear.

She broke the silence. "Do you really think heaven is in the desert?"

He set his cup down, avoided her eye, and stirred the few swallows remaining in the cup. "Desert?"

"There at the cemetery, you said something about camels and sand and all. Do you really think God looks down on us from a desert?"

"Don't know, it just sort of came to me. Likely not, but I fought once in a swamp during the war that could have passed for hell. You know religion well, do you?" he asked.

"I know a little about the Bible, but I'm not as sure of my religion as I'd like to be. My mother died when I was ten. My daddy left me with a preacher's family in Gainesville. When I got to be fifteen, I left."

Bones noticed the helpings the waitress brought were not as big as Sally's, but the steak looked good. "How come you to leave?"

"The preacher decided I looked better to him than his wife … God, too, I guess."

Startled, Bones jerked his head up. "They ain't no conflict twix you and God noways I can tell," he muttered.

Estella sat composed. She tilted her head. "Tell me about Catfish."

"His name's San Tone now. Changed it when he got his free papers. We was born two days apart … me first, a soon to be orphan, then him, son of Azalea Jones, queen of the delta. Grand-daddy Malone and Momma lived at the big house. Azalea took care of it and lived in the quarters. My daddy died a few months b'fore this. Anyway, the day San Tone was born, my momma took a fever. She didn't last a week. Azalea wet-nursed us both. Me and San Tone were together until I went to war. Wasn't ever much the two of us couldn't lick."

Estella chuckled softly. "I can imagine."

Bones saw nothing funny in his story. He pondered his words, then felt his face reddening.

"I expect you were fond of Azalea," Estella said.

"Fond of her … hell, she was the only mother I ever knew. What little raising I got, she give me. Taught me how to behave and which fork to use when we had company. When Cat … San Tone misbehaved, she whupped him, and, when I did, she took a stick to me. She was stern with us, but happy with the world. Darkies weren't allowed to dance in the drawing room when outsiders were there, but she near wore out the floors in the rest of the house. My mother had taught her to read, in secret, and she read the Bible to us twice a week. Till it got so she couldn't catch us.

"There were two thousand five hundred acres at High Manor, and more than fifty slaves. I went back after the war. Everything was growed up … the big house just a pile of ashes. A carpetbagger at the courthouse said it belonged to the government then. Granddaddy and Azalea were both killed by Yankee soldiers, and everybody else was scattered. I don't know exactly how it all came about. Hope San Tone can tell me. I sure have rattled on, ain't I?"

"I enjoyed it, Wil."

"You can call me Bones if you want. It don't matter."

"No, you're Wil Malone to me."

"How's that?"

"Bones is OK. It has a friendly ring to it, but it just doesn't quite fit what I consider to be the most honest man I ever met. I like Wil Malone better."

"Called me Bones early this morning."

"I know you better, now."

"There's a road south of town, leads to Seven Wells. Best water in the world, and there's tracks set in rock out there that must have been made by the granddaddies of all buffalo before the stars learned to twinkle."

"That must have been a while back."

"A long time. Under a three-quarter moon, like tonight's gonna be, it's sort of pretty down there. I could get Rosco's buggy hitched to old Barney, and it wouldn't take long to get there."

"I better hang around Charley's tonight, but ask me again."

* * * * *

Bones drank very little during the evening. He played a little poker, listened to Estella's music, and, around 9:30 p.m., saw San Tone wave from the doorway.

"Decide you need something stronger than lemonade?" Bones asked.

"Nope, lemonade's just fine. Don't hit the hard stuff. Jest thought I'd find a place to unroll this blanket."

"You can share my wagon if you don't snore." Bones waved for him to follow.

"If I snore, I never heard it."

"Where you reckon that gal found them lemons?" Bones asked.

"When yuh live in a banker's house, and he lives by a train, yuh can find anything," San Tone offered.

They unrolled their bedding in the floor of the wagon and stripped for the night—Bones near the tailgate and San Tone near the front. The air was cool and the moon cast shadows. Bones lit his pipe and sat on the blanket. He leaned against the side of the wagon.

San Tone lay on his back, looking at the sky. "That's a mighty pretty sight. That old man in the moon's just a-smiling. Me and Beula studied it quite a bit. Heard a man say once he wouldn't be surprised what all's up there. You ever give it any thought?"

"Never paid it no mind."

The black man's voice was hushed, as if to not disturb the moment. "Wil, did yuh ever get it worked out?"

"What?"

His friend's faint words drifted out of the night. "The meaning of old life."

"Never had a wife, but, for sure, I'd favor sweet and young."

San Tone looked at him, rolled over, and tucked his arm under his head for a pillow.

"Bought a saddle. You can have it for twenty-seven dollars," Bones said.

"Ain't got no horse," San Tone replied. A moment later, his snores rattled off the sideboards.

CHAPTER SIX

The next morning, Barney and Pete settled into a rhythm. San Tone sat beside Bones on the wagon seat. They headed northeast, towards Double Mountain country. Just out of town, the roadrunner fell into his long pacer's stride, sprinting behind them. He cocked his head, looking closely at both the added saddle and San Tone. Apparently they passed muster, and he soon took up his favored perch.

San Tone watched the bird several minutes, then queried: "Where'd that old roadrunner come from?"

"Guess he hatched out 'round here somewhere. Signed on with me a month or so back. Arnold calls them Mexican Peacocks."

"What yuh gonna do with him?"

"Do with him? I don't know. Maybe I'll eat 'im if I get too hungry. Have I got to do something with him?"

San Tone shook his head and pulled out a plug of tobacco. He busied himself with the chaw and spit a stream of brown, instead of answering the question.

Two days later, at daylight, they harnessed the mules after bedding down at a place Bones called Hazard Springs. He pointed. "My last load came from a pile I'd stashed over there. An old rabid wolf bedded up in them and almost et me when I come to pick them up."

"He'd likely 'a' spit yuh out after one bite," San Tone commented, grinning. He buckled a collar strap, shaking his head and chuckling softly.

For a brief moment, Bones wondered if Charley and San Tone had set him up on the wolf story. But, hell, it wasn't possible. They didn't even know each other. Just showed what a man had to expect when he was careless about the kind of friends he made. Damned if he'd try that story again.

"Yuh do any good … hauling these old skeletons?"

"Hope to clear a thousand dollars this year, after keeping a little something in them mules' feedbag, not to mention mine. Beats wages. Thing is they're about to play out around here. Farther west and north, though, there're plenty just awaiting."

San Tone hooked a thumb towards Sundown City. "That old town's got more bones than a starved sunfish. Stack by that railroad's higher my head."

"Yeah. It's a helluva thing … trains hauling more bones than cows."

"One of them boys back at the cemetery said yuh've made a name up and down that old cow trail to Kansas."

"Well, I probably did that. Pushed a bunch of 'em north. Oh, we rode cyclones and spit at prairie fires. I helped a few of them drovers build what's been called empires. Helped others take the lid off Dodge and Abilene. Mostly, though, the ones come to mind are those we left out on that lonesome prairie." Bones climbed to the wagon seat, wagging his head.

San Tone waved at the mule's tails. "Sure couldn't be no worse than working behind these things."

Bones found the words tumbling out over each other. There was much he wanted to tell this man. "I had a part in a lot of it, but, to tell the truth, I got to the point I was glad when the rails came. These days I'm about half scared of horses. The darn things are always falling down on me, squashing me, or trying to walk on me."

San Tone crawled on the wagon, laughing. "Yuh ain't never seen that day. Yuh stash them bones in piles, do yuh?"

"This one we're going to is the last one. We ought a make it by midafternoon. Probably get them all loaded on the wagon before dark. Tomorrow we'll head for the Crooked Letter I."

"What's that?"

"It's the brand Wade's starting. Told you I ran into a waddie works for him."

"Yuh reckon Wade's gonna be friendly to us?" Concern showed on San Tone's face.

"Shore he'll be friendly. Why wouldn't he?"

San Tone shook his head. "Don't know. Yuh an' him always fought 'bout something. Now, it's twenty years later, after he married your sweetheart and everything. How come yuh to go off to war and leave Sassy, anyway? I thought sure yuh two was fixin' to marry up."

"It was on my mind, but Uncle Phillip called me in. Said he'd fixed it with the commissioners that one of us, Wade or me, could stay home, if he paid the Cause four hundred dollars. Agreed to pay me three hundred if I'd go. He clinched it by saying he'd give me that sawmill I was running for a wedding present after the war. You know me … hell, I jumped at it like one of them catfish you was always catching."

"Your Uncle Phillip pampered that boy something fierce, didn't he?"

"Aw, Wade's all right. He'd just always figure a way to get us to do the sweating. Besides, I never could stay mad at anyone I could whup."

"Reason yuh was mad at me so much?" San Tone laughed.

* * * * *

The next morning, Pete warily cocked his ears, studying Bones' approach. How an ignorant brute read sign that keenly beat all. How did he know a saddle was to chafe him today, instead of yesterday's collar? Bones decided on a flanking move. He stopped and turned to San Tone.

"Tell you what." Bones pointed. "See that peak over to the left, then the other to the right. Them's the Double Mountains. About halfway between them is where Wade and Sassy are supposed to be. We ought to make it in eight or nine hours. Only thing … old Barney here, being the smallest, may have to be led part of the time to stay up with Pete. Me being lighter, I'll ride him, and you can just sit there, nice and cozy on Pete even if I do have to hoof it every once in a while to give Barney a breather."

"No, I'll take the dun … yuh take this old grullo yuh call Pete. I wouldn't feel right, me riding and yuh a-walkin', 'specially since yuh own both of them." San Tone grabbed Barney's bridle and started putting it on. "Can I borrow one of them saddles?"

"Borrow, the devil! I'll rent you that one for ten dollars a month, or sell it to you for thirty."

"It was only twenty-seven dollars before."

"I was in a better mood then, an' you had a choice," Bones said, jumping at Pete, who had laid back an ear and raised a rear hoof.

San Tone handed him a twenty dollar gold piece and allowed laughter to mix with his words. "When we get to the next merchant, I'll even up the seven dollars."

With Pete saddled, Bones stuck his left foot in the stirrup, grabbed reins and saddle horn with his right hand, and Pete's bridle, near the bits, with the left. Jerking hard on the bridle, he managed to get the animal's nose back almost to the point of its shoulder. He swung his right leg over the saddle. Pete humped his back and crow-hopped in a small circle to the left. After three hops, the mule settled down, and Bones looked over to see San Tone smiling broadly from the back of Barney.

Shortly after noon, they crested a rise and looked down on a pool of water surrounded by cattails and salt cedars. A mile past the water and across a plowed field sat a false-fronted general store. Homesteads and scratched fields scattered the landscape for several miles in either direction. Maybe the merchant offered liberal credit or laced his cough medicine with moonshine. Something was afoot. There were too many farm rigs parked around the place for a work day.

Bones never held much truck with those that stole milk from baby calves, but, today, the possibilities offered by that enterprise made his mouth water. "Reckon they got cistern-cooled buttermilk to wash down our ole hard cornbread?"

"Or rock candy," San Tone added.

Bones' head bobbed as they kicked the mules into a trot. Drawing nearer, he saw a group of men in the shade of a wooden-wheeled windmill. One man wore a white shirt, vest, and an apron around his middle. The garter around his arm sleeve said he had to be the merchant.

"Mister, I don't guess you got a crock of buttermilk in that store of yours, do you? Barring that, maybe a bottle of hooch? And ole San Tone, here, has his heart set on hard rock candy." Bones pointed his thumb at his pal while finishing his remarks.

"Don't deal in spirits. Missus probably has milk over at the house." The merchant looked at a boy standing behind him. "Alvin, go see." He motioned Bones to follow him to the store.

San Tone eased himself from his saddle at the side of the building. "I'll wait out here," he said. An old lady dragged a wooden crate beside him and sat. Stepping on the porch, Bones heard her reliving her life story to San Tone in great detail.

He returned to their side a few moments later with a fist full of candy in one hand and a crock jar of buttermilk in the other. He handed the candy to San Tone and removed his hat to the lady. "I'm Bones Malone, ma'am. Me and him keep each other out of trouble. We hail from Mississippi. Can I get you something?"

"Nope. I'm fine. Just call me Granny ... everybody does. These folks here are helping celebrate my birthday. I'm eighty-four tomorrow, providing I make it through the night."

Bones raised the jar to his mouth, tilted it, then wiped at the buttermilk mustache with the back of a sleeve. "Well, I'll say."

San Tone offered the sack to the woman. "Ma'am?"

She shook off the offer and nodded at the crowd of revelers about them. "Was a time a good twelve inch rule was all I needed to handle that bunch. Those I didn't spank the life into, I taught to read and write. Had to take care of both them chores for most. Now a person can't hear themselves think, when they get started a-carrying on." Granny swelled with pride and continued. "They're all good people, though. We're too tough to let this old droughty country best us now we're here. We're proud of what we were in Arkansas before we left Fort Smith, and we're proud of what we done here in Texas these last two years." She nodded at Bones. "Mississippi, you two boys come to see us sometime." She stuck her hand out, and Bones helped her stand. She looked him in the eye and winked. She made her way to the last buggy, and a young woman helped her board. A stern-looking man controlled the horse. "If you're ever back through Welcome, look us up ... everybody knows us."

Bones walked to the nearby merchant. He'd learned the man's name was Merle. Together they watched the buggy drive away.

"Them her kids taking care of her?" Bones asked.

"Nope. Man's her grandson." Merle continued watching the buggy, adding: "You boys want to use it, there's hay in the barn you can throw your blankets on for the night."

Bones handed the buttermilk to San Tone. "Maybe we're not too full to make a couple more miles before dark. We're obliged. But we'll just mosey after we rest a spell. You really call this place Welcome?"

"It's what we decided to put on the church."

* * * * *

Bones jerked from his blankets, wet with sweat. He shook. Dark shadows threatened. Salt cedars—the shadows were salt cedars—around the nearby sump. He lay back on his blanket. His mind attempted to trace the events and images that had awoken him.

The dream seldom varied, but it came more frequently now. It started with a man's image standing with a raised ax while the last of the Confederate Army stepped from a suspension bridge. He was the man. Faces of hundreds of Rebel soldiers passed before him. Marked with fear and defeat, they looked over their shoulders at the Union Army advancing on the bridge's other end.

Forty yards away, Stonewall Jackson stood with raised saber. Bones waited—waited for the order to cut. It never came. One slash of his ax and they would be saved. The general's features registered only pain and helplessness. Always just before Bones woke, he and Jackson wandered aimlessly behind a wagon—a wagon loaded with bloody limbs.

Nothing was clear. He knew he had spent part of a year in the hospital in Memphis, and he had left there with shambles for a memory. God, he was scared. Then he pictured High Pockets' smallest youngster in Erma Lou's strong arms at the grave site. The two-year-old snuggled safely against her mother's breasts, her face showing confusion, but no fear. He had seen someone reach out to touch her, and the child instantly retreated deeper into her mother's folds. Seemed to him, he had never known that kind of security. Shaking, he wished for a drink. Finally sunlight washed him, and he shook himself.

San Tone spit tobacco juice, a coffee cup in his hand. A small fire separated them. San Tone nodded. "How's bacon sound?"

After breakfast they muddied the sump water, bathing. They dried with their old shirts, pulled on clean ones, and rode toward the twin hills rising out of the rolling plains. Pete worked well, and

Bones was refreshed after the sump bath. He shut one eye, raised the other brow, and looked at San Tone. "Seed through me back there about old Pete, didn't you?"

"Boy, I been watching and seeing through yuh ever since yuh had me thinking them tadpoles were baby alligators."

Bones laughed, remembering how round his pal's eyes had become when his alligators learned to hop instead of crawl.

CHAPTER SEVEN

Irene Malone stood on the huge porch of the recently completed main house of the Crooked Letter I. The odor of new pine lumber reached her. The breeze it rode pressed her riding skirt firmly against the front of her legs and sent the material billowing behind her. A flat-brimmed Mexican hat shaded her eyes from an adolescent sun, and morning moisture diluted the dryness of the air. For the past two months she had withstood the racket of new construction. Now she gloried in the result. Being mistress of the largest house west of Fort Worth served as her reward.

To her left, men worked on the framework that would become the crew's bunkhouse. Beyond that a huge barn sat surrounded by corrals of differing sizes. She'd give Wade one thing—no matter what other shortcomings he might have, pinching pennies was not one. Perhaps that accounted for her following him on this fool move to the Texas wastelands. A few months would be enough for him to grow tired of this game of playing cowman. Then it would be back to Galveston, or, this time, maybe New Orleans. He'd called most of the shots on this move. She'd call the next.

Her thirty-nine years had taught her to keep inner thoughts

and emotions contained, but today an excitement dwelt within her that threatened explosion. It seemed a month, but was in reality only yesterday, that Peaches and the herd from Goliad had arrived. It was then that the little straw boss had told Wade of his encounter with Wil Malone. She wanted to laugh and giggle, muss her hair, and dance on the banister of this huge porch. She'd love to see the expression on the men's faces if she did such a thing. If it wasn't for her son, she believed she'd do it. To hell with Wade!

A picture of the swarthy and handsome Wil Malone of prewar High Manor danced in her memory. To think he was here in this godforsaken country. It was almost too much. The past had been such a fairy book time, so long, long ago. Dare she think of the chance to recapture even a momentary fragment of the excitement and grandeur of those glorious days?

She knew he would still find her to his liking. Wade's enthusiasm for her certainly hadn't waned. Men watched her wherever she encountered them. Her figure still reflected back at her, trim and curvaceous. Standing here now, she glimpsed men at the corral sneak a look when Wade and Ruben were out of view.

A tremble coursed through her at her own recklessness. Was she only a tramp? Surely the last twenty years as faithful wife and caring mother had not been just an act, a facade covering an energy that would not be stilled.

OK, there had been the one slip with the captain during the war, but that hadn't been her fault. Everyone at the ball had been drinking, and he had been so persistent. It had no meaning, just a dumb thing that shouldn't have happened.

She walked to the end of the porch. Thank goodness, she at least had possibilities for a change from all this. This barren country had her near hysterics. Wade should know better than to think she could endure this kind of existence.

The young cowboy called Juan rode toward her, leading

Maude. "*Buenos días*, Missus Malone," he mumbled, looking everywhere but her direction.

"*Buenos días*, Juan. That's OK, don't tie her. I'm ready." She stepped to the ground and took Maude's reins.

Juan held the mare's bridle while Sassy mounted, and then rode side-by-side with her to the corral. He smiled shyly once and quickly looked away. She tried desperately to think of something to say, some way to break the ice, but there was nothing. Their worlds were too different.

At the corral, Peaches was speaking to Wade. "I got you. Go north to the Salt Fork, then upriver. Drop off a hundred ever' five miles. Think you're right. Scattered like that they ought to be able to rustle on their own through the worst winter." The cowpuncher removed his hat. "Morning, Missus Malone," he finished.

She nodded, but Wade's words overrode her greeting. "When you're down to where you can handle the rest of the cows without them, send Juan and Jesse on up to Hayrick."

Peaches waved as he moved out, five cowboys following him south toward the herd just coming into view.

Wade looked at Sassy with that deep concern in his eyes. "Hon, why don't you let me send one of the men with you. I keep trying to tell you, it may not be safe riding alone. This ain't San Antonio or Galveston."

"I'll be all right. Just going to be over yonder."

Ruben, their son, came crossing the lot rapidly. His bounce displayed the youth of his filled-out body. It always amazed Sassy that Ruben was now a man.

"Where you off to on this pretty day, Momma?"

"Don't you start on me, too. I'm going to ride over to the nearer of those two mountains. Been curious to see what all this looks like from up there. Want to join me?"

"Naw. Dad wants me to check that fencing crew up at Hayrick. Now that's a hill for you to climb." Ruben mounted. "Mom, if you get off, tie Maude good. Peaches said he saw a black mustang stud, drifting a band of mares this way. He might like to upgrade his herd with a thoroughbred like Maude."

"Yes, Son." She feigned childlike obedience.

The boy was another reason Wade's ranching idea rankled. Ruben wasn't interested in cows. He liked to build things. What would become of him out here? She could see it all now—just another dirty young man on a horse. *God knows West Texas has enough of those*, she thought.

* * * * *

Southwest of the Crooked Letter I, near shadows of the Double Mountains, Bones and San Tone rode across a flood plain. The silted lowland was a half mile wide, its nourishing river fifteen feet of ankle-deep water. Salt cedars separated the two.

Bones nodded at the river, offered a statement. "A branch of the Brazos."

San Tone looked down river. "Is there still Indians in this country?"

"Used to be Kiowa hunting grounds, but they're all gone now. Why?"

"I don't know. I still don't feel right about this trip. Thought I heard noises down that river. Yuh say them Kiowas is all gone?"

"Mostly. Oh, every once in a while a few of the young bucks will sneak off from the territory and come this way, sort of paying their respects to old Lone Wolf."

"Who's Lone Wolf?"

"A Kiowa chief. Half this country's named after him, Lone Wolf this, Lone Wolf that ... bloodthirsty old vinegarroon. Him and Quanah Parker of the Comanches got together and made buffalo hunting pretty scary for a while." Bones gave Pete slack to move forward.

"Saw a man once that had been scalped," San Tone said. "This Lonesome Wolf, do he scalp folks?" He rode Barney to the middle of the water and twisted, holding his hand up for Bones to be still. "I'll swear, I hear sumpthin'."

Bones heard a turtle dove, a crow, and Pete, stomping flat-footed at the water. "Hell, San Tone, I can't sit here for long. This damn Pete's itching to take a bath. What do you hear?"

"Voices from downriver. Maybe Indians … maybe cowboys hollering at cattle."

Bones jerked Pete's head up and spurred him to the other side. "Let's go on down there. Bet it's some of Wade's bunch. Could be old Peaches." After a moment, he heard the voices. Whoever they belonged to worked cattle. He slowed, and San Tone fell in beside him. He pointed at his friend's belt gun. "Your iron loaded?"

"Yuh know darn well it's loaded. Why?"

"Growing cautious … too old for surprises. Old country's pretty raw this far out. Probably only Wade, or some of his men, but let's look them over before we go lollygagging in."

They crossed a wash and stopped in a clump of cedars on a slight rise. Downriver, men pushed a bunch of cattle toward them.

"That's a passel of men for such a small herd," Bones observed.

San Tone leaned slightly forward and spit. He nodded at the cattle crew. "They're working them cattle this way. Why don't we jest let them come to us?"

Bones nodded, pulled his Winchester, and laid it across his saddle. "Good idea. Watch yourself … I don't think that's anybody I know."

Well concealed by the cedars, the knoll offered additional comfort. Since Gettysburg, Bones found high ground preferable in tense times.

The strangers moved closer. A spotted longhorn cow held the lead behind a point man that sat, slouched and a little twisted, watching the stock behind him. Eight riders, all bristling with weapons, pushed the cattle. Fifty yards away, the cow stopped and threw her head up. She sniffed the wind and turned to her followers. A lone rider approached the herd from the left.

The drovers watched the approaching rider, forming a curved line. They moved slowly forward, then stopped thirty yards in front of the knoll.

Bones turned his attention to the approaching rider, and caught his breath. It was Sassy. He glanced at San Tone and saw the recognition on his friend's face. He lifted the reins to ride forward, but stopped upon hearing the point man's voice.

"Morning, ma'am. Nice day for a ride. My name's Emit Rose." He lifted his hat, looked briefly at Sassy, then stood in his stirrups and looked in all directions. He slumped back to the saddle, apparently relaxed. "Tell me, hon, does your name fit you like your seat sits that saddle?" A thatch of brown hair curled from under his tilted hat and stubble smudged his grinning face.

"Mister Rose, perhaps my husband can arrange a proper introduction for us later. We are always anxious to meet new neighbors." Sassy's toss of the head wasn't unlike Maude's chomp of the bit.

The spotted cow turned, and Bones made out Wade's brand.

"This husband of yours, he let you ride around all alone, does he?" Rose asked.

"I don't believe that concerns you, sir," Sassy retorted. She seemed to hesitate, then turned, examining the milling cows behind Rose. She glanced at the other riders.

Blood pounded in Bones' forehead. Sassy always stirred him this way, but one would think she'd have learned a few things in twenty years. She was perky as ever. Didn't the little fool know she played with fire? Those boys didn't have dance cards. They grew up under a different fiddler. They were rough, uncivilized, and woman-hungry. A blind person could see the blamed beeves were probably stolen. That ought to temper her some. Even aggravated, he secretly acknowledged her wild recklessness was part of his attraction to her.

Rose threw a chaps-covered right leg across his horse's neck. He indolently rolled a smoke while admiringly scanning every inch of Sassy's form.

She squared her shoulders. "Mister Rose, can you explain how it is that men I don't know are moving cattle that wear my husband's brand?"

"Fact is, sweetheart, we picked these old strays up for him over near the Buffalo Gap range, by Deep Creek. Guess maybe he lost track of them. Thought he might want to make it worth our while to bring them back. Why don't you an' me just mosey along over by the river and I'll tell you how it all works?"

Bones raised the rifle to his shoulder. He centered the Winchester's front sight inches below Rose's chin. A nudge of his knee put Pete around the brush. San Tone remained hidden with his colt cocked. Bones spoke in a loud voice. "Neighbor, you got so much respect for the man's cows, seems your manners with his wife would be better. I can't abide your mouth. You can eat crow or bite dirt. It's your call."

Rose straightened at Pete's first step. He sat now, slack-jawed, with cigarette dangling, obviously weighing his chances. He stared at the barrel of the Winchester.

The rifle neutered the pistols leathered at the man's hips. They were a lifetime away, Rose's lifetime. The seven that rode with him would make the final difference in any shoot-out. Likely some would see its end. The question Bones counted on keeping them at bay was just who.

San Tone's voice came from behind the cedars, almost friendly. "There's more back here."

Rose blinked. "My apologies, ma'am. Tell your husband we'll call on him later and talk about how to handle the strays." He motioned to the men he rode with. "Bring them on."

A few steps of his sorrel brought Rose directly in front of Bones. He sat at the bottom of the low bluff. Blood flushed beneath the old leather color of his sunburned face. His eyes glowed with anger. "What's your name, old man?"

"Name's Malone ... some call me Bones. You can call me Mister Malone." He nodded in Sassy's direction. "If her man wants them cows, I'll know where to look."

A second rider, the smallest of the lot, pulled to a halt behind Rose. He looked at San Tone, who now sat Barney in full view. "Where'd you get that saddle, boy?"

The scrawny cowpuncher was likely ten years younger than San Tone. Bones figured his use of the word "boy" had just bought all of them a war. Funny, it sounded a lot better to him than "old man."

"I bought it, trash. Do it mean something to yuh?" San Tone's Colt pointed at the ground, held loosely by his hand resting on the saddle horn.

"That's Allen's saddle. How'd you come by it?" The little man fidgeted nervously with his reins.

"Allen ... don't know that name. Buried a ... boy in Sundown City. Might have been him. Somebody said he didn't play smart cards. Might be he lost it b'fore he died. Expect it's time you move out." San Tone motioned with the pistol.

Seeing both Rose and the other rider kick their ponies to a trot brought a sigh of relief to Bones. Sassy came toward them, standing in her stirrups and peering intently into his face.

"Wil, is that you? San Tone, is it y'all?" Her voice conveyed excitement.

Bones spurred Pete down the bluff. He saw recognition confirmed in Sassy's eyes and wanted to grab her. She reached for him.

"Later, Sassy ... we gotta get out of here. Which way's head-quarters?" Behind the drags, the last rider trailed out of sight. "They'll be back. Let's see what that mare's got, and we'll follow you." He hit her horse on the rump with the bridle reins.

The thoroughbred bolted, and Sassy gave it slack. She directed her downriver. After 100 yards they angled left. The thoroughbred widened her lead on the mules.

San Tone twisted, and hollered. "They're coming …!"

"How far to help?" Bones yelled to Sassy.

She pointed. "Over there! Five miles to the ranch house. Oh, Wil, thank goodness you're here!"

CHAPTER EIGHT

Bones turned in the saddle, measuring the five riders giving chase. "San Tone, we got a quarter mile on them. They won't get close to Sassy on that jack rabbit she's riding. Not so sure about these mules … but Pete's moving easy."

San Tone lashed Barney. "The next half mile will tell. We make that … we got a chance. Mules is tough."

Shortly afterward the rustlers turned from the chase. Sassy slowed the mare to a lope, allowing the mules to move alongside. The roof of a huge house appeared beyond the next ridge. A balcony with unpainted balustrade followed, rising above Pete's shuffling ears. Gradually the entire house rose before them.

San Tone was first to speak. "Lordee! Miz Sassy, you and Wade doing it proud, ain't yuh?"

"Oh, yes, San Tone, do you like it? Wil, what do you think?"

What he thought was he'd wasted a lifetime. Wade had all this, and Sassy, too. Against that, he could muster two mules, a wagon, a little money in a bank in Fort Worth, and a few card-cheating friends too scattered to find.

"Shore is big, ain't it?" he said.

Bones allowed his winded mount to walk. With heads bobbing,

the two slowed beside him. For the first time, he relaxed and looked at Sassy.

She differed from his memory only slightly. She had filled out, matured; now a full-figured woman, her beauty remained intact. Faint crow's feet around the corners of her eyes failed to dull their sparkle. Gray had yet to find her red hair. Strange, even with his fickle memory, her image had always remained vivid. At the moment, her face flushed with excitement. She looked good.

"Never figured Wade for a cowman," he said.

She gave him a curious look. "Me neither."

As they approached the yard, Bones recognized Wade standing halfway up a ladder. His cousin added his hand to a narrow-brimmed hat, trying to shade the sun. He retreated to the ground and walked briskly toward them.

"Wade, look who's here! It's Wil and San Tone!" Sassy exclaimed.

Her husband looked bigger than Bones remembered, his face less the shape of a pear, more round. A full sweeping mustache, below his straight nose, shaded the small chin. Wrinkles grew from noticeable puffiness surrounding his eyes. His shoulders slumped, and it looked like he had a little grass belly starting. Still, he gave the appearance of prosperity, like he'd be right at home dining at Old Man Quinley's table.

"Howdy, Cousin." Bones dismounted.

"Wade, how do?" San Tone greeted.

Wade wore a big grin. "Wil, San Tone, we'd 'bout given you both up for dead. Where in the world you been all these years?" They pumped hands.

"Been different places. Met up a couple of days ago at Sundown City. Picked up this stranger between here and Welcome." Bones grinned at Sassy.

Wade waved to a teenage boy to take the animals. "C'mon, let's go to the house so we can talk."

"OK, one thing, though, bunch of old boys lit out after us just before we got here. How many men you got on the place right now?" Bones explained their run-in with the riders, and ended with: "Sassy thought them cows might be y'all's."

Wade stopped and looked in all directions. "You think anyone meaning harm would have the gall to ride right in here?"

"Wade, they're eight of them boogers. If we'd had their guns at Gettysburg, cotton would be seventy-five cents a pound, and the Stars and Bars would fly in Washington. If you're gonna live in this country, you gotta understand that. The law here, right now, is what a man's big enough to make. Them boys will go where they want this side of Abilene, and do what they please. Let's go somewhere and sit in the shade and have that powwow." He grimaced, measuring the walking distance to the house.

San Tone dropped behind as they neared the porch. At the first step, he halted.

Sassy noticed him holding back. "San Tone Jones, don't you do that! You know better than to stand there and act like a darky field hand. You got as much place in this house as anybody. Just forget that colored stuff around here. It wasn't that way at High Manor. It still isn't. Besides, your momma taught me to waltz in the ballroom of the big house. Get on top of them steps before I find a broom and sweep you up there." Sassy waved her arms in mock sweeping motions.

San Tone laughed, and beat Bones up the steps. The men moved to the shade of the east porch. They sat while Sassy went inside. A Mexican maid with just a touch of gray showing in her pulled-back hair brought water and whiskey. Wade referred to her as Sylvia.

He did the honors with the whiskey, but San Tone shook him off and worked on straight water. Bones loaded his pipe and searched for a match. He made the rounds of his pockets twice and started on the third trip, when San Tone tapped his own forehead. Bones reached to his hatband, found a match, and lit up. Wade puffed on a cigar. San Tone whittled a chaw from a plug of tobacco.

The three of them had never been easy together, and now the quiet made Bones itch.

"Sassy looks good," he said, fiddling with the rowel of his left spur. Wade and San Tone both nodded and grinned self-consciously. *They feel the strangeness, too*, he thought.

Wade tossed down his whiskey and trailed it with water. "About these men … you think they were working our cows?"

"They wore your brand. Has Peaches got that bunch of his here yet?"

"Yeah, they come in yesterday. Said y'all ran into each other at Sundown City."

"Well, I 'member he mentioned a bad run over near Deep Creek. Said he lost some there. Bet a pocket watch to a biscuit, them sons of b's started the run just to snake off a few. Use to be a bad bunch holed up over near them hills." He looked at San Tone. "You hear anything about 'em while you was over at Abilene?"

"Come to think, did hear that Rangers had cleaned out a mess of bad 'uns several weeks ago, over southwest of Buffalo Gap. Some shooting took place. Think they said it was the Potts bunch." San Tone paused.

"Potter's gang, that's it!" Bones shouted. "The way that old boy talked, I'd bet my hat, they're gonna try to sell your own cattle back to you. Was I you, I'd keep a sharp look out. Them boys movin' into your country, they won't be room for you both. When I think on it, seems I heard of this Potter in Dodge City. Jack Wilson, ramrod of the Lazy YR, had a run-in with him in 1879. Potter claimed a toll of fifty cents a head for passage through Buffalo Gap. When the smoke cleared, Potter had the herd, and Jack Wilson had six dead men and bad memories."

Wade called to one of the carpenters and motioned him to the porch. "Larry, meet Wil Malone and San Tone Jones. Missus Malone and these men ran into some strangers, four or five miles out, this afternoon. There was trouble, and there may be more. Keep your guns as close as your hammers the next few days. If anyone needs them, let me know, and I'll loan you some rifles." He waved the man away—a little arrogantly, Bones thought.

"Wil, I got four riders working out of headquarters. They'll be in directly … then there's six fencing up near Hayrick. Peaches has five with him, and he'll be back in a couple of days. We got enough to take care of the eight, plus a few more, if we're together. Trouble is we're spread over lots of country."

"How much?" Bones asked.

"Thirty-five miles across and eighty miles northwest to the Cap Rock. Close to two million acres." Wade waved expansively.

San Tone whistled softly.

Bones looked at Wade. "You're gonna need more men. They'll steal you blind."

"Don't you worry about it," Wade said testily.

Bones shrugged and looked at his glass. "Pretty good whiskey."

Sylvia showed them to separate rooms and informed them dinner would be in an hour. Bones washed, then shaved using a small mirror over the washstand. He felt the bed, looked at his dusty trousers, and sat in a stuffed chair. Sleep came quickly.

A light knock woke him. A small, stern-faced Mexican boy stood in the hallway.

"Dinner, señor," the child said, making no move to leave.

Bones moaned and sat upright. He looked steadily at the boy. The child returned the gaze as deadpan as it was given. Bones closed one eye, not taking the other off his visitor. Still, the child stared, showing no trace of emotion. Bones switched eyes and got no reaction. He removed his right boot, took the foot in both hands, and placed his heel behind his right ear. With considerable pain and more effort, he raised his head enough to view the boy while crossing his eyes. Nothing! He gently removed the foot from its awkward position and asked: "Live around here, or ride an elephant?"

"You awake?" the kid asked.

"I'm awake," Bones responded.

The child sprinted a few feet down the hall, and Bones could hear him repeating his dinner announcement to San Tone.

A few minutes later the imp blocked his passage at the foot of the stairs. "I got a guinea hen," he said.

Bones stopped, feigned disbelief, and tried to look serious. "Can she run?"

"Fast," the kid said.

"Bring my roadrunner next time and we'll have a race," Bones replied.

The boy darted for the kitchen.

Wade sat, drinking coffee, at the head of a long table. Bones counted eighteen chairs. He took the second one down from Wade's right. San Tone sat opposite him. Maybe Sassy would sit next to him.

Taking a closer look at the table, he realized it had come from High Manor. "See you got Granddaddy's table," he said, knowing Wade had misread his meaning from the look on his face. It honestly pleased him that a bit of High Manor still existed.

"Nobody else to take care of it. I've had to drag it all over Texas. Tried my best to find out what happened to you."

"It's good, Wade. Glad you got it. I came through Grand Gulf after the war … may have been near a year after. They told me Granddaddy and Azalea were dead. Uncle Phillip, too. Place all burned up and grown over. Don't know how …" He was going to say more, but was suddenly out of spit. Seemed it had gathered up around his eyeballs. "Either of you know how it all happened?" Bones finished, looking from one to the other.

"Daddy got the fever, second year of the war," Wade answered. "We brought him and Momma to Vicksburg. He never was strong after that. Then, during the siege, they both passed." Wade lifted a spoon and stirred his coffee, adding: "Judge Austin told me about Granddaddy, but you were there, weren't you, San Tone?"

"Uh-huh. Me an' Mother was with him. Y'all was gone, and the colored had all left the quarters and scattered no tellin' where. Mother had a pot of hominy boilin' when they come. Six Yanks, with a sergeant in charge … they thought your granddaddy had gold buried. You know how that old story went around. I started up from the barn and seen them. They drug him out of the house, hittin' and cussin' him. One pulled out this big old pistol and held it to his head. The shotgun was in the barn … I ran for it. Just as I come out, the pistol fired. It liked to blowed y'alls Granddaddy's head plum off. I shot one, and they took off a-horseback. Mother come from behind the kitchen, runnin' toward your granddaddy. One of them Yanks tried to grab her and carry her off. He came up from behind and grabbed her from his horse. She fought, and he weren't as strong as he thought. He had her half on by this time and was runnin' full out. He dropped her. When I got to her … her head hung funny. She was dead. I buried them … him in y'alls plot … her down 'cross the fence with her daddy and momma. I locked the big house and started walkin' to Vicksburg that evenin'." San Tone looked out the window, sighed, then laced his fingers together on the edge of the table and inspected his thumbnails.

Bones fiddled with his pipe, stuck it in his mouth, and then put it back in his pocket. Wade stood, faced the window, and clasped his hands behind his back.

CHAPTER NINE

Musical notes drifted from the doorway. "*La-de-da*," Sassy said. She curtsied. She raised her head and extended her arms. "How do I look?"

Bones almost knocked his chair over getting to his feet. San Tone and Wade stood.

"You look jest perfect, hon," Wade said. "She does, don't she, boys?"

"She do that," San Tone said.

Bones wanted to store her picture, run back the clock to a time when the world had meaning. Her hair was a bit shorter, but her skin seemed as soft and smooth as in her youth. There might be a bit of stiffness around the mouth, but the years had treated her gently.

Afterwards, sitting in comfortable chairs, childhood memories washed over Bones. Laughter greeted incidents kindled from old memories. He relaxed.

Sassy idly fanned, Wade poured a whiskey, and San Tone broke the momentary silence.

"They call Wil 'Bones' out here."

"Why's that?" Wade asked.

Bones jerked his gaze from Sassy back to his cousin. "Make a business, hauling the darned things. 'Course, my lean beauty may have more to do with it."

"What do you mean business?" Wade smiled. "I thought you hauled freight."

"Do, but it's mostly buffalo bones."

"Heard there's money in them," Wade said.

"Was ... think it's about petered out in this country."

Sassy frowned. "I don't care. I don't like it. Bones sounds common. You're Wil Malone."

"Don't matter what they call you, long as they holler it loud at dinner time." Bones winked at Wade.

"Well, Bones ... Wil ... whichever one you're going by, I need some barbed wire hauled. How many wagons you got?"

"Just the one." Bones could tell by his cousin's voice they were talking serious commerce now.

"Tell you what ... you get another wagon, and I'll keep you busy the next three months, hauling wire from Sundown City out here."

Here it comes, Bones thought, *the old Wade Malone skin game. You get the game, and he the skin.* "What you paying?"

"Seventy cents a roll. You ought to haul at least twenty rolls to a load. Thing is ... you got to have two wagons. I've got a train-car load due in Sundown City tomorrow, and we're gonna start a second crew fencing next week. You sleep on it, an' let me know in the morning."

"Tell you what," Bones announced. "For ninety cents a roll from the depot to that barn out yonder, you can sleep on it. Be extra, you want to go on north. Some of that country's pretty rough on a wagon between here and town. Besides, I ain't real fond of barbed wire, anyhow. Let me know at breakfast."

San Tone looked from one to the other, then started a shrug that grew to a yawn and a stretch. "I'm turning in," he said.

Bones stood, too, then, limping slightly, headed for the stairs.

He could feel Sassy's eyes on him as Wade asked: "Are you all right, Wil? Seem a little gimpy."

"No. It's OK. I'm pretty limber, except when I'm stiff. What you say, San Tone? After breakfast you and Wade want a little game of jump the broom?" He stopped and turned at the door. "You ain't told us about the boy. Where's he?"

"Oh, my goodness!" Sassy exclaimed. "Wade, we ought to be ashamed. Wil, don't tell him we were this long in telling you. He's the finest thing ever happened to us." She pointed to a picture hanging on the wall.

Bones moved, positioning himself before the handsome young man's likeness. The serious face of the boy looked over a top hat held in his left hand.

Wade raised his voice. "That was made a year and a half ago. He's a day's ride from here. Up at Hayrick with a fencing crew. His mother spoils him, but he's a good boy."

Bones leaned closer. "Looks like Granddaddy, don't he?"

"He does," Wade agreed.

* * * * *

The smell of coffee pulled Bones to Sylvia's kitchen the next morning. A pot steamed on the stove. She had her hands in biscuit dough up to her wrists, and the odor of yeast filled the room.

"Can I beat you out of a cup?" he asked.

"Help yourself." She tilted her head toward cups in the pantry.

He found a large mug and poured the coffee. Looking at her, his mind imagined an earlier time, before the wisps of gray had found her hair, and he could see her in her youth with all the young hombres tossing there hats in a ring and stomping ants. Suddenly he realized where he'd seen those smoldering eyes.

"That little boy yours?" he asked.

"My youngest. Sugar's on the table."

"Bet you're proud." He added one spoon of sugar, a bonus he seldom enjoyed. "Your man about?"

"He's with Juan and Peaches."

"Juan's a good man. We rid together … two trips. They don't come no better'n old Peaches, neither. I'm obliged for the cup." Coffee in hand, he backed out of the kitchen, then tiptoed upstairs. He found the balcony and sat in a straight-backed chair. The balustrade railing provided a resting spot for the cup. He filled and lit his pipe, then picked up the coffee, admiring the colors of the sunrise.

Near the barn, four cowhands worked at catching their day's mounts. The tallest caught his own nag, then those of the other three. The man's skill tossing a lariat, underhanded and up, was a tonic to Bones' senses. Often he had used the trick himself. He admired the cowboy's mastery. Some smart horseman had learned that horses dodge better down than up and it didn't take long for word to get around. With the loop coming from the ground up, the ponies lost a certain edge. The Crooked Letter I had good hands in these four.

His gaze moved to sweep the surrounding mesquite and grass-covered slopes. Moments later he noticed the cowboys mounting and moving out. Out to the west, he saw a wolf—or was it a coyote?—cross a rise a half mile away. From the confident way the animal traveled, he decided it was a wolf. A glint of sunlight from a hill beyond winked. Reflected light meant people. He stood and removed his pipe. Tapping the bowl against the palm of his hand, he dropped the ashes over the railing and watched the hillside intently. Then he saw them. Riders coming—more than a few.

He hollered as he ran to his room. "San Tone, Wade, get up … get your guns!" He hopped on one foot as he pulled on his second boot, then he strapped on his pistol. His rifle leaned near the door. He checked both guns and added a sixth shell to the empty chamber he kept under the Remington's hammer.

San Tone met him in the hall, fully clothed, calm. They went down the stairs two at a time. Wade and Sassy stood near the front door, looking out. A frightened look covered Sassy's face.

"There's riders coming," Bones repeated. "Unless you're expecting company, I'm betting it's that bunch we saw yesterday. Wade, they're probably gonna demand a finder's fee for bringing your own cows back. We ain't got much time. They're coming in pretty fast."

Wade ran to the porch and hollered at the carpenters standing near the bunkhouse, waiting for breakfast. "Boys, come here!"

Four men started casually, then, seeing their boss continue to wave, sprinted to the porch.

"Riders coming. They may be cow thieves. Get your guns. Three of you get in the barn, two in the loft, and one under the shed. If shooting starts, you're on your own. They try to enter the house or barn, or even take cover, shoot hell out of them. Alfred, I want you in the big house, back there by the kitchen."

Bones was surprised at the firmness in Wade's voice. His cousin fit longer stirrups than he'd thought. Of course, he had always been good at giving orders.

"Wade," Bones said, "this is your party. I'm gonna be on the balcony … that is, if they ride here to the front. I'll follow your lead, but, whatever the hell you do, don't let none of them within fifteen yards of the house. Where you gonna be, San Tone?" Bones asked.

"Here, with Wade, in the living room. Is there a shotgun around somewheres?"

Wade pointed. "Through that door. There's buckshot in the right desk drawer."

Bones counted nine riders about a third of a mile away. "Wade, them boys will try and take us if they think we're weak. Most likely, though, they're checking us out for later devilment. Why don't we take some of them long guns from the rack in there and poke them out the windows. Make them think we got an army."

San Tone headed for the gun rack. Bones started for the stairs, but stopped when he felt Sassy's hand on his arm.

She took a deep breath, then said almost in a whisper: "Be

careful." Her face blanched at the same time that Bones realized Wade had noted that she held his arm. She dropped her hand, and he bounded for the stairs. At the doorway to the balcony, he stopped and chambered a shell into the rifle.

The riders continued their approach at a lope, but slower now and strung abreast in a ragged line. His view swung to the loft opening and the rifle barrel showing there. Good, a show of force was what they wanted.

They were forty yards away when Wade yelled from the house: "That's close enough!"

A man near the middle of the line raised his hand and pulled his horse to a stop. The group halted. It came to Bones that he'd seen the dandy leading this bunch before. It was the hombre that had been using crutches in Sundown City when he was picked up at the train. A walking stick swung from his saddle strings. Most of the others had been with the herd yesterday.

The lead man spoke and edged forward with one other rider. "My name's Virgil Potter, and I got a bone to pick with Mister Wade Malone."

"That's me." Wade's voice came from inside the house. "What's on your mind?"

"Like to look a man in the face when I talk to him," Potter said. "Think my boys got off on the wrong foot yesterday. I come back with them today, to explain things."

Below, Bones heard steps cross the porch and knew Wade now stood at its front. *Dumb*, he thought. He would have to make himself visible to give them something more to think about. He felt good about his position, though. The floor of the balcony would shield him if he had to back away from their guns. He walked to the railing.

Emit Rose and the little man who had been so interested in San Tone's saddle yesterday both glared when he stepped into view. The small man wore a clean, white-and-red-striped shirt.

"Say your piece," Wade said.

"On our way back from San Antonio, week before last," Potter said, "we come across these cows with that Crooked Letter I on them. It was near Buffalo Gap. They was lank, tongues a-hanging out like maybe they made a run. Folks in Abilene told me they were yours, and what you're doing out here. We gathered them for you."

"How much?" Wade asked.

Potter oozed confidence. "They been a right smart of trouble. They're a sour bunch. Fifteen dollars a head delivered, there"—he pointed—"to them lots. Hate to ask anything, 'cause we all got to help each other, but we got ourselves to look after." He had trouble playing his role seriously, sitting there, fighting back a smile, with both hands near the handles of his Colts.

Surely Wade knew this parley was only an excuse to size up their firepower. If they saw weakness, these men would kill them all, then add what cattle they could to those they'd already stolen and move the whole outfit to Mexico. Still, it surprised him they'd try the sham with odds this even. Seven well-armed men with cover were a handful for nine on horseback.

"I tell you what you can do, Mister Potter …"

"Just a minute, Wade," Bones interrupted. He hollered loud enough for the men in the barn to hear. "Everybody, hold on … I'm going to shoot in the air. Wade we're forgetting our manners. Think we ought to get them four hands back here so Mister Potter can meet them." He pointed the rifle skyward and fired three evenly spaced shots, then levered in another shell, and said: "Sorry, Wade, you was saying …"

Wade's voice came, loud and strong. "Potter, you can go to hell. Before I pay you a nickel, we'll swing ever' damn one of you. If I have to hire a hundred riders and call out the army, we'll clean you out. There's fifteen guns pointing at you. You've bit off more here than you can chew. Now get!"

No one moved. Maybe there was hope.

"Old man"—the small rustler with the striped shirt pointed at Bones—"we got word last night of how you gunned down Allen in Sundown. He was my kid brother. I'm calling you out for the yellar dog you are. Step away from that rifle, and let's settle this even … just you and me." The rustler shook with anger, one hand resting on the butt of his pistol.

Bones tilted the barrel, bringing it to bear on the man's nose. "Why would I do that? You're the one dressed to die, peppermint stripes and all. You either ride out now, or these boys can carry you."

The red of anger disappeared from the little man's face and was replaced with the pale paste of fear. He started to speak, but made only a gasping noise.

The sound of running horses reached Bones and he knew the signal had worked. He held the cards, but in a way felt trapped having to play this man's game. Revulsion at what could happen here swept over him. Surely this fool would back off, but he'd seen grief, big talk, and bluff send more than one to an early grave.

The rasp of panic filled Rose's voice as he warned the small man: "No, Luther, this ain't the time."

Bones saw Luther's shoulder jerk to pull his pistol. Immediately he squeezed the trigger of his own gun. Luther's head wrenched backward. The barrel of the Winchester kicked up, blocking Bone's vision, while its blast rang out a slashing pain through his ears.

Luther's body fell from the blood-splattered saddle over the rump of the shying horse, and Rose's hand started for his pistol, but stopped at the sound of the rifle lever. Staring at Bones' gun, he raised his hands and nimbly dismounted with only his boot touching rigging. He squatted beside his fallen companion and straightened with the dead man in his arms. He looked up at Bones. "His name was Luther. Remember it. I'm the third brother. We gonna meet again. Remember … the name's Emit Rose."

"I know your name, Emit, an' I know you'll be the luckiest man alive, if you get Luther's body a-horseback and outta here."

Emit lifted Luther's body in front of his own saddle, mounted, and wheeled his horse. He didn't look back as he spurred to a dead run.

A frown had replaced Potter's grin. "What you think, Walt?" he asked hoarsely of the rider beside him.

"Too many guns, Virg," the hard-faced rider said. "There's some in the house and more in the barn. There'll be a better time."

Potter, followed by the remaining riders, pulled his horse's reins and backed away. After several steps, they all spun, leaving in a high lope.

Bones watched the riderless horse trailing the disappearing rustlers. So that was Virgil Potter's bunch. He noticed his cup still held coffee. *Probably still warm*, he thought. Killing was a quick business. He'd never get used to it. He shuddered. From the look on Emit's face, he knew he had one more Rose to take care of. He silently cursed himself for letting tomorrow's trouble ride off.

Wade stood at the foot of the stairs with San Tone, as Bones descended.

"Damn you, Wil, why'd you put this on me?" Wade said irritably. "I had them ready to leave, an' you start shooting. Now you'll have to kill Emit, and, could be, the rest of them will take it out on us."

"You did good today, Wade. San Tone, meet my cousin, old Fifteen-Gun Malone." Bones walked toward the door. "Which way you say that boy of yours was? Think while I'm alive, I'll go meet him."

CHAPTER TEN

Wade posted guards after the riders faded from view, then joined Bones and San Tone for breakfast.

Bones cleaned his plate with the last of a biscuit, then studied his cousin. "You still perturbed with me?"

"Way things were, don't guess you could have done much different," Wade admitted. "Been thinking about that wire, and I'm gonna let you haul it, if you want."

Bones studied him over the rim of his coffee cup. "Ninety cents a roll?"

"If you get a second wagon."

"There's another one in Sundown. How about it, San Tone? Want to start freighting with me fifty-fifty?"

"Hauling bob wire?" San Tone studied both men. "I dunno … haul wire, keep y'all from fightin' … worry with an old team … seems layin' track would be more peaceful. If we do, yuh promise I ain't gonna have to break up no fights?"

"Like as not," Bones said, "but I don't think either one of us is dangerous no more. C'mon what do you say, San Tone? Beats working for wages." He didn't mention it would also give them a chance to see Sassy again.

"I'll think on it," San Tone said.

"Wade, about that bunch out there a while ago, and them cows of yours," Bones said, "… ain't my business, but I'll lend you a hand if you want to try to get your beef back. Now's the time, while they got the herd gathered. You don't … they'll likely move them plum out of the state. You take them back, then, once they're out to graze, it'll make it tougher for anyone to sneak them off your range. We can do that, then start hauling your wire. It's your call."

"How would we find where they are, and how many of us would it take?" Wade asked.

Bones lit his pipe. "There's a place out by the Cap Rock, near your west line I expect. Bet they're heading for it. You get out there, toward Yellow House Draw, there's places to hide an army, plus water. That's all a bad man needs. They had them cows angling in that direction when Sassy and us met them yesterday."

Wade downed a sausage in one bite. "Damn me, you're right. While they got them gathered, they're just a couple of days from being gone for good. You want to meet Ruben. How's this sound? I'll draw you directions to Hayrick. That's where he is. You get him and his crew of six. I'll take one of these here … Owen, I guess … and catch up with Peaches an' his five. That'll leave three cowboys and four carpenters here to protect Sassy and the place. The nine of you cut across and join us on the Salt Fork. We'll give Potter a lesson."

Bones looked at San Tone. "What d'you think?"

San Tone tilted his head at Wade. "What yuh payin' us while we're chasin' around all over the country?"

Wade got a pained expression. "I'm paying these punchers thirty dollars a month and keep … I guess the same for y'all."

San Tone scratched the back of his neck. "A even dollar and two bits a day sounds better. Another thing, if we gonna be runnin' around after gunmen an' stuff, you better give us sumpthin' to ride besides Wil's old team. It was nip an' tuck gettin' to this ranch yesterday."

Sounded like San Tone had joined the business. Bones warmed

inside, rejoicing that a bit of Mississippi sun had moved to Texas.

"That remuda behind the barn's got fifty head. Take your pick," Wade said.

San Tone interrupted. "Wade, Potter probably set somebody to watch this place. Might be a good idea to wait till after dark to ease out of here."

Bones slapped San Tone's back while getting up from the table. He retrieved his hat from a peg by the door, then turned his attention to Wade. "Ain't he something? Darned if he ain't right. Be safer for Sassy and the bunch here, too. Won't hurt our odds for surprise none, either."

"I'll tell Sylvia to fix your grub," Wade said.

"Come on, San Tone, let's go check them broomtails. Ought to be one or two out there I can fit a rocking chair on."

Wade motioned Bones aside. "Go ahead, San Tone, he'll catch up." Wade tilted his chair, letting his heel dangle on a lower rail, while Bones packed his pipe.

"Wil, I know how it was with you and Sassy before the war, and I know you ain't out here 'cause of me. Know, too, what you're offering for this manhunt's mostly for her. But I want you to know I'm obliged."

"Aw, hell, that was all a long time ago," Bones declared. "I'd come to see you once ever' twenty years if you'd married Polly Bingham." He smiled, wondering how he'd come up with her name. The youngest Bingham girl's homeliness had been almost as scary as her persistence. "Besides, we was all just kids then."

"Sassy maybe, not you an' me. We was as full grown as we'll ever be … nearer thirty than our teens. Another thing … what Daddy did about you going to war … I didn't know about that till years later. The judge told me after Daddy passed. You may have always been the doer, but I want you to know, I'll fight against you or with you, but I never intended you to fight *for* me."

"Ain't never give no thought about you running from a fight,"

Bones responded. He surprised himself by putting a hand on Wade's shoulder and squeezing. "I'm just glad you weren't in it."

Wade looked intently at him.

"See you in a few days along the Salt Fork," Bones said.

As Bones walked away from the house, he realized for the first time that, although he had never cared much for him, the man was his nearest living relative. He had always been a puzzle. If Wade ever laughed out loud, Bones couldn't remember it. As boys, he and San Tone attracted dirt like dogs gathered fleas. Wade shined. His cousin had avoided chores, other kids, and adventure. In Wade's mind, God made the big river to flood, hide water moccasins, and drown little boys. According to him, lightning killed, blinded, and turned some people pigeon-toed. In his world, frogs gave you warts, sweat caused measles, and, if you got a nosebleed on Sunday, a mad dog would bite you on Tuesday. He liked grown-ups and things in their proper places. He and Wade might be kin, but they were opposites. He felt a smile cross his face. Opposite about all but Sassy.

* * * * *

They selected their horses, then rested. In the afternoon, San Tone's snoring woke Bones from his nap. They lay on the porch. He crawled to a rocker and pulled himself aboard. He lit his pipe, and Sylvia completed his happiness by bringing him coffee.

A few minutes later Sassy joined him. She asked: "Now that you've had a chance to look around … what do you think of our spread?"

"Far as headquarters goes, it's a dandy. I'll know more about the range after this trip." The joints of the rocker grated slightly as he shifted.

Sassy's perfume smelled good, and strangely he thought of Estella. *Bones*, he thought, *you're a peculiar piece of work. No matter what woman you're with, you're always thinking of another.* Looking at Sassy came easily, and he realized he was staring.

She returned his look. "You've never married?"

"No, no," he blurted. "Wanted to ever' time I saw a woman dressed for town. They was always too fast, though." He smiled.

"Are you happy, Wil?"

"Happy …?" He realized he'd never connected that possibility with himself. "Never thought of it, one way or the other," he replied honestly. He reached with a toe to kick the snoring San Tone.

Sassy shook her head and made a face. "Have you seen Bonnie Glen?"

"Who?"

"Bonnie Glen, our thoroughbred stud."

"Naw, where's he?"

"C'mon," she said. "I'll show you. Let San Tone enjoy his nap."

He followed beside her toward the barn. His gimpy ankle warmed slowly, and he limped in spite of himself.

"How'd you do that?" She looked at his ankle.

"Fell off a rock at a place called Little Round Top in Pennsylvania."

"Fell?"

"Well, actually an old Billy Yank shot me. I was running along, jumping from one big old rock to another when he winged me. Broke the ankle when I fell."

"Bless your heart. Wil, I worried so. We got little news, and what we got was so bad. It must have been terrible for you."

He said nothing. How could he tell her death would have been a welcome relief to her letter? That, after the shot she sent through his heart, Yankee bullets held no fear.

"*Aw*, it wasn't so bad as all that."

She stepped into the shadows of the cavernous barn, and led him down a long hallway. The scent of fresh hay, leather, and horse droppings mingled with that of new lumber. Tack rooms, stalls, and hayracks bordered one wall, and rays of light filtered through cracks in the barn's walls. Near the far end, the heads of horses protruded from stalls. One whinnied softly, another chewed at a chain across its gate, and Sassy jerked from the thunderous boom of a kick against the barn's wall.

The horse that kicked was a bloodred bay, preened and pampered till he shined. He was stud of the walk, and his muscles rippled as he stood, straight and proud. If an inch, he measured sixteen and a half hands. His neck arched down into withers connecting a short, well-defined back ending in muscled hips. He was the last word in horseflesh and, to Bones, the least interesting thing in the barn.

Damn thoroughbreds, he thought in disgust. He liked his horses a little tougher, and with a lot more sense. "Where did you say he's from?" he asked, trying to show interest.

"His daddy came from Scotland. We had him sent down from Nashville." She talked of the horse, but tilted her head to look at Bones.

He realized the thoroughbred had failed to hold her total interest.

Sassy reached and took both his hands. "Wil, I'm so sorry. Have you forgiven me? When I told you I'd wait, I planned to. Then you were gone, and I had no one, nothing. I loved you so much I thought my life would end. Wade was so kind." She stopped, waited. "Say something."

"What you want me to say? Good for y'all! Sure, Wade was kind ... so kind you were in a family way before my dust settled down the road. I got used to it a long time ago. You fell in love with old Wade. That's it."

"No." She put her arms around him, her head on his chest. "That's not the way it was. I'm telling you, I did love you. I still do. My love didn't change. I was just ... just weak." She raised her face to be kissed. She pressed against him.

Nervously he looked around the barn. He had wished for this

for twenty years. The feel of her body, the smell of her. This was it. No more dreaming. Life wasn't over. Too bad about Wade. So … why was he just standing here? Why didn't he kiss her? *Damn it, Bones! Don't spoil this.* He pushed her back. "Guess I forgave you for loving Wade. Now I gotta think on it … you not loving him. Gal, you know you're all I wanted. You've rid in front of my mind for twenty years. Hell, they thought I was crazy in the war, trying to get killed so I wouldn't have to think of you and Wade." From the corner of his eye, he caught a glimpse of the stud's bared teeth shooting toward his left shoulder. His ears were flattened, and his eyes held a devil's glare.

The horse's timing was good. Bones found action a relief from the words that stuck in his throat. He doubled his fist and jabbed in a reflex motion at the animal's soft nostrils. The sharp edges of the horse's wide-spread teeth collided with his fist, and pain coursed through his hand and arm. Blood spurted from his knuckles. He wind-milled his hand in the air, then bent and stuck it between his knees. Blood flowed.

"Oh, shit-fire-damn!" he cursed. He yanked his hat off and threw it against the wall of the barn.

Sassy untied his neckerchief and wrapped it around the hand. "C'mon, let's go wash that."

He couldn't tell if he heard fire or blizzard in her voice. He picked up his hat and followed her out. Served him right. Whatever she was thinking … what kind of fool went into a dark barn with a pretty girl and ended up picking a fight with an 1,100 pound horse?

CHAPTER ELEVEN

Bones and San Tone rode from the night shadows of the barn. Two days of hard riding would put them in Ruben's company at the Hayrick Mountain camp. A cloth bandage wrapped Bones' hand causing him to reflect on the dangers of mixing cold-blooded women and hot-blooded horses.

San Tone yawned. "What happened in that barn yesterday?"

Bones looked down at the bandage. He looked again at his partner. Did he know, or was he just fishing? "Told you, their fancy stud tried to bite me."

"Must have been more than that. Sassy looked like she's ready to throw a conniption fit."

"San Tone, if I ever figure it out, we'll talk." The man was right—Sassy had been fit to be tied. Bones' feelings were scattered. Sassy had shuffled the deck and everything was out of order. Over the past twenty years, he'd thought he had it put together, found a slot for every piece. The way he worked it, Wade and Sassy fit together, and he and the rest of the flotsam in the world wrestled for what was left. Now, why wasn't it simple? She wanted him. God knew he wanted her. Why wasn't that enough? Of course, Wade's being a part of it messed it up, but that shouldn't stop him. It was hard, though, to figure how he could be so darned lovable in her presence, and so easily forgotten when he rode over the hill.

The next day, the blue haze of Hayrick greeted them in early afternoon. It rose over heat waves from multicolored banks of clay and yellowing short grass prairies. Its peak aimed at drifting clouds.

San Tone lifted his hat and wiped sweat with the back of a sleeve. He pointed. "Yonder's the start of the fence."

Light reflected from new wire. Minutes later, they stopped to examine the stoutly braced end post abutting a mesa drop-off. Five strands of shining wire stretched railroad-straight, rising and falling with the lay of the land as far as the eye could see.

They rode closer. The horses approached the fence, ears erect, eyes widened, and their nostrils flaring in the presence of the unnatural invader. With spur and tight rein, Bones forced his mount to quit sidestepping and get close enough for him to lean over and pluck the top strand.

The wire *twanged* like a bow, and San Tone's horse shied, almost unseating him. He got the gelding under control, anger flashing from his eyes. "Wil, why don't yuh just keep your hands in them pockets. Yuh're a threat to yuhself and everybody around."

For a while they rode in silence beside the fence, dodging washouts and cedar thickets. When San Tone sulked, it sometimes took hours to work him back to friendly. He reminded Bones of Charley in that regard. At other times, San Tone's mad could be cut off before it got a full head of steam. Bones estimated the posts were spaced thirteen feet apart.

San Tone said: "Twelve."

Bones wondered aloud if the braces for a section of the fence that mounted a particular slope were on the proper side.

His friend responded: "Yup."

"It's an embarrassment to mankind. That's what it is," Bones said. "Damn fence's just a shame on us all."

"Just some old posts and wire, that's what it is. What yuh talkin' about?"

"If the good Lord had wanted it where things weren't free to move about, he'd have put a fence along here."

"I guess we'd have been born with that railroad already to El Paso, too. Is that what yuh think?"

At least San Tone was talking to him again. "No, that's different. That's what they call progress. It helps people go places. See this damn fence just stops things from going anywhere. What if I wanted over there on the other side? What about that?"

"Guess you'd have to ask Wade to put in a gate."

"See what I mean. It would embarrass me to have to ask a man if I could go somewheres … 'specially Wade."

* * * * *

Shortly before sundown, smoke announced the location of the fencing crew's camp. They stopped 100 yards away.

"Can we come in? We're friendly!" San Tone hollered.

Bones saw several men moving about the camp. "We're kin," he added.

"C'mon in," a voice invited.

He recognized Ruben from the picture they had showed him. From beneath his Stetson, tangled hair showed above clear gray eyes. He stood straight, looking intently as they rode toward camp. His face, like his father's, was wide at the cheekbones and narrowed to a small chin. His lips were fuller than most of the Malone clan's. He was brown as old leather and trying to look stern.

"Ruben, we just come from your daddy's. I'm Wil Malone. They said we would find you up here." Bones leaned and stuck out his hand. "This old boy the sun's worked on is San Tone Jones, known at High Manor as Catfish."

Ruben shook their hands. "Momma's told me about y'all … she

and Daddy both. They about give up on you till Peaches come in a couple days ago. Y'all light. We got coffee."

Bones had never seen a more tattered group of six than this crew. Their clothing had stitches over the stitches and patches two and three layers thick. Scratches and ripped hide showed on every exposed part. When they moved to shake hands, elbows and knees played hide-and-seek through torn clothing.

"Y'all look like you forgot to dodge a passel of bobcats. Think this fencing business is gonna catch hold?" Bones asked, trying not to let his amusement at their wretched appearance show.

"Not with me, it ain't," said a heavyset cowpuncher named Perk. "Most aggravating damn stuff I ever saw. If it ain't wrapping 'round your legs and wrestling with you, it's slapping blood out of your face."

"I've seed rattlesnakes uncoil a lot friendlier than it do," added another. "Getting a little tired of dancing with them posts, too, but Cecil says they getting prettier ever' day we're out here."

"Yeah, we caught him trying to slip one under his blankets, the other night," said a redheaded hand.

Cecil smiled and his one remaining tooth made his ragged clothes less noticeable. A round of laughter at his expense ended the fencing talk. Bones and San Tone tethered their horses and returned to find the crew eating. Cecil, apparently having drawn cooking detail, dished stew onto their plates.

Bones sat, cross-legged, near the wheel of a wagon, his plate in his lap. "You make up this stew did you, Cecil?"

"What's wrong with it?" Cecil asked.

"Not a darn thing. Best I ever had. I was just gonna say, if you can stand to leave your cedar post here, you can bach with me anytime."

Cecil gave Bones a hard look, top to bottom. Bones knew he was in trouble, but there was no way out.

"Believe the post is fancier." Cecil's face remained deadpan, his good tooth hidden.

Well, he'd asked for it. Nothing to do but take it.

San Tone slapped his knee, and the crew guffawed. Ruben chuckled, and Bones grinned. Life was a hoot. Hell, that one line was worth the ride out.

Evening settled around the fencing crew, and shadows tempered the smoldering heat in the arroyo. After supper all the hands, except Ruben, reached for tobacco. The heavy smell of dry cedar mingled with that of burning mesquite from the campfire. Talk resumed.

The crew, tired of their own inbred stories, hungered for news from beyond the Crooked Letter I. Bones brought them up to date on happenings in Sundown City. He finished with: "Ruben, you don't mind, come an' help me move those ponies to a fresh graze. San Tone, you want to come with us?"

Away from the others, he relayed to Ruben all that happened at headquarters and what he knew, or had heard, of Potter's gang. He included Wade's request that they meet with Peaches on the Salt Fork, and ended with: "Ruben, I didn't want to come riding in here hollering orders an' making a general ass of myself, just wanted to tell you what's going on. Did I forget anything, San Tone?"

"Guess, that covers it." San Tone looked at Ruben. "Son, I ain't sure about nobody else, but if your granddaddy was doing it, these boys would know they had a choice about going into this."

The look on Ruben's face had grown more serious with each word the two men spoke. "You sure everybody's OK back there?"

"Were when we left," Bones said.

"These are good solid men, San Tone. I'll see they understand the danger, and, sure, they'll have their choice. I'm obliged to y'all for thinking of us," Ruben said.

Bones blurted: "Thinking of you! It ain't that way. We need your guns." Doubts caused by his nephew's youth crossed his mind.

Ruben hesitated, then made a motion with his thumb toward

camp. "Y'all go on back ... I'll be right there and tell them."

They finished moving the horses and headed for the fire. Looking over his shoulder, Bones saw Ruben back in the shadows. Looked like the boy was fooling with his tether stake, while kneeling on the ground. After a few minutes, Ruben joined them.

Ruben poured coffee. "Men, Dad sent word he wants us to meet him and Peaches, soon as we can get there, over on the Salt Fork. There's rustler trouble, and we got some cows to get back. A bunch, led by a man named Potter ... least eight to twelve of them ... are the ones that stole them. Ain't none of you got to go, if you don't want. You'll still have a job, no matter what, but we want all of you we can get. 'Course, there may be shooting. Your lives likely gonna be at risk. On the other hand, you may have to take the life of one of them. We need to know now, I guess."

The redheaded cowpuncher poked at the fire. "Boy, just tell us what you want. We may not be much when it comes to fencing ... ain't studied it like you have ... but when I ride for an outfit, I see it through."

Cecil looked from one to the other of the remaining men. "Reckon we'll all ride, Ruben. We stayed after you sicced that bob wire on us, don't reckon rustlers is gonna run us off."

"Thanks, men," Ruben said. "We'll move out at daylight. We'll just leave the wagon here."

The men asked questions about Potter's bunch. San Tone surprised Bones by telling in detail what weapons each of the bandits had been carrying at their visit to the ranch house. After satisfying their curiosity, the crew brushed debris from sleeping spots and rolled out bedding.

Ruben sat alone by the fire, reading a book by the light of the last flames. Bones squatted beside him and filled his pipe. He plucked a live coal from the edge of the fire and juggled it into the air. With the pipe in his left hand, he caught the ember in its bowl. He licked the fingers of his right hand, and said: "Don't use 'baccy, do you?"

"No, 'course I tried it, but me and it didn't get along." Ruben put the book down and smiled.

"What you reading?"

"The Bible. Try to read a little of it 'most every day."

"Well, I'll swun!" Bones studied the matter a moment. "That's good. Well, I declare. You the first I met since Stonewall Jackson, excepting a parson or two, does that. Now, there was one for you ... Jackson, that is. Bravest and fightingest man I ever saw. And he could 'cite verse and scripture for near ever'thing that went on. You're in good company, boy. Try to live by the Good Book, do you?"

"Wil, I been busting to talk to somebody about that. Look's like you're it."

"Fire both barrels. That's what kin's for."

"Are you religious?" Ruben asked.

"Naw, I ain't. Guess I'm what you might call a first-class sinner. Ain't that I want to be, it's just ... things tempt me bad. You know, like the feeling I get around women, and I can't hardly turn down a good drink to save my hide. Naw, ain't nobody ever put that brand on me. I know some of the word. See, San Tone and me was raised pretty much by his mother. She read the Bible to us near ever' day, till we got big enough to stay hid out on her. I believe in good, it's just I got so much of the other that works on me."

Ruben held up a hand to stop him, and Bones felt embarrassed at his own eagerness for confession.

"Well, it's this way," Ruben began. "I made a decision about six months ago that I wanted to be a minister of God's word. I ain't really told nobody ... just me and God ... but I think these boys here got a pretty good idea of where I'm headed."

"Well, they shore ain't nothing wrong with that. No, siree! So that's what you were doing at that stake."

"What I got to talk about is ... like I said ... I ain't told Momma or Daddy. I don't think they'll mind, but I guess I'm just not sure enough about it. Anyhow, on this trip, getting our cows back, Wil,

I can't shoot a human being over a cow. You reckon folks are going to think I'm a coward?"

Bones' pipe was suddenly cold. Working on it offered a good cover while he tried to think what to say. He got the pipe going at the same time he realized he hated serious talk. And thinking on it, this was about as serious as it got. "Ruben, I've knowed a lot of young men to worry about courage. Spent a smart deal of time thinking on it myself. Seems to me, what you're wrestling with is between you and him up there, and what the rest of us think don't matter a … don't matter. I've learned the last two days that I really don't know your folks. I know what I 'member, but we've lived almost more time apart than together. Think they gonna be like me … just proud as a new pup that one of the Malones amounts to somethin'."

"Wil, it's scary, and I need any advice you got."

"Advice, boy, you don't need none from me. You just follow the one you're tracking. This old world needs your kind, and you want my thoughts on it … I ain't met many brave enough to tell me what you just did." Bones stuck his hand out, and they shook. "You rest good, and don't pay no heed to nobody except that Book."

Bones made his bed and rested with his head on his saddle. Near him, he heard the rustling sounds of Ruben preparing for sleep. He reviewed their conversation in his mind, and it carried him back in thought to his old leader. "Ruben," he said, "old Jackson was partial to lemons … you got a taste for sour fruit?"

"Barely ripe plums and tart lemons, you bet."

CHAPTER TWELVE

Bones' smoke-colored mount's ears kept rhythm with his gait, one swishing forward, then the other. His interest seemed more on the long early morning shadow of Hayrick Mountain to his rear than the trail ahead. He twisted in the saddle. True to his range birth, the grullo seized the opportunity and ducked his head and exploded into action. Bones rode the sunfishing outlaw into submission, then took a deep breath and waited for Ruben and San Tone to ride up.

"Dad's told me what bronc riders you two were, when y'all were young."

"What you mean ... *was* young?" Bones said. San Tone smiled. Ruben grinned. "I didn't mean ..."

"That's all right, Ruben, you mark us right," San Tone said. "And your daddy was right, too. We could get the job done with green horses. You ride the rough ones?"

"Not much, but Peaches told me about this mustang stud he'd been seeing, and I got a look at him a couple of days ago. He's a hoss. Had six mares in his band."

Bones had seen mustang fever before, and it was easy to see the boy had been bitten hard. He couldn't blame him. As much as he feared the damned things, every once in a while the old urge to test himself against the worst tempted him. It had gotten a lot easier to push it back, though. "You thinking about having a go at him?" he asked.

"I'd sure like to, but not sure what I'd do with him, then." Ruben looked from one to the other.

"Where'd y'all live when you growed up?" Bones asked, surprised at the boy's lack of experience.

"Galveston, mostly," Ruben answered.

"I bet they're men in this crew could give you a hand with him," Bones said.

* * * * *

The next day, they joined forces with Wade and his crew. Peaches and his men were with them.

Owen, one of Wade's men, led Pete and Barney. Wade motioned in their direction. "We brought your friends along. If things go well, you can cut across to your wagon and not have to go back to the house."

Bones detected no hint of anger in Wade's voice. Still, San Tone had sensed something had happened in the barn. He knew Wade had seen Sassy grab his arm when the Potter's group rode in. It was easy to see his cousin didn't want him around headquarters. Could be that the happy Wade Malone family had a spat after he and San Tone rode out.

The following day Bones pulled near Wade and asked: "Reckon we ought to put about three riders in front to act as scouts? Be embarrassing, were that bunch of boys to start shooting and us not knowing they were around. I'd go, but it'd be better was it somebody could hear thunder."

Wade waved a rider forward. "Owen, if you don't mind, take a lead out about a half mile yonder. San Tone, you wanna take the right over there. Ruben, you might get out about a mile straight ahead."

"Sure," Ruben said, and turned to ride out. Like the others, the boy had a saddle gun swinging beneath his right leg. Unlike the rest, he carried no pistol.

"Here, just a minute," his father said. "I got an' extra handgun in this saddlebag. You better take it."

Ruben twisted in his saddle, looked first at Bones, then his father. "That's all right, Dad. I don't need it."

Wade fastened the bag he'd just loosened and, as his son rode off, he looked at Bones with puzzlement.

"Did y'all talk last night?" Bones asked.

"Naw, what about?"

"Nothing, he's just proud of that fence, thought he might have told you about it. It's good." He guessed he wasn't the only Malone that stayed away from serious talk.

Later, Owen rode back with the other scouts and halted the group. He motioned over his shoulder. "Boss, some of them boys are holed up with your beef in a box cañon up where that creek feeds the river. The cañon is about three miles up and a natural holding spot."

Bones studied the group sitting their horses in a loose-reined circle. Not the hardened killers he had with him at times during the war, still they were cowhide tough. They slouched in the saddle, some with a leg draped in front of their saddle horn across their mount's necks. Others sat hipshot, their weight on one stirrup. None showed signs of nerves.

Wade looked at Owen. "You know the lay of the land. What do you think's our best bet?"

Owen lifted his hat and ran his fingers through sweated hair. He looked around the group. "There's three of them. They're gonna be hard to get close to in daylight. 'Course, ain't no place they can run, once we get in the opening of that cañon. It's shaped like an old mule shoe, narrow through the front, but deep. That opening on this end is only a couple of hundred yards wide. Good place to hold cattle, bad place to escape from."

"Sounds like a hell of a place for grown men to let themselves get trapped," Bones said. He looked at Wade. "Your call."

"We wait here till after midnight, then ride up close. Three men will stay with the horses, and the rest of us will sneak in afoot. At daylight, we jump them." Wade looked at Bones, then swept the rest with a glance. "Anything else?"

Owen answered: "I'm good with it." The rest of the crew nodded ascent.

"Boys, it'll be Perk and Shorty who'll stay with the horses. Wil, you, San Tone, and Peaches' men, move in from their left, me and the rest will take the right. Ruben you and the fencing crew ride up the middle."

Bones tried to keep his voice soothing, like talking to a green colt. "If you're dead set on it, we'll do her that way, but I'd ruther not. We split up in the dark, we're liable to end up shooting one another. A crossfire is fine, set up right, but, if it ain't, somebody can sure catch a stray slug. Think we'd be best served with just a single front."

He thought he saw impatience in his cousin's eyes, but Wade kept it out of his voice. "OK, that's probably best. We'll do it your way."

The men dismounted. Bones squatted and gnawed on jerky while watching Ruben and his father in deep conversation a short way from the group. They talked earnestly, then Wade put his arm around his son's shoulders and squeezed.

Returning to the group, Wade walked to Bones. "Said he told you a couple of days ago." He looked back at his son and scratched his chin. "Ain't he a card?"

"Know you're proud," Bones said, then added: "Hell, I'm proud. Guess I'm gonna have to clean up my old dirty mouth, though."

Wade stopped and raised his voice. "Men, there's another thing I want you to know … Ruben's made a decision about his life. Wants to follow the teachings of the Bible. What that means, for the moment, is he wants no part of gun play. 'Course, I honor that decision. You all know I generally push him harder than the rest. Just thought you was entitled." He looked at his son proudly. "Cecil, you lead the center line. Ruben will help Perk and Shorty."

Ruben looked embarrassed, and Bones wondered why Wade hadn't given the boy a chance to talk. He heard some of the men near Ruben joshing him, but could only pick up parts of it. Something about "sprinkling" or "dunking," and another accused him of only wanting out of fencing. It was easy to see that, to a man, this bunch thought a lot of Ruben Malone.

Later, they sneaked into position and spent the last half hour of darkness sixty yards from the three sleeping rustlers. The sky lightened. Daylight touched them. Along the creek, outlines of trees and the forms of three horses took shape. One held its head high, looking in their direction. Its ears were erect. Shooting light was a couple of minutes away. A startled pony could cause a lot of trouble.

At that moment, one of the animals snorted and wheeled with both front hoofs off the ground. It awkwardly lunged away as fast as its hobbles permitted.

The figure of a man's upper body rose from the dark shadows along the ground. He, like the horses, looked in their direction. His voice rang loud with fear, yelling "Wake up, we got company!" then he dropped from view.

Wade hollered: "Don't none of you move, we got you surrounded!"

Bones worried that his cousin's words rang a little weak for this job.

Three guns barked from the creek. Darkness hid the shooters, but not the muzzle flashes. Rifles blasted from either side of Bones, and still he had no target. A horse squealed and fell thrashing to the ground. It struggled to rise, only to fall back into the shadows. He caught a glimpse of a man running among the trees, going up the creek. Too quickly Bones snapped a shot and knew he missed. San Tone and Owen raced after the man.

Bones ran toward the thieves' camp, beside Wade. He shifted the rifle to his left hand and drew his pistol. A figure fired at him from behind a tree, and Bones dived to the ground.

Wade fired, and the man stepped into the open, almost went down, then righted himself and pointed his weapon at Wade. From his knees, Bones brought his pistol to bear on the man's chest. He squeezed the trigger. The gun bucked just as Peaches fired pointblank at the same outlaw. Their target hit the ground and, unbelievably, bounced up, running from Peaches. Cecil stood a short distance away, calmly sighting at the running man. The outlaw dragged one leg. He carried his pistol in his left hand, his other arm flapped, broken. The fencers' cook pulled the trigger. The outlaw buckled in the middle and fell. His face rooted the ground. Sight of Cecil's ragged tooth spoke to the improved quality of light.

Bones heard someone shout: "Don't kill me!" Several yards to his left, four cowboys disarmed one of the rustlers. San Tone and Owen walked behind the third outlaw. It was the man named Lathum Ferrell he had played cards with in Sundown City.

"You're a long way from the Santa Fe Trail, ain't you, Ferrell?" he said.

Then the sound of running horses reached them. As instructed, following the sound of gunfire, Ruben and his two companions raced in quickly.

Ruben brought his horse to a tail-sitting stop. He looked pale in the morning light, as his eyes searched the group. He sank comfortably back to the seat of the saddle when he saw his father.

San Tone examined the rustler Cecil had shot.

"How many times he hit?" one of the cowboys asked.

San Tone held up five fingers.

Owen looked at Wade and pointed with his thumb over his shoulder at the two prisoners. "What do you want to do with them, Mister Malone?"

Wade scanned the area. "That cottonwood, over there, looks about right for the job."

Owen went to his saddle and slipped the loop from his rope. He tossed the lariat to the redheaded cowpuncher from Hayrick. "Fix a noose on both ends, Pete. I'll cut it for two when you're through."

San Tone rubbed his neck. "Wade, you gonna hang 'em?"

It seemed a cruel way to die to Bones. Oh, he'd seen it often enough. It was a tough business. He'd never known of thieves stealing again after it happened.

"Ruben, Peaches, y'all take about half of these men with you an' drag that cañon for them cows," Wade ordered. "We'll scatter them along the river on the way back. Rest of us got a hanging to tend to."

Juan and Jesse were first on their horses. It seemed they'd rather limit their ropes to cow work. Four additional men joined them. Ruben twisted and looked back. Bones thought he read uncertainty in the boy's face.

Cecil led two horses up to the outlaws, and another cowboy took pigging strings and started to tie their hands behind their backs.

"Tie them hands in front, to their belt. Give them a little more than a foot of slack. They're gonna need to hold onto the horn to stand on that saddle," Owen said.

"Gonna have them stand?" Wade asked, the glint in his eye getting even brighter.

"Old Ferrell, if that's his name, has a little leg on him. If that rope stretched or the limb bent, he'd be kicking dirt. Yeah, we better get them up in the air some," Owen answered.

The fresh morning air turned root-cellar stale, and the whistle of bobwhites took on a haunting, unreal sound that made Bones uneasy. He had no qualms about passing out cold hard range justice to men. But the ashen-faced youngest prisoner was no older than Ruben.

"Owen, how you gonna keep them standing on a horse long

enough to get a noose around their necks?" Wade asked.

"Cowboy can't stand on a still horse, ought to be hung," Owen grunted.

Cecil and another hand prodded the condemned men into mounting up, then led their horses beneath the tree. It had a large limb almost parallel to and fifteen feet above the ground.

"Wil, move another of them saddle horses over here for Owen to stand on," Wade said.

"You're doing OK … don't think I want a part of this," Bones said.

Perk brought the extra horse, and Wade glared at Bones. Owen and Wade sat on either side of the two rustlers. The gathered Crooked Letter I men looked curiously from Wade to Owen. Few met the eyes of the two men with tied hands.

Ferrell stared sullenly straight ahead. "You think I'm gonna stand on a horse for my own hanging, you can rot in hell." He threw himself from his horse and tried to run, but Cecil, Perk, and Pete grabbed him. He twisted left and right, fighting desperately. They dragged him back to his horse and tossed him into his saddle.

Pete picked up the rope he'd dropped and handed it to Owen, who cut it in half, and then stood on his saddle beneath the chosen limb. He tossed the ends of the ropes over the limb and tied them so the noose of each was just below his shoulder.

"Pete, take them branding irons from back of that saddle yonder, and put them in the coals of that fire," Wade ordered, his eyes burning with a strange shine. "I'm gonna need them in a minute."

My God! thought Bones. *He's enjoying this.*

Owen stepped from the saddle on his mount onto the hips of Ferrell's horse. With one hand he held onto the rope just above the hangman's noose, and with the other he grabbed Ferrell's collar.

Wade shifted his position to one in front of the rustlers. Neither of the doomed men looked at the men around them. The younger condemned man's eyes rolled. He wet his lips. Tears streamed down his face. His mouth opened, then closed. He finally forced out the words. "I ain't done nothing to y'all. Just punched them cows from Abilene. Let me go, and you'll never see me no more."

"You punched the wrong cows, boy," Wade said.

Bones had changed his mind—Wade might be tough enough to run this spread.

"I'll see you in hell!" Ferrell's voice was shrill.

Wade's face darkened, and muscles twitched in his jaw. "Stand up there!" he shouted at Ferrell.

"Don't do it," the youngest one begged.

Wade pulled his pistol. "Get your feet in that saddle and stand. You want to die with both feet intact, do it now." He cocked and pointed the pistol at Ferrell's boot.

The kid held his saddle horn with bound hands and put one foot at a time in the seat. Bending over, he stood, then straightened. Owen put the noose around his neck.

Ferrell gritted his teeth, then spat in Wade's face. Wade fired. The outlaw's foot jerked as the bullet passed through and on into the left back leg of his horse. The pony's scream mixed with that of Ferrell. Both horse and rider fell in a heap. Owen jumped clear and landed standing up. The kid's horse bolted and left its hapless rider swinging by the neck.

Anger flashed from Owen's eyes. He glared at his boss. He threw both hands upward in disgust, and stalked off.

The young rustler's eyes bulged, and a strange rasping sound came from his open mouth. His body gyrated in wild convulsions, before all movement stopped.

Ferrell's horse spun on three legs, six feet from the crumpled form of its rider. Perk pulled his pistol and shot the animal between the eyes. It somersaulted backward, thrashed a moment before lying still.

Wade tossed the loop end of his lariat to Cecil. "Put it around his neck." He nodded to indicate the half-conscious Ferrell. "Gimme your rope," he said to Pete. He tied the ends of the two ropes together, threw one end over the cottonwood limb, and, riding to the dangling end, dallied it around his saddle horn. He turned his mount to face the downed man at the other end of the rope and backed the cow pony away. Ferrell slid like a sack across the ground, gaining consciousness just as the ever-tightening rope lifted him skyward. Wade stopped his horse when Ferrell's twisting body was about the same height as the kid's.

"Some of you men come and tie off this rope," he said.

Three men took the rope and tied it without looking at the thrashing object at its other end. Bones stared at the bulging eyes and distorted faces of the two men and turned away. A cowboy to his left ran three steps, bent over, and a geyser of vomit erupted.

Wade sat his horse ramrod straight, eight feet in front of the dead men. His face no longer showed emotion, but his eyes still shone. When Ferrell's kicking stopped, he rode forward, and, grasping the outlaw's collar, ripped open his shirt front, exposing the rustler's chest. Next he did the same with the kid. He reined his mount to the fire, and Perk handed him the two hot branding irons.

He rode slowly back to the dangling bodies. First, he pressed the "S" iron onto the chest of each. Next he took the straight iron that formed the "I" in the bared flesh of each outlaw.

The hot iron hissed as smoke curled. The odor of burned flesh made Bones gag, and sent the hapless cowpuncher with the weak stomach to his horse and away from the group.

Bones pushed his chestnut to Wade's side. "What the hell … don't you think that's enough?"

"Stay out of it! We ain't kids no more. There ain't nobody to say … 'Let Wil do it.' *I'm* doing this." Wade wiped at a trickle of spittle that had wet his chin and glared at Bones. Then he turned back to the bodies. "Potter can look on this for a spell. Thinks he can run roughshod over me, does he!" Wade's whine had a childlike quality.

Bones' cousin had always been prone to tantrums, but he'd never seen him this wild. He reined the horse to the creek, dismounted, and washed his face. San Tone joined him. Kneeling, Bones slung water from his hands and looked at his friend. "Ain't that the goddamnest thing you ever seen?"

San Tone shook his head.

CHAPTER THIRTEEN

Virgil Potter's back muscles stretched drum tight as he loped from the Crooked Letter I headquarters. From the moment he wheeled his buckskin and turned to ride away, he had expected a bullet between his shoulders. Distance now lessened his fear and changed it to smoldering anger.

The youngest Rose brother—now a face-down corpse stretched across a saddle—had joined them only recently. The older brother, Emit, wouldn't have made that mistake. He would have waited and settled the score at a time of his own choosing. He should have talked to Emit when the boys brought in word about Allen. Should have told him to keep the younger brother in line.

Potter spoke from the corner of his mouth to the man beside him. "Walt, that makes three times that old goat's pulled down on some of us, and he's still kicking."

"We'll get him, Virg … him and that other smart-talking, high-handed son of a bitch that owns the outfit. We'll just do it in our own sweet time."

Potter slouched sideways in the saddle and pulled his sore foot from the stirrup. Walt Hanover was always calm. He stood out like a broken horse in a herd of broncos. Counting the hands with the herd, there were eleven now. The death of the kid left them a little light for the Cap Rock country. It was dangerous. A man needed a full deck when he rode such a land. His bunch had been well set up, totaling nineteen at Buffalo Gap. That was before Rangers had hit them. You needed a lot of men to take over a herd.

Potter reached into a saddlebag, and pulled out a bottle. "Hold up, boys." He raised his voice, looking at the last of the Rose brothers. "Emit, it ain't over. We'll see they pay."

Emit viciously spurred his horse to Potter's side and took the offered bottle. "You damn right, it ain't over." Hours out of sight of the Crooked Letter I's guns, he and the others had joined the men left in charge of the stolen cows.

Potter raised and circled his arm. "Gather 'em up, and let's move."

* * * * *

Two days later, they herded the cattle into a box cañon, and Potter assigned three men to remain with the herd until his return. He would come back for them after finding a buyer among the wastelands of the plains. But first he'd scout the dim trails of the Llano Estacado looking for traders with short memories and a need for cheap cattle. Years earlier, he had drifted the herds into the High Plains country until he found a buyer. But that was the old days, before Goodnight had settled along the Canadian and the railroad had passed Abilene. Now, you never knew which side of the law stirred dust in this country. He would tuck these cattle away until he found a buyer. If that didn't work, he'd move them west to New Mexico or north to Tascosa. It paid to read a man's sign before letting him see another's marks on the hides you pushed.

* * * * *

After an overnight rest at Yellow House Draw, Potter, Walt, and three companions sat their horses on a slight knoll. A few yards away a wagon zigzagged its way toward them, dodging greasewood and salt bush. A walking plow was lashed to its sideboards. A man rode a horse a few feet ahead.

Potter removed his hat and swung a leg over the saddle horn. He rubbed a hand through his damp forelocks. As the wagon came closer, he smiled. The mounted man stopped and sat his horse. Potter nodded toward the traveler. His voice purred softly: "Mister, I gotta admit you got me buffaloed."

The woman handling the team pulled to a halt. The dry *squeak* of the stilled wheels quieted, leaving only the sound of hurrying wind and the team rattling harness while fighting flies.

The traveler folded his hands on his saddle horn. "How's that?"

"Westward wagons is common, but heading East is strange."

The man coughed and spit. "I been West. Wasted four years. Now, we're headed back to Jack County." Tobacco stained the corners of the farmer's mouth.

A barefoot boy in his early teens sat a bay mare on the offside of the wagon. He carried no gun. The bay had a large collar scald on her neck and limped slightly on her right forehoof. A girl, four or five years of age, sat on a milk cow tied to the back of the wagon. She wore britches rolled to her knees.

Something about the farmer's wife seemed out of place with this bunch. She was too clean—too young—to fit here. A closer look under her bonnet showed tired features that belied the earlier thought. She held the mule's reins tightly and peeked from beneath her headgear, measuring each man.

"Whereabouts out West you been?" Potter asked while wondering why any fool would wander around the country with a beauty like that?

"Lincoln County, New Mexico. Went out there with two hundred head of cattle, a hundred and sixty acres of valley land to farm, and seed money." The farmer dropped his reins and stepped from his horse. "A Dutchman named Knapp ended up with the land and an old cowman from Texas ended up with the cattle. Too many that tangled with them two disappeared. So I lit a shuck." He pointed at his family, starting with the boy. "Zeb and Sarah, and the gal back there's Alice. I'm Sam Matlock. You boys light if you want. We're stopping here for the night." Sam turned his back and reached for a dipper tied to a barrel in front of the plow.

Potter shifted his hat on his head. Three shots rang out. Sam Matlock's knees buckled and his face slammed into the water keg. His back turned to blood.

The little girl never made a sound. She sailed through the air, then fell in a heap at the end of a trail of her own blood.

The third shot knocked the boy out of sight, beyond the mare. The animal pivoted around the boy's body as his arm convulsively jerked on the rein. The kid hit the ground and bounded up. Potter jerked frantically for his pistol. Jumping to the seat beside his mother, the youngster pushed her to one side. He whirled to enter the wagon. Walt's revolver roared again and the wagon's canvas bulged from the weight of the small body inside the wagon falling against it. The rippling bulge down the covering's length telegraphed the boy's journey. The kid came out the tailgate feet first, but his legs failed to support him. From his knees, he tilted a shotgun's barrel toward Potter. Walt's third bullet hit him between the eyes. He toppled sideways, his legs jerking, then he lay still.

The woman vaulted from the wagon and knelt beside the little girl. She lifted the child's face to her breasts and rocked back and forth. Her bonnet tilted skyward, and she moaned: "Oh, God!" Lowering the child back to the ground, she stood, ignoring the pointed pistols. She walked to the wagon. She lifted a stuffed doll from inside it. A polka-dotted red dress covered it. She clasped it tightly and walked slowly toward the distant horizon on the other side of the wagon. Segments of a faint lullaby trailed behind her.

Potter eyed the large opening of the shotgun's barrel and shuddered. "Sid, kick that scatter-gun away from the kid's hand." Seeing the task accomplished, he holstered his pistol and nodded at the rope of another rider. He twitched a thumb in the woman's direction. "Ira, wrap her up, and get her ready to travel."

Walt replaced spent shells in his six-gun, studying the boy's twisted body. "Just a hank of hair and a slip of rawhide, but he were a tough little knot, weren't he?"

"More trouble than this whole outfit's worth." Potter forced anger into his voice, hoping to hide any sounds of nervousness. He released the gunny sack tied to his saddle and tossed it to one of the riders. "Sack up any trinkets, fire the wagon, and bring the stock with you." He motioned for Walt to follow, then rode past Ira and the man helping overpower the hard-fighting Sarah. "Turn her loose, boys. She's no good to us, touched in the head is what she is."

Released, the woman gathered herself, retrieved the doll. She took halting steps, moving away. She removed her bonnet, placed the doll inside, and held it near her breast. She cradled the bonnet, rocking it side to side while walking away.

Potter freed his .45. He winked at Walt and pointed a finger at the back of his own head to indicate the location of the woman's bun. He cocked the pistol as it arched downward. Its roar rolled across the prairie. The bun exploded. The woman collapsed forward into the prairie sod. Its grass smothered her last breath.

* * * * *

Bones' head hurt. Other Crooked Letter I riders rode silently, scattered about the prairie. He wanted to nudge the gelding into a lope and put distance between him and the rustlers' hanging site. He tried to think about something other than death. Nearby, the queasy cowpuncher that had emptied his stomach a moment earlier stared at his horse's mane. He rode to the cowboy's side.

"Bet you're Sylvia's old man," he greeted.

The man forced a brave smile and nodded. "Angel."

Bones extended his hand. "Met your littlest one. He's a pistol, ain't he?"

At mention of the youngster the man's eyes brightened and some of the stiffness left his face. He offered no reply.

Good, thought Bones, *we're a pair*. "Mind if I poke along b'side you a ways?"

Angel shook his head. They rode side-by-side.

Beyond the cañon's opening and out of the herd's path, the riders stopped. Cecil built a fire and made coffee.

An hour and a half later, Ruben and Peaches pushed the cows through the gap, and all hands took up positions alongside the herd. There had been little talk during the wait.

Bones and San Tone rode near Ruben. From the boy's tight-lipped look, it was a good bet he'd stopped by the hanging tree.

Bones asked: "How'd y'all get them wires so tight?"

"We got wire tighteners … stretchers they're called. They're just ropes with pulleys wound through them. We got two. Sometimes, if you got a wagon, but no stretchers, you can just pry up a wheel, and tie onto the spoke with your wire. The wheel rim gives you good leverage."

"B'darn, where'd you learn about it?" Bones swatted at a mosquito.

"Went to Denison on the train and stayed with the hardware man there. Folks that make wire sent a man to explain it. He talked two days."

"Denison, Texas?"

"Uh-huh. You see, thing about fences is, they got to be straight and tight." Politeness rather than a desire to discuss stringing wire appeared to force Ruben's answers. His coloring was a little blanched and he cast frequent glances toward his father.

"I guess so," Bones agreed. "Where you gonna learn about Bibling?"

"San Antonio's got a good place."

"Good, you go there."

San Tone closed from the other side and squinted at the herd through a veil of dust.

Ruben looked back toward the box cañon. He put his hand out and touched Bones' arm. "Wil, those men hanging back there ... it's a bad thing, but I know in this country it's done. Did Dad give them a chance to make their peace with God? You know ... pray."

Bones looked at San Tone's blank expression, then back to Ruben and the yearning in the boy's face. He stood in his stirrups and feigned an interest in a sore-footed cow. He slumped back into the seat of the saddle. "He did. Your daddy asked them right out, had they any last words."

"That's good. I know the whole thing must have been hard for him to witness."

Bones nodded. "I 'spect so."

Ruben squirmed. "Wil, just one more thing, and I'll let you go."

"You go right ahead and ask. I don't mind."

"Somebody desecrated them bodies, put a brand on them. Who did that?"

Bones found his pipe and put it in his mouth. What could he say? From the other side of Ruben, he heard San Tone's whisper.

"I did that, boy. Your daddy tried to stop me. I know it ain't right, but I guess ... just the old savage nigga took holt of me."

"San Tone, you?" Ruben gaped.

"I know it was wrong. Maybe yuh'd say a word for me?"

Ruben's eyes misted over. He spurred and reined his horse away from them. His voice came from over his shoulder. "At noon, I'll say a word at noon."

Bones stared after Ruben. He shook his head and put his cold pipe back in his pocket. "He talks to them others, he's gonna know we lied."

San Tone tugged at his hat. "Damn Wade."

A couple of hours later with the sun straight above and shadows shrinking beneath the overhangs of rocky outcroppings, the men allowed the cattle to mill near a creek. The crew gathered for an hour's rest on a low hill. They loosened their cinches and dropped where they found thorn-free ground. Ruben was last to join the group. In his hand was a Bible. He dismounted, removed his hat, and placed it on his saddle horn.

"Any of you men want to, you can join me," he said.

Everyone stood, bared his head, and, to a man, made efforts to blend into the barren landscape by sidling behind his neighbor.

Ruben's voice was firm. "Father, today we were forced, by the evil of others, to perform an act that goes against the way we want to lead our lives. Men were killed ... two hanged. If we sinned, forgive us. One among us committed a particularly barbaric act of paganism. Forgive San Tone, Father. His instincts are different from ours and his training in your righteous ways is limited, otherwise, he would never have put that hot iron to those not yet cold bodies. In your son's name we pray. Amen."

A look of disbelief reflected from every tilted face as it lifted upward. Most of the men stared at Ruben. Some glanced toward Wade.

Bones read confusion on his cousin's face, saw it change to understanding, then shame. "Now ..." Bones started to speak, then San Tone's grip tightened on his arm.

San Tone's "Amen" cut through the shimmering heat. The men's eyes moved from Ruben to lock on the big man as he turned to squat in the shade of his horse.

* * * * *

The next day, after a noon rest, Wade stepped into his stirrup. Over his shoulder, he asked Bones to join him. They rode a short distance from camp. No words had passed between them since the hanging.

"Wil, after y'all left for Hayrick, Sassy told me you tried to bring up the past 'tween you and her, out at the barn. Said you was a gentleman about it, otherwise I'd be wanting satisfaction."

"You'd be wanting what? Satisfaction! I'll accommodate you, but you won't find it satisfying. You'll find me as bitter to swallow now as a while back. Man, you got anything else on your mind, just say it damn easy." Bones shifted his weight in the saddle to his right foot and twisted sideways to face Wade. His pulse throbbed in front of his ear. He fought for control.

Wade tensed, appeared ready to run. He jerked his horse to a stop. "Wil, no need getting hot. I want you to know you're still welcome, 'cause your kin, but hell. Let's face it, we never did get along. Just do your hauling, like any other hand, and stay away from Sassy when you're at headquarters. Your mules are nearby. No need going back if you want to cut out for your wagon."

Bones' impulse was to shoot the arrogant son of a bitch where he sat, but there was San Tone and Ruben sitting their horses and looking at them. Hell, he'd made enough orphans, no need making another in his own family. He started to speak and realized, if he started, he'd likely go beyond words.

He turned to San Tone and raised his voice. "Let's take our mules and head for the wagon." He pointed. "It's yonder some-where."

Wade handed a paper to San Tone. "Here, take this letter to Hank Oliver at the depot in Sundown City. He'll unlock that car for you, so you can get to the wire. Y'all keep them horses with you, if you like. On back of that letter's a map to the place near

Welcome where Ruben's gonna be fencing. Just bring these first two loads to him."

The fool didn't even know how hard he pushed. Bones looked at San Tone. "You still want to haul wire?"

"Might's well," said San Tone.

A few minutes later they had Pete and Barney in tow behind their horses. Almost a mile separated them from Wade and the crew, and Bones had found a new cuss word for every foot they covered. Cussing came hard for him. Ordinarily he got a soapy taste in his mouth if he used Azalea's forbidden language, but in times of real anger he made a pretty good hand at it. Today the words came easily.

"If yuh got so mad at him, why yuh gonna work for him?" San Tone asked.

"I was too mad to quit. 'Fraid I'd shoot him," Bones answered honestly. "Didn't want to leave Ruben without a pa. Some things don't never change, do they?"

* * * * *

They found the wagon the second day. With the mules in harness, San Tone wiggled on the seat beside him. His friend was cheering up. "Where'd yuh get these mules?" San Tone asked around the chaw in his cheek.

"Abilene. A feller from Palo Pinto had 'em. Said they belonged to his brother-in-law. His story was that the man died from a bad 'pendix."

"They're coming along, ain't they?"

"Barney is … don't know if I'll ever be proud of Pete. Bought him as green broke, but he's greener than broke. Feller's sister must have been partial to drummers or store clerks. Sure no cowboy had his hands on these two."

San Tone spit. "Pete'll be fine, once he learns a little."

"Yeah, an' once this desert gets rain we'll have cantaloupe for dinner." Bones searched the sky as though looking for rain clouds. No showers came, but during the late afternoon of the next day they sighted the river at Sundown City.

CHAPTER FOURTEEN

Bones left San Tone studying his likeness in a trickle of Lone Wolf Creek water. Earlier he had soothed the larceny that periodically gathered in his innards by wetting his cargo of bones from a deeper pool. The penalty A. J. docked him at the boneyard for the weight of the moisture cheapened his labor, but the scheme appealed to his inner spirit.

"Going down to that burg and see a man about a dog!" he hollered over his shoulder to San Tone. "Who knows, maybe somebody down there that remembers me. Want to go?"

"Go ahead. I'll mosey in later."

Quinley's National Bank was closed for the day, and shadows from the false front of the Sea Breeze lay across the street. The three ponies fighting flies at the saloon's hitch rack said Charley had customers.

Piles of buffalo bones glared a dirty white near the depot. A buggy stirred dust in the street, while three male dogs vied for the number two spot in a line of four. Maurice's wheelbarrow and shovel sat deserted near the front of the General Mercantile Store. Bones concluded civilized people were home for supper.

He found an empty lot at Rosco's and pulled the saddle and

bridle from the chestnut. He gave the horse a half gallon of oats and noticed Quinley's wagon was still for sale at the yard.

Across the street, curtains blew in the open windows of Sally's Good 'Un Café. He crossed and entered. Erma Lou Pinella stood behind the counter. Her sad face broke into a big smile. He stood, hat in hand, just inside the door, letting his eyes adjust to the light. He placed his hat on a rack and took the hands she extended.

"You doing OK?" he asked.

She nodded. "It's good to see you, Mister Malone."

"It was Bones to your man."

"Bones," she agreed.

"You buy this place?"

"Me and my partner," she said.

At that moment Estella stepped through the kitchen doorway. "Erma Lou, we're going to need more potat—" She saw him.

A wisp of hair hung in front of her nose, and a red and white apron drew his attention to the curves above and below its strings. He saw recognition change to an instant smile, and something deep within those beautiful eyes put a curb strap on him no amount of fighting could remove. He hadn't realized how much he'd missed her.

She reached out and came toward him. He didn't know if a handshake, a hug, or what was on her mind. He dismissed the first possibility, and, instead, grabbed and kissed her. She returned the kiss with a force that spurred him. In his mind the band played "Dixie," cannons roared, and Bones Malone was home at last.

When he released Estella, Erma Lou had vanished. He thought they were alone until he saw Maurice standing just inside the door. The woman with him had to be his wife. Beside them a shiny-eyed girl of about ten held her hand across her mouth.

Maurice stood stooped, his straw hat in his hand, and turned toward the door. "We'll come back," he said quietly.

Estella's face reddened, and she jumped to place a hand on

Maurice's shoulder. "No. No, stay … I'm sorry. Please forgive me. Mister Malone's been gone … and …"—she looked at Bones and laughed—"we sort of got carried away."

Maurice's expression remained a little uncertain, but he allowed Estella to direct them to a table.

Bones sat nearby. "Been hot, ain't it?" he said. He noticed the little girl still looking at him, giggling behind her hand.

Erma Lou brought cups, and Estella followed with the coffee. She poured for Maurice's family, then filled Bones' cup.

Erma Lou tilted her head toward the sign behind the counter. "Try the beans and tamales, Bones." She pointed at Maurice's wife. "Juanita makes them and Maurice brings them in on Fridays and Saturdays."

"Looks like y'all about got the whole town in on this," Bones said, and looked at Maurice. "Your missus, huh?"

"*Sí, sí.*" Maurice held both hands open, palms up, one pointing at Juanita, the other at Bones. "Bones Malone, *mia señora*, Juanita."

Estella brought her own coffee and sat with Bones. "How was your cousin?"

Bones examined his cup. "Fine … fine."

"And Sassy?"

His coffee went down crooked. There was no napkin on the table. He grabbed his neckerchief with his right hand and covered his nose and mouth. With his left hand he worked at undoing the knot under his chin. He coughed through his nose, and tears streamed down his face. The knot loosened, and he managed to get a breath, then wipe his face. Erma Lou took the bandanna and handed him a damp towel. He used it, noticing the little girl's interest had turned to a frown of disgust.

"Doing … good," he said between gasps for air. "Where'd you hear about Sassy?"

"You mentioned both of them … and Charley added some," she said, taking up her coffee cup and heading back to the kitchen.

What did Charley know about Sassy? Bones wondered. *What did I say when I was drunk?*

He ate, then paid for his meal. "Can I see you later?" he asked Estella as she counted out his change.

"We close at eight. Why don't you come walk me home?"

"I'll be here." He stopped halfway to the door and came back. "Have I done something wrong?"

"Yes."

"What?"

"I'm not sure … why don't you tell me?" She turned to the kitchen.

Bones nodded to Maurice's family on the way out. A few moments later, he stepped through the batwings of the Sea Breeze. Charley had his back to him, but nodded to him in the mirror. Three men played cards. Another drank alone at the other end of the bar. Alice Marie worked on her nails at a table across the room.

Charley met him with glass and bottle in hand. He poured a half inch of amber fluid, then set the glass in front of Bones. "How was the family?"

"You an' me ought to be so good. Think somewhere down the road, they got rich." He looked into Charley's eyes. "You been mentioning stuff to Estella I told you as a friend?"

"Damn it, Bones, you ain't got no friends. Anything I hear a drunk say, I want to chew it over with somebody else, I do. If it ain't about no lady, that is."

"This may've been about a lady."

"Couldn't've been. Estella's the first lady you ever knowed."

They locked eyes, and Bones took a large swallow of whiskey without allowing his gaze to waver. He put the glass down, still looking at Charley. "I might punch you right in that gut, but you're so damn windy, you'd probably blow this burg away."

"The day you try'll be your last." Charley's eyes twinkled. "That drink's on me."

Bones had the feeling the old salt would, in fact, relish a fight. Even cautious men got bored sometimes.

"Just told her you had said something about being sweet on the gal that married your cousin."

Bones leaned low with his arms on the bar, his chin on his hands, and examined the whiskey in the bottle. "That was too much." The drink burned pleasantly inside. He'd make it right with Estella. Funny, when his head didn't hurt, he couldn't stay mad more than ten minutes with nearly anyone—well, nobody except Wade. "There's varmints in this whiskey," he said.

"Ain't no such a darn thing. 'Sides, if there was, I didn't charge you for them. Just bits of charcoal and flakes of a wood barrel. Nothing on this earth can live in that stuff."

Charley took a fresh bottle to the poker players, and Bones examined the painting behind the bar. It was no use. Estella had ruined it for him. There had been a time, only a few days ago, he could spend hours studying it. Now, no matter how innocent or interested in art, he still felt guilty for ogling the thing.

When Charley returned, Bones motioned to the painting with his head. "We gonna have to take her down."

"Take who down?"

"That woman. We named her one night, but I can't remember what. We're gonna have to take her down."

"Like hell we are! I paid fifteen dollars American for her in New Orleans, ten years ago."

"It ain't fitting no more." Bones downed the last of the glass. "We got ladies come in here now."

"You know what I think?"

"What?"

Charley held to the top of the bar and roared with laughter. Great burbling fountains of merriment rolled up from deep inside the man. Everyone in the saloon stared. Smiles brightened their faces, and they, too, chuckled at the pure happiness of the moment.

Charley raised his head and caught his breath. Alice Marie walked toward them, a look of curiosity on her face. "Yeah, it's true. I'll be damned. You're in love!" Charley exclaimed. He cocked his thumb at the painting and looked at Alice Marie. "He says we gotta take her down, 'cause ladies come in here now." Still laughing, Charley shook his head.

Alice Marie swung a haymaker blow that hit Bones' stomach. "What the hell does that make me?" she asked.

As licks went, it wasn't that much, but being unexpected it took his air and bent him over. Bones held his stomach and wheezed at Charley: "Told you a while ago, you talk too damn much."

Charley's face held no mirth as his gaze followed Alice Marie's back across the room. Her shoulders quivered, and her head drooped. Charley's expression had changed to one of sadness. "What are we gonna do?" he asked Bones.

"For starters, you can quit making news out of my private talk." Bones rubbed his stomach. He was not sure what Charley and Alice Marie meant to each other. He knew she had followed him up from the coast, but that may have just been business. She had a kind heart, always loaning a dollar to whomever needed it, and sticking up for whomever was getting badgered the worst. She once chewed out a railroad hand for kicking the old red sow that prowled the town. No one raved at her beauty, but she wasn't homely. She had a way of looking better as the night wore on, or as the coal oil got low in the lamps. Always before, she had treated him good, and he didn't like seeing her hurting any more than did Charley. She wiped her face and looked across the room at him. He crossed to her, but stood far enough away that she couldn't hit him. "Alice Marie, you know I wouldn't make you part of no talk in this place."

"I know, Bones. Sorry I hit you. You was just handy."

"Anytime," he said, relieved. He returned to his bottle. He told Charley the details of Virgil Potter's gang and the hanging of Ferrell and the kid. He mentioned the fence building and that he had a load of wire contracted to haul to a spot past Welcome.

At the mention of Welcome, Charley interrupted. "Didn't know they was such a place till two guys come in this week. Said that was where they were from. Had two mules … a Georgia Stock and a saddle horse. Said they'd plowed a twenty-five mile furrow from Welcome so folks wouldn't get lost between here and there."

"Did they buy a drink?"

"Funny thing … one wanted to, but the other looked down his nose at him, so they both had soda water."

"Figures, they're big on quoting scripture. They're decent folks, though," Bones said, and then he thought of Ruben. "Guess what. Wade and Sassy's boy's gonna be a preacher."

"Huh," Charley grunted.

The clock by the piano said ten till eight, so he paid for his last drinks and told Charley: "So long."

* * * * *

Erma Lou left the café early to go home to the kids. When Bones took a seat, Estella poured him the last of the coffee. He watched her wash the pot and do the last bits of tidying up. She looked a little tired, but seemed happy. He blew out the lamp while she waited at the front door. He kissed her lightly on the cheek, and she seemed pleased. She took his arm, and they headed for the hotel.

"No, this way. I'm renting a room from Erma Lou." She directed him up a darkened road.

"Got tired of Charley's, did you?" Bones asked.

"I guess that's about it. I'll miss the piano, but not the rest. Sometime you men just don't want to take no for an answer."

A knot tightened in his throat. He grasped her by both arms, stopping her. "Somebody bother you?"

"No … no more than usual. Settle down, you don't have to go

mark a territory. Like they say, I just got tired of it." She squeezed his arm. "Besides, me an' Erma Lou are gonna make some money at the café."

They moved on toward the pale lamplight glowing from Erma Lou's window.

"I'm just as glad," he said. "I would probably have gotten angry, then ended up hurting somebody, if you'd stayed." He wondered if he should tell her about Alice Marie, but he couldn't think of a way to avoid looking as dumb as Charley. Instead, he told her about the men plowing a furrow twenty-five miles from Welcome.

The memory of her kiss escorted him back to camp. San Tone had obviously gone to town. He smoked and relived the evening. His last thought before sleep brought thankfulness that Estella had pushed away the nightmares. It was good to think of the present, still better with her in it.

CHAPTER FIFTEEN

The next morning he awoke to San Tone waving the skillet. "C'mon, yuh want any of this?"

Bones filled his plate and looked at his friend. "Where'd you get eggs?"

"Colored lives down on the river has chickens. Beula told me 'bout him."

"How's she doing?" Bones asked.

"Fine … except that old man's pestering her to death." San Tone's answer carried a note of anger, and his face grew hard. "Yuh know 'bout that?"

"You mean the ladder?"

"Yeah, an' what all goes with it."

"Think everybody knows except Missus Quinley," Bones said, "and maybe even her."

Later in the morning Bones finished his bone dealing with A. J. at the tracks and drove to the bank. He hitched the team and held the door for San Tone.

Old Man Quinley greeted them before they had time to remove their hats. "Mister Malone, I've been hoping you'd come by. Been hearing lots about that cousin of yours." He judged San Tone with a horse trader's eye, but made no effort to shake after releasing Bones' hand. "This your man?" He motioned toward San Tone.

The "Mister Malone" had surprised Bones. It took a minute to adjust. The question that followed angered him, and he made no effort to adjust to that. "Ain't got no man. This here's San Tone Jones, the freight haulingest scoundrel west of the Mississippi. He's looking to buy a wagon."

The banker grabbed San Tone's hand. "Come in, Mister Jones." He led both men to an alcove with a low railing bordering it, and gestured for them to be seated. Twisting his paunch from left to right, he settled behind a large desk.

"Mister Jones, I have a wagon at Rosco's yard I expect you'll like. It's a new Studebaker. Hate to lose money on it, but I'll let it go for three hundred and seventy-five dollars. Cost me a little more than that, but the bank needs to help commerce, you know." He looked dubiously at San Tone. "If you need to borrow some, just put down a hundred dollars, and, if Bones cosigns for you, you can take out a note for the balance. You going to haul bones with Mister Malone?"

"Bob wire mostly," San Tone replied. "Mister Quinley, I saw a wagon like that sell for two hundred and ninety-five dollars in Abilene. I'll give yuh three hundred, and we can both get back to work."

Bones twirled his hat by the brim. He wondered if San Tone had fifty dollars, much less his bargaining price.

"Now, just a minute, boy, don't sass ..." Quinley was talking to San Tone's back.

"Good day to yuh," San Tone said over his shoulder.

Bones stood, searched in his pocket, and handed the banker ten dollars. "Put that on what I owe you, Milton. Have a good day." He put on his hat while shutting the door and trotted to catch San Tone.

They went to the depot and showed Oliver the letter from Wade. The depot man unlocked the boxcar and returned to his sidecar. Bones and San Tone loaded thirty spools of wire into the wagon.

At the twentieth roll, San Tone straightened. "Thought Wade said we could only haul about twenty spools."

"That's all he knows about the freight business." Bones shaded his eyes and guessed the time to be near 10:00 a.m. "I'm going to Charley's while you figure out what to do about a second wagon."

"I can catch the train to Abilene an' get one cheaper'n foolin' with that old goat Quinley." From the sound of San Tone's voice, Bones knew this mad was not one to be talked away. San Tone untied his saddle horse. "I'll stop at the livery and see have they got a team that's anywhere near reasonable."

* * * * *

Bones played poker till noon, then cashed his chips and headed for the café. After a short exchange, Estella placed a fried ham sandwich before him. Her fingers strummed a rhythm on the tabletop. A blind man could see the excitement in her.

"What?" he asked.

She showed him a letter she had received from a girl in Wichita, Kansas. The young woman wrote that a Dr. Clerence Emory had contacted her trying to learn Estella's whereabouts. The man was looking for his daughter. Somewhere he had learned of the two of them working together in Fort Worth. He said he'd been forced to leave his child in Texas after a fever had killed her mother, and he'd been trying to locate her since the war. The doctor was old and in bad health. He lived in Memphis, Tennessee, and the letter included his address.

Her face showed uncertainty as well as excitement. "What should I do, Wil? I'm so frightened and at the same time excited."

"Seems to me you're two lonesome people looking for each other. Time to fix that. Believe I'd start scribbling." He didn't know if it was good advice, but he figured it was what she wanted to hear.

She rushed to the kitchen, wiping at the corner of an eye with the back of a finger. In a moment she stuck her head around the corner of the door. "Thanks."

"Hey! Reckon Erma Lou would let you off a little early tonight? Remember, you promised to see Seven Wells with me."

"Seven-thirty!" she called.

Minutes later, Bones' team struggled up a steep incline. They made the rise, then turned east toward the camp on Lone Wolf Creek. In front of the Quinley place, Bones heard a cry, but couldn't tell where it came from.

"Help!" There it was again. Someone was in trouble. "Help!" The word was full of panic, and much louder now, coming from the direction of the Quinley house.

He did a quick twist of the reins on the brake handle and jumped to the ground. Built on a hill and the largest in town, the Quinley home consisted of two stories. To his right was a curved gravel buggy path, and at the hitch rack stood San Tone's horse, beside the Quinley rig.

"Can't hold … much … longer. Help me!" The voice came from back of the house.

Bones rounded the corner at full speed. He dodged to avoid running into San Tone. His big friend stood calmly, looking up at Old Man Quinley.

The banker hung by two hands from the maid's second story bedroom window. Framed in the next window stood Abigail Quinley. Little more than two feet separated her window's opening and the one in Beula's room. The ladder was slanted to the right, resting on one leg on the ground, and the top tilted to Mrs. Quinley. Milton Quinley's foot searched futilely for the safety of a rung. His body hung suspended, straining with exertion from surrendering to decades of dining pleasures.

"Milton, why aren't you at the bank?" Abigail scolded.

"Move that ladder over here, woman. I can't hold on much longer." Milton sounded like a man with a horse on his toe.

"What are you doing in that girl's room? That poor child! You're just a dirty old Lucifer, aren't you? Go ahead, fall! Think I'll get the gun and shoot you." Abigail looked down at the ground. "Oh, excuse me, Mister Malone, when did you come up?"

"I'm just passing, ma'am. Matter of fact, it's best I just go on." Bones turned, starting for the corner of the house.

"Bones … thank … God … man!" Quinley stated. "Move the ladder a little this way. I'll be in your debt forever." The banker wheezed, coughed, and spit what Charley called an oyster.

"Sure thing, Milton, me an' old San Tone here will get it right now," Bones answered.

"Just leave the ladder be, Mister Malone," came from Abigail Quinley. "Mister Jones came by and woke me. Said he thought Milton was home, and he needed to speak to him about a wagon. Well, I thought he was just looking for an excuse to see Beula, till I saw Miltie's buggy."

"Bones … help." Old Man Quinley's voice was weaker.

"Milt, about that wagon. Does two hundred and seventy-five sound OK to yuh?" San Tone asked.

"Move that ladder and it's a deal."

San Tone grabbed the ladder and righted it in position for Mr. Quinley's salvation. The banker got both feet on a rung and breathed a sigh of relief. His knees shook, and one hand slipped, when he released the window. He caught himself just before he fell. Rivulets of sweat streamed down his pudgy face.

"Mister Jones, Mister Malone, y'all know anything about banking?" Abigail said. "I may be needing new partners." She turned to her husband. "This ain't the end, Miltie. Didn't think I could still get up those stairs, huh? Dry air helps arthritis. Guess you forgot that's why we came here in the first place." Her shrill voice continued even after Milton hit the ground and scurried for his buggy.

"No, ma'am, we don't know banking, but I'm learning. What you want us to do with this ladder?" San Tone asked.

"Just put it on the ground. He's through with it." Abigail paused to get a breath.

Bones looked up at the maid's window. Beula watched San Tone's broad back and smiled.

When San Tone straightened, Bones said: "Get your horse, San Tone. Think these people're too tough for us Mississippi boys."

Milton came around the corner of the road in his buggy with his horse at a fast trot. San Tone ran and cut him off, waving money in his hand. The banker stopped, took the money, counted it, and sped on down the road.

San Tone walked to his horse, mounted, and sat waiting by the roadside.

Bones had a dozen questions, but, before the team pulled even with his friend, he asked the most obvious one. "How'd you get mixed up in that mess?"

"Think I sort of egged it on."

"How's that?"

"Well, Beula told me last night, the old man said he was coming to her room at two this afternoon whilst Missus Abigail napped. Coming by, I saw that ladder and just moved it over a little bit from her window. Then, like Missus Abigail said, I went around front and knocked. Guess I woke the lady. She did the rest. Reckon her miseries are getting better."

"You ain't been up that ladder, have you, pardner?"

"No, but it go both ways," San Tone answered, smiling. "Found a team at the livery. I'm gonna go get my wagon." He rode toward town.

"I'll be back, an' meet you at the boxcar. Help you load up. Guess we can leave come morning!" Bones called to his friend's back.

* * * * *

That evening, with little daylight remaining, Bones and Estella arrived at the great sandstone slabs of Seven Wells. The rock formations huddled fifteen feet above seven distinct natural springs. Everlasting in the parched environment, they gave the ravine its name. A few yards downstream, the water flowed into Champion Creek. Parallel paths, worn by wagons, crossed through the draw. To the west, a low ridgeline cast shadows over the wells, adding to the contrasting coolness of the spot.

Bones tied Barney and hurriedly led Estella the few steps to the springs. On the way, he showed her fossilized imprints of buffalo tracks, once mashed into mud and now preserved in sandstone. Cold flowing water rose from the depths and ran of its own accord into the stream.

"They're so round. How wide would you say?" Estella asked.

"A good hop. Four feet maybe," he said.

Someone had placed a dipper in a crevice of a stone outcropping near the springs. Bones filled it and handed it to Estella.

She took it, and walked back to the tracks. "You can tell this rock was soft when they stepped here. How'd it all happen? Isn't it wonderful to think about?"

"What about petrified wood? See it all the time, and I ain't got a notion of how it happened," he said.

She looked off into the distance. "Do you wonder about it? Does it bother you that when y'all get the last bones this will be all that's left of so many thousands and thousands of those animals?"

"Hadn't thought about it. Know some Injuns that are pretty upset." He leaned against the buggy. She moved and stood beside him.

Bull bats fluttered high above, then swooped down into the darkening valley. She leaned with her back against his chest, and he rested their weight against the buggy wheel at his rear. He clasped his fingers together in front of her waist and savored the nearness of her.

"Be nice if we had your piano up there on that rock … could sort of send this old day out with a lullaby."

"I couldn't add anything to this," she whispered.

His special feeling of loneliness crept into his consciousness, and he wanted to tell this woman of his memory loss, the nightmares that tormented him. If she cared about him, she had a right to know. It had sneaked up on him in this calm, safe, and beautiful spot. Now it pounded at him, but, as always, he could not bring himself to voice what he considered his weakness.

Estella stirred, and he realized he'd lost track of time with his daydreaming. "I told you it was nice out here," he said.

She turned and put her head on his chest. "I wrote my letter."

"What did you put in it?"

"I told him where I am, and about Erma Lou and the café. Said I'd like to see him."

"Did you tell him about knowing this good-looking young fellow name of Malone?"

She laughed. "I'm afraid I'll have to get to know both of you better before that."

He took her arm. "We better get in the buggy, or the darn snakes are liable to eat our toes."

When she was seated, he released the mule and sat beside her. A short distance across the darkened prairie, a half dozen lights twinkled from town.

Estella cuddled against his shoulder. "Tell me about Wil Malone."

"Ain't nothing much there to talk about."

"No, come on, Wil, I'm serious. I want to know."

"Well, old Wil, he's reformed since he met you."

She laughed.

"No, it's true. Like somebody once said, I was feared of living and skeered of dying when you come along. Wasn't going no place, just spending my time wondering if I missed where I'd been. Planted more friends than I'd kept alive. Didn't have nothing or nobody, and the thing was, I didn't care."

"And now?"

"Now, I'm ... guess I'm sort of friendly."

"I'll be your friend." She kissed him.

He wrapped Barney's reins around the brake and put him in charge of getting them home. Thirty minutes later, he looked up at the pale glow of Rosco's lantern hanging above the "S" on the sign saying STABLE. Estella slept beside him. He slapped Barney on the rump with a rein and headed them toward Erma Lou's.

CHAPTER SIXTEEN

Shaded by a bush, the roadrunner scanned Barney and Pete. He cocked his head. It had hardly given San Tone's lead wagon a blink during its earlier passage. It followed the bone wagon a short distance, took flight, and landed on the old Studebaker's tailgate. Seemingly satisfied that bugs shunned barbed wire, it turned its attention to the grasshoppers startled into flight.

Wade's map identified Ruben's location four miles north of Welcome. Bones hollered and pointed to the route marked by the farmers' plowed furrow. San Tone nodded and reined his team alongside the gash that knifed through the sparse turf.

That night they camped at Hazard Springs. After supper, they cooled a second cup of coffee, then propped, elbow down, near the wagon.

"Wil, they's sumpthin' we need to talk on."

"What's that?"

"Yuh ever hear your granddaddy say anything about the paper?"

"Paper … what paper?" Bones asked.

"Not many days before the Yanks killed him, he called me over under that old oak, and we sat, and he talked 'most an hour. Like he used to with the two of us."

"Wish I'd been there." The words came without thought, but cinched tight with feeling.

San Tone gave him a knowing look and continued. "That story about him being a pirate with old … what's his name?"

"Jean Laffite."

"Yeah, he told me it's true. Said he was old Mister Laffite's first mate. They both left New Orleans about the same time. Him to Grand Gulf, Laffite to Galveston. Said your grandmother cured his itch to travel."

"I knew she came upriver with him. Well, I'll be."

"Yes, siree, that's what he said. He thought Laffite was a fine, brave man."

"What about that treasure everybody's always talking about?"

"I asked him, and he laughed. Said they wasn't nothing buried, but that, when he passed, me an' yuh, an' your Uncle Phillip should find the paper. He said we'd find it behind that iron plate to the side of the fireplace. Said the paper told everything we ought to know. What d'yuh think?" San Tone looked like he'd dropped a heavy weight.

Bones divided the last of the coffee. "That fireplace was rubble when I came by. You reckon Wade knew about the paper?"

"Don't know. His daddy wuz still alive when your granddaddy told me. May never been no paper. Some thought the old man just rambled. But if they wuz, what you expect happened to it?"

Bones shrugged and watched Pete toss his feedbag up and down, trying to find the last kernel of grain. Memories flooded from his childhood. His grandmother had been a fiery Creole girl who had captured the heart of his sea-faring granddaddy. The contents of his granddaddy's chest in the attic of the big house had verified its owner's ties to salt water. It contained a sextant, a compass, maps, and sailor clothing. As a boy, he often overheard men talking about his granddaddy using gold and silver jewelry to pay expenses.

"Next time I see him, I'm gonna ask Wade. He may know

sumpthin'," San Tone announced as he rose and went to his team, removed the feedbags, and watered them.

He returned and sat by the wagon, wiggling his back like he was trying to substitute muscle for bone in contact with the wheel he rested against. "Your granddaddy worried about yuh being off in the war. What was it like?"

"What was the war like! San Tone, I 'spect you know. War's about death. Every day's the first cold day of winter. You know hawg-killing time. Things die … people, animals, crops, and other things … countries. Sometimes it seems maybe even God. A saddle empties, then, before long, fills again. Some eager-eyed youngster or tired old man crawls up and sets his jaw and you ride on. Afterwards it's like that buffalo slaughter a few years back. All you got to show for it is old drying skeletons like me and them relics I haul." He paused, his own words ringing in his ears. He needed to stop, but how do you stop flames once the range is afire. "I thought I'd be glad when it was over, but then I was at Appomattox when we called it quits. It turned out to be the saddest day of my life." Bones took off his hat and dried the sweatband with his elbow.

Holding his hands parallel and straight, several inches apart, Bones sighted through them at the prairie. He motioned up and down, trying to pump words up from the depth of emotion welling inside. "Those times … about God dying. Well, that's true, there were times like that. Somehow they passed, just like me and these old bones out on this prairie are gonna pass." The words were coming together and pain flowed out with each one. "That boy of Wade's and Sassy's, I see him and all that strength he's got, and I know God pulled through without a scratch. All them drum beats, the bugles blaring, us a-marching, we didn't know where. It must have had some purpose, otherwise, why would that boy be here now, a-looking so fine. Tell me that, San Tone-Catfish Jones!"

"I knowed the answers, I wouldn't be asking the questions."

"That boy knows what it's about … goodness and kindness …

yet he ain't soft. Why, I bet he could pick the two of us old gobblers up and throw us over this wagon. His daddy hung two men and looked weak doing it, while he wouldn't even carry a gun and he stood out like … like old David." Bones took a deep breath. "And you know them boys just keep coming."

San Tone looked at him, strangely quiet. "I reckon yuh're right."

Bones had no more words or energy. He felt a little foolish. How long had he rattled on? The feeling wasn't all bad though. "San Tone, I'm sorry, I didn't mean to wear you down, leaning on you so. It must be a craving for whiskey or something."

"Sumpthin', I expect. Anyway yuh ain't said nothing I can't abide by. That boy, Ruben, he do make a man think on good things. Wouldn't Mama like him? They could quote that Bible till the sun went down."

* * * * *

The next day they tracked two miles of standing posts to the fencing crew. Ruben, Cecil, and Perk had three new men working with them.

"Y'all showed up just right. We were about to run out of wire," Ruben said.

"We smelled Cecil's cooking the last fifteen miles. Sorta spurred us on," Bones said.

"No, you didn't. I'm off that chore now. 'Course, we all getting a little weak, depending on old Perk's grub." Cecil nodded at Perk and winked.

"Another crack about my cooking, you'll be eating alkali pie," Perk said.

"Ruben, where we gonna unload this wire?" Bones asked.

"We can put half of your load here, on them rocks, and the rest in our wagon. Daddy said for San Tone to bring his load on to headquarters while you go back for another."

Bones wiped frothy sweat from Barney's shoulder, slung it on the ground, and silently cursed Wade for being so obvious about not wanting him around headquarters. "The other crew still fencing at Hayrick?" Bones asked.

Ruben nodded.

With the help of the crew, it took only a few minutes to unload the wagon. They watered the team, unhitched, and fed them the last of the oats brought from Rosco's, then settled by the wagons. Perk called them to supper.

Bones pushed the conversation. "That old single string of wire looks lonesome there by itself, don't it? 'Pears tight as a fiddle, though."

Cecil gestured with a swipe of his hand. "She's tight. We got her stretched so thin yesterday, we broke her. It was scary as hell. That stuff sang out like a banshee and lashed back into coils for a hundred yards. Only thing I ever saw move like that was an old blue prairie racer, whipsawing around. See it wasn't stapled fast, just tightened. It'd a-cut a man in half like that. Darn near got old Al." It seemed Cecil had become the self-appointed voice of authority on fencing matters.

Bones noticed Ruben trying to enter the conversation several times during the meal. Obviously the boy had news to tell. After supper, talk lagged enough for him to get it out.

"Fellows, guess what." He didn't slow to let them guess. "We caught that mustang stud I was telling you about."

Bones leaned back in real surprise. "The heck you did." He would have bet against such success so quickly. "How'd you do that?"

"Well"—Ruben's eyes were bright, and his face beamed—"it showed up the second day we were here. Owen had mentioned we might try stationing relays to run him down. Next morning three of us took up spots two miles apart along a ridgeline Perk thought he might favor. He picked the right path. Only thing was, he didn't tire down." Ruben's pride showed.

"Yuh mean he wore down all three nags?" San Tone said.

"He did," Cecil confirmed. "He's a hoss."

"Anyway, making a long story short, Perk was the last relay man, and he was fast losing him, until the mustang got himself trapped up against a cutbank of the river. The rascal wheeled and leaped over a bluff into knee-deep water." Ruben smacked his hands together. "The bottom was quicksand. That horse went down to his belly and stuck tight as a drum. Took the three of us an hour to get him dug out of there, but we got him."

"Where?" Bones asked.

"He's tied to a log back there, a mile and a half," Perk said. "You need to go by and see him, boys. He's good. I'd rather have him than that thing they call Bonnie Glen."

"Is he eating and drinking?" Bones asked.

"Started yesterday. Skipped his meals the first day, then started back," Ruben said. "I'll show him to you on your way out tomorrow."

"Good, always like to look at a good hoss," Bones said.

"Yeah! Me, too," San Tone said. "But I ain't got no interest in mules."

"Why's that?" Ruben asked.

"They sort of replaced pork at Vicksburg when the Yanks were starving us." San Tone's mouth turned downward.

CHAPTER SEVENTEEN

At first dawn, Bones wiped leathery bread through the last smear of molasses on his plate. "Ruben, let's go see that mustang you boys been mistreating."

Earlier, he'd agreed to meet San Tone en route in four days. Both of the Crooked Letter I saddle horses were tied to San Tone's new rig for delivery to the ranch. Ruben tied his horse behind Bones' wagon and climbed aboard.

"Why does your dad want a fence here?" Bones asked. "It ain't gonna connect with that one coming down from Hayrick, is it?"

Ruben pointed at a dove feigning injury to lead the wagon from her nest, then answered: "Oh, it's just a drift fence, six miles long between us and that Welcome bunch. It's to keep our cattle out of their crops. Dad's afraid they'll get in those fields and the nesters will start butchering them."

"He's right. Say, Ruben, did I ever tell you about my road-runner? Traveled with me till yesterday. He liked my company when I hauled bones, so he could get bugs, but he gave up on me after pecking on that barbed wire a couple of days. Think San Tone wanted me to give it a name." Bones chuckled. The morning air was cool, his head no longer hurt, and there was just something about being with this life-loving young man that lifted his spirits. He handed Ruben the reins and loaded his pipe.

"Bet you was glad to run into San Tone again, huh?" Ruben said.

"For a fact, and I'll tell you, boy, I'm glad we've had a chance to get to know one another."

"Same here," Ruben said. "We're gonna turn left at that crick up there. He's about a quarter mile up it."

Minutes later, Bones decided the black mustang was a sorry sight to behold. His flanks were gaunt, and caked salt mixed with dirt discolored his body. His head drooped, and his long mane and tail were tangled. The rope, tying him to a log, gave him twenty feet of movement, and hobbles made him clumsy. Of all his features only his flashing eyes told that his spirit was unbroken, and that a wild animal lived in his scarred body.

"Kinda looks like me, don't he?" Bones said.

"You'd make a pair, all right." Ruben chuckled while dismounting. He untied the stud, and half led and half dragged him to the creek. Bones used the wagon to move the log to fresh grass. After drinking, the mustang's flanks rounded out, his head lifted. His nostrils flared and his muzzle still dripped water when Ruben tied him back onto the log. Bones waved and headed the empty wagon toward Sundown City.

Two days later, he pulled into Rosco's wagon yard with a new load of wire from the boxcar already aboard. He put the team in the liveryman's care and headed for the café. There his spirit could feast on Estella while beef and potatoes revived his body.

Heavy, dark clouds loomed beneath threatening thunderheads northwest of town. Veins of brightness swept across the level prairie beneath clouds from a lowering sun. A strong front of blowing wind and sand whipped the street in blinding gusts.

A man stepped from the door of the café and walked, leaning forward, into the blowing gale. It was Emit Rose, and he headed for the Sea Breeze.

Bones scanned the streets through the blowing dust. He pulled his pistol, checked the load, and added a shell to the empty chamber under the hammer. Maybe it was Emit's doings, perhaps lightning flitted about, but, regardless, the hair on the back of his neck tingled. Emit crossed the street and entered the saloon.

Bones tugged his hat brim tighter, tilted his head from the blowing sand, and walked to the Sally Good 'Un. He peeked in the window, making sure the last Rose brother hadn't been accompanied by a slow eater.

Estella had her back to him as he entered. He stepped inside and closed the curtains at the window. He took a seat facing the entrance. A smile spread across Estella's face at sight of him. "When y'all gonna do something about renaming this place?" he asked.

"Be with you in a moment," she said.

Bones shifted the holstered pistol resting just above his left groin and thought about Emit. His shoulders felt a heavy burden, and even the smells from the kitchen failed to lift his gloom. It seemed something always came up to put a damper on things. For the first time in months he'd reached a point of being able to make it through his days without a belly full of rotgut, then this bad penny showed up.

Emit would slap leather at first sight, bound for blood payback for his brothers' wasted lives. For his part, the best he could hope for was ringing ears and a bouncing stomach. Ruben was right: life had to mean more than some drunken officer's battle plan, another man's cows, or some kid-like idea of family honor.

Estella interrupted his thoughts with a coffee cup in her hand. "You all right?"

"Rowdy as a pup," he lied.

"Look a little peaked to me," she said, peering closely into his face, and put a hand on his shoulder. "Hungry?"

"What's good?"

"Got a good stew with cornbread," she said.

He nodded and moved his view to the front door and windows.

A moment later she returned with his food and sat down beside him.

"Where's San Tone?"

"He went on to headquarters. Guess he's there by now. I came back for another load." She was right about the stew. "That fellow just walked out, seen him before?"

"Yeah, he was here yesterday. Ate with us last night. Claimed he's a friend of yours." She raked crumbs from the tablecloth to her hand. "Where did you know each other?"

"Met not long ago, northeast of here. He say anything else?"

She looked concerned. "No. Wil, who is he?"

He didn't want to tell her. Still, she and Erma Lou, especially Erma Lou, had a right, maybe even a need to know. "He's a brother to that one that shot High Pockets."

Estella looked quickly at the door, then toward the back where Erma Lou worked. "You've got to get out of town. He's looking for you, Wil. He'll shoot you on sight." Her words came quicker the longer she talked. "He may be out there now. You come with me." She took hold of his elbow.

"Hang on. I ain't going nowhere. Just got here. Settle down … he's over at Charley's." He gently removed her hand from his elbow.

"Wil, he'll kill you. He's a gunfighter. I've seen them before. He carries two guns, for God's sake! He's twenty years younger than you."

"He is that, but hold on, girl. You starting to get personal now." He smiled at her. "Don't measure me for no box, yet."

Estella went to the door and looked toward Charley's. Through the open door fading light and blowing sand hid the other side of the street.

Bones lifted his empty bowl. "Got any more of this?"

She took the empty bowl to the kitchen and brought it back, with Erma Lou two steps behind her. "Tell her," she said, nodding at her friend.

Erma Lou wiped her hands on her apron. "Tell me what?" Erma Lou asked, eyeing Bones.

Bones' tongue felt dry. He wet his lips. "The man who shot High Pockets had a brother, and he's here. Estella wants me to hightail it." The words had a bad taste.

The widow's hand went to her mouth.

"It's that man with the two guns that was here yesterday asking about Wil," Estella said.

Erma Lou started to say something, then tears came, and she strode quickly back to the kitchen.

Bones had heard enough about guns, how old he was, and the fact Emit Rose could probably chew him up and spit him out. He stood and reached for money.

Estella's face showed fear, mixed with anger. "You're gonna stay and see him aren't you?"

"I ain't gonna turn tail, if that's what you mean. Hon, you can't run from trouble. Tried it once in the war. You can run to it, but you can't run from it. It's faster'n us." He shook his head. "No more."

She stood in front of him and placed her hands on his arms. "I just found you. I don't want to lose you."

"Have you heard from your daddy?"

She shook her head and gave him an angry look. "Don't change the subject. And don't treat me like a child."

A smile worked at his face, but her frown said it wasn't a good idea. What had he done? It was a simple question. He stepped around her and shut the door as he walked out. He stared into the dark. Sand stung his face. His teeth ground grit, and somewhere off to the left a bucket, or maybe a tub, *clanged* against wood. Charley's window glowed between gusts. Bones felt with his foot for the edge of the sidewalk, then stepped to the street. A dull glimmer of lightning flashed, then retreated. Thunder beat around him. The air turned cold and smelled of ice. He stood in front of the door of the Sea Breeze. The light inside was low, only a glow.

Charley and two cowpunchers watched the storm from the door of the saloon. A shadow, maybe Emit's, moved near the window.

Bones stepped inside, ready for whatever Emit had in mind. He hated to meet a man on his own ground, but damn it he wanted a drink.

He walked to the bar. Emit matched him, stride for stride, ten feet away. Their eyes locked like a couple of barnyard dogs. Emit took a spot down the mahogany bar, in front of an empty glass. The two cowboys went to a table.

Charley showed no sign of knowing Emit, but seemed to sense the storm played second fiddle to the suddenly tense atmosphere inside his saloon. "Some blow, huh?" he said.

"Makes a man want to find a hole, don't it?" Bones said. "Give me about three fingers, then add a hand and a half."

Charley poured the drink and tilted the bottle at Emit. "You boys know each other?"

Emit nodded for a refill. "We met, but ain't much acquainted."

The painting behind the bar faded in and out with the swing of the lamp. One of the cowboys walked to the door and closed it. Emit's face showed blank. For a minute, Bones hoped nothing would happen—hoped letting the man live had not been a waste.

Emit spoke through a grim smile. "We both got an eye for that lady across the street, though." He held his glass with his left hand. His right rested on his belt.

Bones realized that hope was unfounded. The challenge lay heavy on sand-laden air. Fear jolted Bones with the familiar smell of death. The hard fact that he had no chance against the clear-eyed gunman washed over him. He stepped away from the bar, feeling naked. His drawl came back to him as if spoken by someone else. "So you're one of the Rose boys, huh? Just how many were in your momma's litter?"

Bones watched the smile die on Emit's face, could see the meaning of the words sink home. The gunman's eyes widened, then narrowed. His right hand blurred in motion toward the butt of his six-gun. The weapon cleared leather. Bones' movements seemed mired in mud.

Beat before he started, he tugged at his hammer while Emit's Colt belched smoke. Searing fire stung the left side of his head. His hat flew off, and instinctively he jumped backward. Both feet slipped. He sprawled with legs flailing. The Colt fired again, and Bones' right boot jerked and twirled him in a circle. He came to rest on his left side and saw Emit crouched with a smoking gun in each hand. His own six-gun pointed between the two revolvers. He squeezed the trigger. The *bang* of the heavy Remington knifed pain through his ears.

The gunman's shirtfront flattened, then turned red. Emit bent forward and stepped backward. His mouth opened. Both of his pistols fired.

Needles of pain gouged Bones' cheek. More burned his hip. His sights rested on Emit's chest. His trigger finger tightened, and his thumb dropped away again. The handgun roared. No longer afraid, he fought because the battle was here. How it ended mattered not. Chancellorsville, Dodge, and Sundown City were all the same. Killing was what he knew—what he did best.

Emit spun and flopped over a table. The two cowboys scampered behind him. The gunman struggled erect, tried to raise his six-guns. He took one step, and both weapons fired into the floor at his feet. He slowly fell to the floor.

Charley walked to the dying man. He rolled him on his back and lifted the revolvers from his hands.

Bones raised to his knees. He swayed. "Is he dead?"

"He's dead," Charley said.

At the end of the room, the two cowboys dragged themselves to chairs and sat, quiet and ashen-faced. Bones tried to rise, but the pain from his right hip forced him back to the floor. He lay on his back.

The noise from the storm increased, and hail beat loudly. He felt Charley examining his head, then his face. The barkeep yelled, but Bones couldn't hear. The hail lessened, then slowed to an occasional bang.

"Am I done for?" he asked.

Charley reached over and picked up Bones' hat. "Hell, I can't find where you're hit." He pointed at a rip in the hat that ran from the base of the brim halfway up the crown. "You got a crease from this that barely broke the skin, and some wood splinters in your face from the floor. Where do you think you're hurt?"

"My left hip hurts fierce, and my right one don't work."

Charley undid Bones belt and pulled his pants to his knees. He pulled a splinter from Bones' left hip, but found nothing on the right side. "I don't think there's anything wrong with you." He stood, got behind Bones, and lifted him up under his shoulders. "See if you can stand."

Bones stood fine, but lop-sided. "He hit my damn boot heel. No wonder this hip hurts."

Charley looked at the heelless boot and laughed. He bent over, tilted his head to see into Bones' face, and slapped his knees. "Am I done for?" he hollered, and laughed.

Bones smiled sheepishly.

CHAPTER EIGHTEEN

The next morning, sporting new boots and a dun-colored 4X Stetson hat, Bones rode high on his wagon seat toward Welcome. Following the plowed furrow, his shadow glided beside the rig. The new headgear smartly topped off the image.

Through the second day, his emotions matched the up and down contours of the plains he traveled. Comparing Wade's wealth to his own poverty drove him to wallow in gloom. His part in the recent killing only added to his remorse. The only upside he'd found was Estella's concern, in front of Charley, when she had entered the saloon after the storm. Embarrassed, still he secretly gloried in the fact she cared for him.

Now traveling beside Ruben's new fence, he noticed what he first took to be a loose post dangling in the wire ahead. He cautiously approached, then gasped for breath when close enough to recognize Cecil's body. Shot in the chest, another time in the forehead, the old prankster hung as stark evidence of someone's bloodlust. The killer's zeal had fermented into overkill and had wasted lead. Facing away from the wire, Cecil's arms, both nearly shot away, looped behind him over the top strand of the fence. His mouth gaped, showing his sparse teeth. Both legs had been shot through.

Tracks marked the ground down the fence line. Bones whipped the mules in that direction. Beyond the next rise, buzzards circled low. He stood, feet spread, bracing against the wagon's bounce. It tilted, almost turned over, then brought him into view of the vultures feeding on the fencing crew's remains.

They were all there, Perk, the new men, and the last, Ruben, still bleeding, strung in wire, and moving feebly to ward off the flapping birds. A post supported him, imprisoned by wire wound around his limbs.

Bones jumped from the wagon. Tears streamed from his eyes. He ran to the boy. Ruben bravely moved his head and tried to smile. His right arm hung, almost severed. Wire curled around his neck making a gash from which blood weakly pulsed with each heartbeat. Bones twitched involuntarily, feeling the barb's bite as if it wrapped him. He reached to grab the youngster, then pulled back realizing any movement would cause the razor points to bury and cut into his nephew's flesh.

He raced to the fencing wagon. Bedding and tools flew about until he finally located the cutters he'd seen at Hayrick. In an instant he was back at the boy's side, clipping wires. He turned his head, tearing his view from Ruben's dangling arm. A tornadic funnel of mixed visions, some present reality and others images from the past, churned about him.

Ruben tried to speak, but no words came. Bones supported the almost lifeless body with his left arm and shoulder and cut through the last wire. It had buried deeply in the youngster's groin. He gently lowered Ruben to the ground and held his head in his lap, rocking back and forth. Did he breathe? Was that the sound of life, or the rattle of death? He cursed his own bad hearing. An eyelid fluttered. He placed the boy's head on the ground and brought blankets and a canteen of water from the wagon.

He covered Ruben with one blanket and made a pillow with another. Next he used his own hand for a saucer and dampened the boy's pale lips. Ruben smiled and moved his head. He made a noise, and Bones lowered his ear to the quivering mouth.

Feather-like the boy whispered softly: "It's OK. No longer hurts."

Bones threw his head back and screamed madly. "No, God damn it! No, not again!" How many times had he done this? It was always the young, the innocent. How many lives had he watched slip away? No doctor, no medicine, too late for a tourniquet. He knew the next step, just hold them, watch life fade, and in the end love and remember them until your own soul died, sloughed off a piece at a time.

He put his ear back to Ruben's mouth and again heard the whisper. "It was Potter." The hand Bones held trembled. "He's got Momma."

Ruben's head sagged slightly, and no more blood ran from his throat. Bones gently closed the boy's eyelids and pulled the blanket over his face.

The buzzards had returned, alternating between watching and hopping among the other corpses. He pulled his pistol and, screaming, emptied it blindly at the sickening birds.

They bounced awkwardly, then wallowed through the air like hogs heaving through deep mud until they reached a dead tree. There they sat, with heads slumped almost to shoulder height, watching. He looked back at Ruben's covered form, and realized he had lived this scene before.

He stuck the empty six-gun back in its holster and grabbed his stomach with both hands. He gritted his teeth and fought back the bile. Memory flooded him. Before … that other horror … it was Stonewall Jackson. He had shot General Jackson, the bravest man, the best leader Lee had. His general had caught a bullet from Wil Malone's weapon.

Darkness settled over him. He remained bent over, afraid to move. What had happened here? Sight of the severed arm, so similar to the dreams he hated had forced return of his memory. His bullet had hit General Jackson in the arm, and they had amputated it. Had he caused Ruben to lose his arm? No, he thought, the craziness running together. He groaned, puked, and, in the end, lay with knees to his chest, crying like a child.

Ruben's words came back to him. Potter had taken Sassy captive. Why had he done that? The thought stayed with him only a moment, then he was back in time on a night like this, at Chancellorsville, eighteen years earlier. He remembered it all now, checking the pickets to make sure they were alert, the sounds of horses in the dark, the shooting and the shout—"General Jackson's been hit!" Where had the memories been all these years?

Old scenes flooded back—a visit to a field hospital, the beloved general lying on his bed, a Bible close beside him on his right. On the left, the sheets flat, showing the void where the arm should be.

A wagon filled with body parts had passed him on the road, leaving the hospital. It wasn't a dream, after all. No wonder they had stripped him of his commission. His mind flitted from past to present. Virgil Potter had Sassy!

It wasn't surprising that the outlaw had sought revenge on the fencing crew after Wade had declared war by using that branding iron. But kidnapping Sassy didn't add up. There was no haven for hostage takers. Even the Indians had learned that. Potter had to know that would turn every hand in Texas against him.

But none of it mattered. He, Bones Malone, had to pull himself together, sort out his disarranged madness, come back into the real world, and form a plan like a real man. Sassy had to be freed.

He found Pete and Barney grazing a quarter mile from the scene of the slaughter. The front wheels of the wagon were lodged in a shelf of rocks. Working them free took time—too much time. He would have to go by the ranch, but he couldn't leave the remains to those damned vultures, especially not Ruben.

Bones unloaded the wire near Ruben and struggled in the moonlight, until he had loaded the last corpse. It was Ruben's. He laid it gently on top. Although the boy's body was cold, his spirit seemed to guide him. A short time later, he pulled the team to a stop on a low rise of the prairie. He fought down emotions and gained release in the hard labor of gravedigging. He guessed the time to be near 2 o'clock in the morning when he finished digging and gently lowered Ruben into the ground.

Remembering the Bible, he returned to the fence site and rummaged through bedrolls until he found the book. He placed it on Ruben's chest and buried him. For the first time in his life he felt sorry for Wade. Then his feelings turned inward, and he pitied himself; he'd have the chore of telling his cousin. If she didn't already know, he'd have to tell Sassy, too, and he wasn't sure how he was going to do that, not if he cried every time he thought of it.

"Stop it!" he grunted. "You ain't got time."

He packed down the last clod of earth and stuck the shovel handle up into the grave for a headstone. He mounted the wagon and turned the team toward the ranch. He was going for Sassy, but if men were available at headquarters, he'd take them. If not, he'd go alone. Chances were Wade didn't know what was happening. He wished for San Tone.

* * * * *

A challenging nicker trumpeted across the dark meadow. The shadowy outline of Ruben's captured mustang moved at the end of his tether. Bones had forgotten the animal. He pulled to its side, impatient to be on his way, but was held immobile by his nephew's last boyhood dream. Reflected moonlight flashed from the scamp's eyes.

The stud's quick movements and alert ears spoke of regained energy. After all of Ruben's high hopes for the horse, it seemed a shame to release him, but he wasn't ready to be led along behind a wagon, and he sure couldn't stay hitched to that log forever.

A good horse could save a day's time getting to the ranch. Now refreshed, the mustang had the makings. All he needed was rawhide riding and a limber-jointed cowboy to roll out his kinks before he'd be usable.

Once he'd have been the one to take on such a chore, but truth of the matter was, right now, he was scared to think about it. Still, Ruben had wanted him ridden.

Shit, he thought, *the boy wanted it, and the bronc offers a chance to get to Sassy sooner.*

He had no choice. He reached for the wagon's brake. He unhitched the mules, hung the harness on the sideboards, and released the animals. He grabbed his saddle and bridle. No telling when he'd be back for the mules, or where he'd find them, but, for right now, they were on their own. He approached the bronco, talking to him like a long lost lover.

A front hoof missed his head by a quarter of an inch, settling any doubt about its readiness for battle. He dropped the saddle and threw a loop around both of the mustang's forehoofs. The horse fought until he lost his balance and fell. Bones allowed him to rise, then, forfeiting safety for speed, bridled him before easing his rig on him. He tightened the cinch. The horse snorted and rattled his nostrils. He stood, hobbled, wild-eyed, and humped-back.

Bones took a last look around, tugged his hat down almost over his eyes, stuffed his pistol into its holster, and with the horse's head pulled toward him, swung into leather. In midair, he pulled the hobble rope, releasing the slipknot. The horse was free, he was aboard, and they had flat ground and open sky to work with. The stud used it all.

Bones found his right stirrup, then lost it on the way down. He couldn't get his own head forward or the outlaw's from between his legs. The horse landed, spine-sizzling stiff. Bones' head came forward, the horse's up, then something slammed against his nose. His old saddle sounded like it was coming apart, and the mustang squalled like a cougar. Somehow his right boot kept trying to kick his hat off. The moon darted across the night sky and thoughts of Pete grew sweeter by the second.

Like a gyrating shadow in the night the black sunfished, spun, reared, and lunged. The horse threw him in the air, but bucked back under him as he came down. He lost his hold, his vision, and tasted warm, salty blood. Fear kept him aboard—fear that the bronco would eat him if he got the chance.

The mustang made one last desperate lunge, reared into the air, teetered, then hit the ground at a dead run. Objects swept past, and blood streamed from Bones' nose and mouth. At this rate the two-day trip to headquarters would be over before dawn, except they were going the wrong way. He tried turning the snake, but the iron jaws had the bit in his teeth and was set on going south.

Pink colored the eastern sky and they slowed. Down the slope before them, a light blinked from the window of a nester's shack and smoke drifted from the chimney. Hell, they must be almost back to Welcome.

Bones pulled hard on the off rein and managed to get the horse turned right by kicking him on the left side of his jaw. The stubborn snake likely had a jackass in his tree somewhere. The animal blew hard, lathered and stumbling from exhaustion. A broken curb strap, visible in the improving light explained his lack of control. Gradually Bones slowed the horse by pulling him into an increasingly smaller circle. Finally they stopped.

Bones couldn't think. Pain numbed him. He sat on the trembling horse and gritted his teeth. The horse's breath came in deep, rasping sobs. The horse's heart pounded, and Bones wondered if the mustang would ever fully recover. He had to get off, walk, rest, but if he did, could he get back on? Probably not. He vowed to tough it out.

The horse blew for five minutes. He nudged the animal and it surprised him by responding. The stud walked toward the farmer's place without offering more battle.

Someone had swept the dirt yard around the place and curtains showed in the windows. Two cedar posts had a clothesline strung between them. Bones was pleased to the soles of his new boots with his success in guiding the black around them. He was too tired, the line too low, to duck.

Near the barn, a man moved from the side of a milk cow and waved. He opened the barn door, freeing a week-old spotted calf. It raced from the opening, took a right turn past the milk pen, kicked its heels in the air, and bucked twice. With its tail straight up and at full speed, it made a large circle around the pen, the barn, and back toward the cow. Bones only had time to tense.

The stud cocked an ear just before the calf ran behind his front legs and under his belly. He rolled his eyes as the baby came out the other side and lunged straight ahead. Bones rode air. He saw the farmer waving his arms as the horse's rump disappeared into the barn. The ground jolted against his back and his head banged hard.

From his back, Bones blinked until the two shadows above formed into the little old lady from Welcome and her grandson. "It's OK, cowboy, I shut the barn door on him," the young man said.

"Can we leave him there a spell?" Bones mumbled. As an afterthought he asked: "Are it stout?"

Granny bent over, checking him closely. "Why, bless my soul, it's that nice Mississippi boy."

Bones struggled to sit, then took his hat off in deference to the old lady.

"Mississippi, you been butchering?" she asked, looking at the dried blood on his face and clothes.

"No, burying."

"Did sumpthin' happen to your colored friend?"

The grandson stuck out his hand. "I'm Lester. Looking out the door over there is my wife Judy. Think you know Granny."

"Wil Malone. No, ma'am, San Tone's OK. Lost a bunch of others, though. Pleased to meet you again, ma'am." Bones nodded at Judy. "Lester, you reckon you could tug a little on that hand and help me up from here?" He stood and staggered toward the well.

He drew a fresh bucket of water and filled the wash pan sitting by the well. His nose had stopped bleeding and was caked with dried blood. His breath wheezed through his mouth. He emptied and refilled the pan before feeling clean.

He told Lester briefly about Virgil Potter and the slaughtered fencing crew. He could think of no reason for Potter to bother the nesters, but at least they would be alerted.

Moments later, Granny leaned out the window. "Vittles, come and get it."

"Ma'am, you don't mind, I'm too dirty to come in. Maybe you'd just hand me a plate out the door. Wouldn't feel right in a civilized kitchen."

Granny started to argue the matter, but took another look at him and handed a heaping plate of biscuits, scrambled eggs, and bacon out the door. "Least take one of them chairs," she said.

"No, ma'am, I'm good. Ain't gonna be here long."

Lester brought him a cup of coffee. Bones ate, then smoked. He would let the horse rest a few minutes before hightailing on to the ranch. He fell asleep watching a pup's busy tongue wash his emptied plate.

Minutes later he awoke, rolling to let blood get to his numb hand. He thought of Ruben, Stonewall Jackson, and Sassy in that order. A panicky sense of urgency pulled at him.

The boy they called John Lloyd threw rocks at a Rhode Island rooster while cussing like a camp follower. Bones guessed the boy to be about six. His rocks missed badly, but the oaths were impressive. The rooster had flogged the wrong customer.

Lester was back at the barn. Bones got to his feet and joined him. He peered through a crack at the black stud.

Lester said: "He settled down about ten minutes after you did. I fed and watered him. Oh, yeah, fixed that curb strap, too."

"Guess I was about tuckered. I'm obliged." Bones opened the barn door, stepped inside, and latched it from inside. Minutes later, he opened it and rode the black out.

Granny's clan watched from the porch.

"What do I owe you good people?"

"Just take care and come back," Lester said.

Bones looked at the kid. "Take care of that pup, boy."

"He's got fleas," John Lloyd said, picking through his rocks.

"All good ones do," Bones said.

"What's her name?" Granny hollered.

"Whose?" he asked.

"Your new girl."

"What you talking about?" He couldn't help smiling.

"Cowboy buys new boots and hat the same pay day, there's got to be a petticoat around somewhere." She cackled.

Bones shook his head. He touched reins to the mustang, smooched, and the horse broke into a crow hop. After a few jumps he settled to a trot. Reckoning by the sun, Bones figured he owed the day at least two more hours till noon.

* * * * *

He paid his debt to the sun and stopped at a creek for water. The lacy shade of a mesquite offered limited relief from furnace-like heat. The rain cloud that hit Sundown City three nights earlier had failed to reach this land. The grass was baked to straw and crunched beneath him even in the shade.

Before dark, he spotted San Tone's wagon coming toward him. The big ex-slave began talking before he stopped. "That darn Wade sent me halfway to Hayrick, otherwise I'd 'a' been here yesterday. Yuh look peaked." He pulled the reins. "Whoa, team!"

"San Tone, Ruben's dead."

San Tone blanched. "How?"

"Potter. They … killed the whole fencing crew." Bones voice broke. "Do you know about Sassy?"

"Know she's jumpy as a flea on a dead man, what yuh mean?"

"Ruben got out that Potter had taken her hostage."

"Saw her day 'fore yesterday. She rode with me a ways, then took off toward one of them hills," San Tone said.

"She alone?"

"She was. I think she and Wade's fussing. Neither one of them would hardly talk." San Tone looked toward the west and slowly worked his way back to face Bones. "Don't seem right … that boy being the one to go and the rest of us still here."

"I'm going to the ranch and let Wade know, then I'm going after Sassy. Coming?"

"Might know sumpthin' would come up a day or two after I drop off the saddle horses. What'd yuh do with your team?"

"Turned them loose. Guess I better switch my gear to one of them plow horses of yours. I've about wore this thing out," Bones said.

"That Ruben's mustang?"

Bones wasn't sure, but he thought he saw the big man wipe a tear. He nodded.

They saddled San Tone's team, left the harness in the wagon, and rode toward headquarters. After the first tug on the lead rope the mustang led like a milk-pen calf.

At daybreak, exhausted and dull from lack of sleep, they rode across the deserted grounds and toward the barn at headquarters.

CHAPTER NINETEEN

Angel sat sideways on a top rail of the headquarters corral. He held a rifle in the crook of his arm. His coloring had returned since Bones had last seen him at the hanging. He strode toward them as they approached.

"Mister Malone and the others ... they left yesterday ... before dark!" Angel hollered in halting English, his words flavored with the softness of his accent.

"Howdy, Angel. Does he know about Sassy and Ruben?" Bones asked as they approached the man.

"*Sí* ... Señora Malone ... he's gone after her. What about Ruben?"

Bones started to speak, but had to choke down his feelings.

San Tone nodded in Bones' direction. "He come on Ruben's whole crew. They'd been slaughtered by Potter."

"Cecil ... Perk?" Angel's face wore a mask of shocked disbelief. He took the mustang's lead rope.

"All dead," Bones said. "How'd y'all hear of Sassy?"

"Maude came back to the barn without a saddle. A message had been tied to her halter. She looked like she traveled heavy miles."

Sylvia and the boy stood on the porch of the big house, looking in their direction. Bones turned his attention back to the cowpuncher. "What did the note say?"

"Said if he wanted to see Señora Malone alive, to send a rider to Yellow House Draw on the Llano Estacada with five thousand dollars. Said to come alone and not to try anything because he had twenty-five men. Do you think he has that many?" Angel had one hand on the stud's halter and was about to free it in the lot.

"No reason to doubt it. Best put the mustang in a stall," Bones said.

They carried their saddles to the shed, then Angel led the way to the ranch house.

Sylvia met them at the front door. Her concern showed. "I'll fix you something in the kitchen," she said.

Bones took off his hat and nodded thanks. Angel took his wife's hand and together they entered the hallway. Their youngster looked at Bones and crossed his eyes. He flapped his arms like the wings of a rooster. Bones smiled, tousled the kid's head. He moved on toward the kitchen.

"You bring your roadrunner?" The boy's eyes followed his mother. His words came out of the side of his mouth.

"Think he growed tired of me," Bones said. "Ain't got a guinea you can loan me, have you?"

The boy shook his head and ran ahead.

Sylvia set the table with cold steak and other leftovers. They talked little during the meal, then took coffee out to the porch.

San Tone motioned for Angel to come. "Did Wade have the money?" San Tone asked.

"*Sí*, he took it from the safe."

"They been on the trail, how long?" Bones asked.

"An hour before dark yesterday."

Bones blew on his coffee. "What you think, San Tone?"

"No way we gonna catch them."

Bones rubbed the back of his neck. "Truth is I'm beat to a frazzle. Let's sleep a couple of hours, then ride. How many horses did Wade take?"

"Just what they rode." Angel looked puzzled by the question.

"How many men?" San Tone asked.

Angel studied the sky. He flicked three fingers on his right hand, one at a time. He looked at the barn and flipped out each finger on his other hand twice. "Thirteen."

"We need this outfit's best three horses," Bones said. "It's a matter of life and death. Which are the fastest and longest-winded mounts on the place?"

"Some are one, you know … the speed … others are the other," Angel said.

"No, darn it, a long run … I mean long … like eighty miles. Which ones?"

San Tone looked at Angel. "Does that fancy stud ride?"

"He's a … how you say? … handful. But Señor Malone rides him."

"Needing only speed and distance, he's one," San Tone said. "Then that mare Sassy rides is another." San Tone cocked an eye at Bones. "You know better than me, but the mustang looks like he's got a lot of bottom. He got speed to go with it?"

"He's got it all," Bones assured. "Angel, water and grain them three now, then again at noon. We'll lead them up there, and, if we get lucky, use them for the run back. Riding out, we'll use those four we rode to Hayrick the first time we met you … remember?" Angel nodded. "If you would, catch them up and have them ready. Yeah, and ask your missus could she fix us some grub."

Bones found clothes in Ruben's closet he could wear and others in Wade's room large enough for San Tone. They showered at the pump house, and then slept on quilts laid on the west porch.

Bones woke an hour after noon, and they rode away from the barn a short time later. San Tone led the thoroughbreds, and

Bones led the mustang and two extra saddle horses. An empty saddle, for Sassy, rode the blue roan. The studs cast warlike glances at each other.

* * * * *

At midafternoon the next day, four mounted figures slowly took form through a chest-deep mirage of shimmering water. The objects dipped from sight only to reappear larger than before, moving through wavering vapors beyond the blistering red clay and rocky outcroppings of the badlands.

Bones sat the roan, relaxed and stuffing his pipe by feel, his eyes remaining on the images moving toward them.

San Tone jerked away from the boulder he had tried leaning against. "Thing's too hot to touch." He spit a stream of tobacco juice and returned to watching the figures. "It's riders, all right. I make out four."

"Should've brought Wade's spyglass," Bones said. "They coming this way, ain't they?"

San Tone nodded. "Let me have them lead ropes, and I'll tie off these extras back there in the cañon. We may need free hands when that bunch gets here."

Bones lit his pipe. He took the rifle from its boot and checked to see a shell was chambered. Sitting on the roan behind an embankment, only Bones' head and shoulders were visible to the approaching riders. He hoped these were Wade's men, but they could easily be Potter's. Ten more minutes would answer the question.

San Tone returned. Bones knocked fire from his pipe. The figures were growing rapidly, taking on form with each stumbling step of their horses.

"It's Wade," San Tone whispered. He rode a few steps toward the oncoming riders and waved his hat. "Over heah, men!"

The horsemen rode in slowly. Wade, hollow-eyed and dirty,

rode in front. Under each arm sweat showed darkly, contrasting with the white alkali dust and dried salt on the rest of his clothing. Owen, Peaches, and the cowpuncher named Carl rode beside him.

Wade looked at them with hardly a flicker of recognition showing on his face. Bones handed him a water bag. His cousin put his mouth to the bag's opening and turned it up. San Tone handed Owen a drink while Peaches and Carl waited their turn.

Wade handed Peaches the water and answered Bones' unasked question. "He's still got her." His chin dropped to his chest, and he slumped in the saddle. His right arm was wrapped in a bloody neckerchief, and his holster was empty.

San Tone looked at Peaches. "The others?"

Peaches shook his head and looked away. His arm was in a sling, and a bandage was around his head.

Carl slid from his saddle and hit the dirt with a soft, plopping sound. Bones sprang to the fallen man. San Tone joined him. The cowboy licked at the trickle of blood coming from the corners of his mouth. He looked left, then right, a wild, frightened expression on his face. "I'm kilt," he whispered, and slipped away. The fear in his eyes turned dull and lifeless.

Bones looked back at Peaches' blanched face. "You mean you four are all that's left of thirteen men?"

Peaches made no comment, but Owen dismounted and motioned for the two to follow. Bones trailed the tall cowboy a short distance. Muscles danced up and down Owen's jaw. His eyes narrowed, and his lips formed a tight line. San Tone stood beside them.

Owen kicked a rock, and a great gulping sob broke from his mouth. "In twenty year, since I left home, I ain't never waved a bad tongue at a man that paid my wages. But, Bones, that cousin of yours is loco as a dog with a running fit. He wouldn't listen, or take heed to nothing nobody offered. Led us into an ambush and got us wiped out ... every damn one, but us three. We all knew better, but we let pride, or whatever the hell it was, bully us into staying with him. Thirteen of us rode into a gap, and four come out." He shook his head. "It was a turkey shoot."

San Tone put his huge hand on Owen's shoulder and Bones saw the fingers tighten. Owen reached and grabbed the hand that held him.

Bones spoke. "Owen, I'm sorry, but there's more. The fencing crew at Welcome ... the son of a bitch killed all them on his way up here. Ruben ... all of them."

"Cecil?"

Bones nodded. "I got to tell Wade."

"You got any whiskey?" asked Owen as he sat down.

Bones walked to his saddlebags and pulled out a full pint he'd taken from Wade's cabinet. Owen took a long swig, then Peaches came over and did the same. Bones took a drink and offered the bottle to Wade. He shook his head, but Bones placed it in his hand and motioned for him to take a drink. When Wade lowered the bottle from his mouth, half its contents was gone.

"Wade, there's more bad news," Bones began. "That bunch killed Ruben and everybody in his crew." Bones watched his cousin's eyes lose what little focus they held, then saw his face turn to jelly. Wade sagged, and San Tone grabbed him and eased him to the ground.

"I've caused it all!" Wade's anguished cry tore at Bones' insides. He had to move. He walked in a tight circle, threw his head back, and stared into the screaming quiet of endless sky.

Later, Wade refused San Tone's offer of food, but Peaches and Owen went after the beef jerky like hungry wolves.

"How'd y'all get away?" San Tone asked.

Peaches answered. "Just luck of the draw. We went in that pass to save two miles. About halfway through when the shooting started. The others were all down before they knew what happened. The four of us got our horses turned. We hightailed it. About a dozen came after us. Wade"—he looked at his boss—"Mister Malone took the money he had in the bags and scattered it as we rode. That slowed them down when they stopped to gather it up. By the time the money was gone, so were we."

"When did all this happen?" Bones asked.

"About three, yesterday," Owen said.

"Yuh throwed out all five thousand?" San Tone asked Wade. He got no response.

Bones stood. "Boys, we're going on."

"You two going up against that bunch?" Owen looked at them in disbelief.

"I hope not," Bones said. "But we're gonna try and sneak Sassy away from them."

Wade raised his head at the mention of Sassy's name, then lowered it again.

"Mind if I come with you?" Owen asked.

"You're welcome," Bones said, "but think we'd just get you killed. See … whatever chance we got lies with them three fast horses we're packing. Mounted on any of this other stuff, there's bound to be somebody up there that has got one faster. You wouldn't have a chance. B'sides, if we get Sassy out of there, we'll get up a bunch … sort of a posse … and go pay Mister Virgil Potter a real visit. I'd sure like to have you with us then."

"You serious?" Owen asked.

"If I ain't drinking in town, I'm always serious." Bones smiled. "See you back at headquarters."

He and San Tone tied Carl's body over his saddle and left the horse ground hitched.

Bones shook Peaches' hand. "See you," he said, and handed the little man the bottle. "Here, pour some of this on them wounds 'fore the screw worms get you."

Riding from the group, Bones turned so San Tone couldn't see his face. He felt used up. Until now he had hoped they could join with the bunch from headquarters and all have a chance. That chance was gone. All his talk about fast horses was just that—talk. Far as he knew, they hadn't made one yet that could outrun flying lead.

He thought about Sassy and couldn't decide if he wished he'd kissed her there in the barn or not. One thing was sure. There was a time he'd loved her. Seeing Wade like he was made him glad he'd backed off from her. He was even more pleased when he thought of Ruben. On the other hand, Ruben was dead, and, if he were soon to be, then it'd be sort of nice to have that memory to take with him.

He thought of Estella and how easy she was to be with. Comfortable, she made him feel comfortable. Then Jackson and the night at Chancellorsville pushed thoughts of her aside. Hell, the world was complicated. He forced his thoughts to the arrogant Virgil Potter, no confusion with that thought. The man had killed enough.

* * * * *

Two days later they rode out of the badlands onto a vast prairie. Unending grass swayed before them, dwarfing their senses. Dry hot wind leached all energy.

Bones stood in his stirrups and, twisting, looked in every direction. He spoke aloud, rambling, trying to form a plan. "All looks purty much the same, don't it? That Yellow House Draw's up there a ways, but don't know how far. Only here once, and we were hurrying. Bet they ain't far. If they're holed up, like I think, we may be in trouble. Wander around on this flat ground too long, somebody's gonna spot us. That happens … the jig's up."

"Don't see much choice. Sign all says we on their trail," San Tone said.

"Think we ought to hole up till dark," Bones suggested. "If we travel at night, we might have a better chance of seeing them first. With Wade done in, they think they're safe. They'll have a fire."

"Ain't no place to get out of sight?"

"We can just stop and sit."

San Tone pulled his horse to a stop. "Here?"

Bones dismounted. "Here."

They dozed, swatted gnats, and watched their horses grazing for the rest of the afternoon. After dark, they rode on. Bones wanted to light his pipe, but dared not flare a match. They rode with the North Star hanging above their right shoulders. Clouds threatened, and lightning flashed in the distance.

"With that cloud coming, we gonna lose this moonlight before long," San Tone said.

"We got to be close, San Tone."

"What's so special about that draw that makes yuh think they gonna be there?"

"Water. Nothing unusual other'n that, but, through the summer and after, them old buffalo wallows dry up. That's enough. There ain't no lookout hill or hidden entrance. Distance makes it safe, and water makes it livable."

A mosquito *buzzed* near Bones' ear. He slapped at it, and the mustang shied sideways at the sudden move. The end of the lead rope brought him to a sudden stop.

San Tone stared at the horse. His look showed admiration. "He's getting feisty again while these others are wearing down." His view shifted from the mustang and he threw his arm up, pointing. "Over yonder! Hold it, Wil! Way over yonder, I saw sumpthin'."

"What …? I don't see nothing."

San Tone pointed. "There … see that? Somebody's got a fire."

CHAPTER TWENTY

Bones detected the faint flicker of light. "How far you think?"

"Maybe a mile."

"That far! They seem to be below us. Camped in Yellow House Draw, maybe. We get closer, these damn studs are gonna nicker, especially if there's mares around. What do you think?"

"You tell me. Studs were your idea."

Bones dismounted and sat. "I think from here on ... bad as I hate it ... this is gonna have to be done afoot. We got at least six more hours of dark." He took off his spurs and tied them to the saddle strings. "You stay here with the ponies."

"You gonna leave them old chaps on?" San Tone asked.

"Most of the way, rather be shot than snake bit. I ain't got no idea if there's a chance of snatching Sassy tonight, but, if you would, saddle the thoroughbreds and that old black. Be ready to ride should I get things stirred up."

"We'll be ready. Iffen I hear a commotion, I'm coming that way, trailing them two. Watch yuhself."

"You, too. And, San Tone, this don't work, you ride the hell out of here. Don't look back nor worry about what might have been. You get back, maybe you and Wade can get the army or somebody to help … in case Sassy's still alive. Pard, least I'm glad we got to say hello again."

Distant thunder rumbled as the storm grew across the night sky. Bones made good time for the first half mile, then slowed. The ground was soft and silent underfoot. The fire grew larger, then faded as though running out of wood. He carried his rifle in his right hand and walked, crouched forward.

He paused often, moving only after assuring himself of the safety of the emptiness before him. He lowered himself and used the sky for a source of light to frame questionable shadows. Moving only his head, he panned the darkness before him. Move, stop, search, like a cat he closed until only yards separated him from the fire. He dropped to his knees.

Other fires glowed to his right and left. He was in the middle of Potter's encampment. There was no way he could scout through this maze. He had to find Sassy, but how? Moving from fire to fire was too dangerous. A twig would snap or a bush rattle. These men lived by their senses—senses honed razor-sharp.

Behind and to his left, a horse coughed, and Bones crouched lower and made out the forms of several grazing toward him. Closer to the fire, blanket-covered forms lay on the ground. His heart pounded. Might he yet get lucky? Could she be there, beneath one of those covers? He studied the scene, then realized men's hats and chaps lay near each form. He forced himself to breath deeply.

He sensed movement behind him, and whirled. A horse loomed above him only a few feet away. Bones slowly stuck out his hand to the animal. It moved toward him and sniffed. The body of the animal showed lighter than its mane and legs.

Potter rode a buckskin. It must be his and spoiled—a pet. Easy to catch, the animal was more interested in getting its nose in Bones' pocket than its own freedom. It wore no hobbles. He removed a leather cord from his hatband and bridled the animal, Indian fashion, with a loop behind its lower teeth.

Positioned with the buckskin between himself and the fire, he walked the animal around the next glow. He moved short distances at a time like a free-grazing animal. Two men played cards and shared a bottle. One raised his head, staring, when the horse's hoof clipped a rock.

"You hear something?" he asked, rising to his feet. He walked out of the circle of firelight, looking intently into the dark.

"It's just old Buck, wandering around." The speaker's voice carried relief.

"He's gonna step in the middle of somebody one of these nights. Virgil needs to keep him down there where he belongs," the man said, turning to the fire.

Bones turned the horse and slowly retraced his steps. The man had said "down there." That meant the opposite direction. Virgil was at one of the fires to the left of the one he first approached. He'd likely find Sassy with the outlaw leader. Anxious minutes later, he approached a fire that glowed in front of a canvas tent.

Lightning flashed, brighter than before, creating a strange world of stark, yet vivid black and white detail. By the fire two sleeping forms presented his most immediate danger. Then he saw her, staring at him in pale, wide-eyed fright. She sat on the ground, against a tree.

His first impulse was to run to her, but he stopped himself. There were at least two men here, and he didn't know how many more fifty yards up and down that draw. The light was gone before he could signal Sassy to make no sound.

He circled and approached from behind her. "Sassy, it's me, Wil," he whispered.

Her wrists were lashed behind her back around the small tree trunk. Her ankles were tied before her. She had no gag, but remained silent. He cut her bonds and rubbed life back into her wrists and ankles. She bent toward him and rested her head on his shoulder. A moment later he helped her to her feet and took her hand, turning toward the horse, pulling her behind him.

Sassy's right arm shot around his body, and his holster shifted as she tugged at his pistol. Two steps later, he grabbed her. She was headed for the tent, the revolver raised and cocked. He took the six-shooter and lowered the hammer. In the next flash of lightning, he saw her face was pale, drawn, and that the hate in her eyes needed no words.

"Not now, Sassy, we'll see to it later." Her sob sounded louder than his whisper. He helped her onto the horse's back, then walked slowly beside the horse for a distance before swinging on behind. Bones walked the horse before nudging him into a trot back to San Tone.

He was exhilarated. They now had an even chance, maybe better, depending how soon someone woke and noticed Sassy was missing.

A few minutes later, at a full lope, he hollered: "San Tone it's us! I got her!" He pulled the buckskin to a sliding halt and was stopped from dismounting by Sassy turning to face him. She threw her arms around his neck and hugged him. Before he knew it, she had kissed him quickly, forcefully.

Was this a kiss from Sassy the woman or Sassy the little girl? Was it awe and gratitude, or more? His head floated; happy, he was tired of questions and ready for answers. It was time to take a chance. In his light-headed relief, it seemed proper. He returned the hug. Life was uncertain. He'd be a fool not to squeeze the last drop. He held her tightly just as she threw her leg from around the horse, and her full weight rested in his arms.

Off balance, he followed her down. Falling, there was little he could do. He hit the ground, protecting her from his weight with extended arms. San Tone swerved and slid Bonnie Glen to a stop.

"Yuh all right, Sassy?" San Tone asked.

She jumped to her feet and ran to him. He bent, and she threw her arms around his neck.

"My heroes," she said. She turned and offered Bones a helping hand up.

Embarrassed, he refused it, and quickly got to his feet.

Sassy's voice held hope, trailing to fear with her last words. "Wil, do you know? Is Ruben alive?"

He stiffened, his heart in his throat. He raised his arms and dropped them. He turned, first to his right, then his left. He looked at her and tried to speak. Muscles contracted in his throat; tears streamed from his eyes. He grabbed his saddle horn with both hands and dropped his head on his arms.

"He's gone, Sassy," San Tone said, his voice vibrating with his own pain.

Bones gritted his teeth, raised his head, and took Sassy by the arm. "I couldn't help him, Sassy." He moved her toward Maude. "We gotta go."

She turned on him, eyes flashing, venom and hatred in her voice. "That son of a bitch up there killed my boy. Go? Not till he's dead." She jerked her arm free.

Bones flipped Maude's reins to San Tone and grabbed Sassy by the waist. He lifted and placed her into the mare's saddle. "I'll be back to see he gets his deserts. Now it's time to go."

He swung aboard his shying mustang. Minutes later, he heard shots. Someone had alerted the camp, they had been discovered—discovered and 100 miles from home with only a two-mile lead.

Darkness and good horseflesh were their only friends. Bones placed the mustang in the lead and held a slow lope. It would take a while for the outlaws to get mounted, then they could only guess at the direction. Darkness offered hours of questionable safety. Tomorrow the test would come. Could they outrun the outlaws' horses?

He reached into his saddlebags and removed the pistol he had taken from Carl's holster. He passed it, handle first, to Sassy. She hesitated, then stuck it in the waistband of her riding skirt.

"I saw them ambush Wade and the hands, but I think Wade got away," Sassy said.

"He did. He's safe at the ranch by now," Bones said. Damn, why hadn't he told her that already?

They saw the first sign of pursuit minutes after sunrise. Ant size, the rider appeared on the horizon. At noon, crossing the Salt Fork of the Brazos, the number had grown to ten.

They would ride on the north side of the river for an hour, then cross back to the south bank as the river curved. The horses had been under saddle for a dozen hours, but they traveled easily, ears up and alert. During the night, they had rested for short periods twice. Now Bones looked back. The enemy had gained. They trailed by only a mile.

"It's close to time to let 'em out, ain't it?" San Tone said, nodding at their mounts.

"Let's give it a couple of more minutes. Be back close to the river by then. I swear, I think we can make it. They've been pushing hard. How do you suppose they gathered so many on our trail so quick?"

"You didn't hear them shots they signaled with a while back?" San Tone asked.

Bones shook his head.

A low ridgeline marked the bluff of the south rim of the Brazos River. The nearest of the outlaws closed to a half mile. San Tone and Sassy cast nervous looks, waiting for the signal. Bones nodded. "Now!"

Sassy and San Tone slacked their reins, and the thoroughbreds responded with smooth, easy, and lengthening strides. The mustang matched them with shorter steps. Culled by nature from Spanish bloodlines and conditioned by the necessities of survival, he seemed to float effortlessly beside the larger animals. The enemy slipped farther behind.

Wind flattened the brim of Bones' hat. His ears roared. He thought his hearing played tricks. A rumble surged from the bed of the river. It was not unlike the rolling noise of last night's distant storm. A moment later, in sight of the riverbed, reality gripped him in a vise. Only yards upstream, the bed of the Brazos erupted in a wall of water—a head rise. In its path, they had only seconds. Survival meant crossing before the water arrived. Otherwise, the bend of the river would turn them back toward the outlaw gang.

"You know what's happening, San Tone?" he hollered.

San Tone nodded.

"What?" Sassy asked.

"A head rise ... the damn Brazos is on a head rise."

Ahead 300 yards, the bed of the river lay flat, bare, and dry. Upstream, a similar distance and to their right, a wall of brown, raging water bore down on them. Inside the frothy liquid all manner of tree limbs and debris churned. The rise was as high as a mounted rider and yards wide.

"Can we make it?" Sassy screamed.

"We gotta make it," San Tone answered.

The trio had asked their horses for full speed at the first sounds of the water. Now they spurred, whipped, and demanded that last burst reserved only for life or death. Their course led across sandy riverbed, then on between a narrow opening of dunes and into a few yards of calm, shallow water. Between the water and the bluffs of the south bank a grass-covered embankment formed a barrier seven feet high. The barrier opened for a dry wash that extended upward to higher ground.

San Tone whipped the bay, and he flattened his ears and jumped ahead with Maude at his heels. The mustang followed. The wind roared. Sassy's hair streamed straight behind. The force of sound from the torrent pushed against Bones. Before the water, great chunks of riverbed plowed, rolling upward, then churned back into the froth. The water digested everything before it.

Bones sensed the stud flatten even lower, his speed inching faster. The bay was through the gap in the dunes first, with Maude's nose lying almost on Bonnie Glen's hips. The mustang was only three or four yards behind, and then their hoof beats splashed water head high. Mist from the flood's spray wet them. The wall of dirty froth sent waterspouts clutching madly at the three riders.

San Tone checked Bonnie Glen to let Maude flash through the embankment's opening in front. The stud's eyes glared wide and he shied sideways enough to falter out of line with the narrow gap. As though sensing its own error, it leaped high in the air in an attempt to hurdle the seven-foot embankment.

Looking up and to the side as the mustang flashed through the opening, Bones saw the bay, with San Tone still on his back, claw like a cat at the embankment, then topple backward and into the roiled water.

The mustang leaped from the fast-filling wash to higher ground, and Bones looked downriver. San Tone and his horse rolled and tossed like chaff before the great force. The river coughed them up, spit them high in the air, then swallowed them back into its wet depths. Bones sat the mustang in disbelief. Sassy cried as Maude dropped her head and struggled for breath.

Virgil Potter, 250 yards away, and nine of his men brought their horses to a stop, totally cut off by the surging current. The chase was over.

Bones shuddered.

Sassy eyes frantically searched for San Tone. "Where is he?" she cried.

Their eyes met, and he shook his head. He thought of the waters of the Mississippi and the boy he knew as Catfish. If he closed his eyes, he could still see how his friend's brown skin shining in the sun when he stepped, bare-naked, from the waters of that great river. Only fifteen, he swam it both ways in the same day. Now he lay dead, from drowning, in a desert wash that ran water three or four times a year.

Where Ruben's death had filled him with emotional tears, San Tone's left him drained with a cold feeling of being old and alone.

He loved the black—man and boy—but he'd wait to mourn. He bit his lip. The mustang lowered his head and pawed, as if challenging the waters that had snatched his opponent and carried him away.

Sassy came to him. "Is he gone for sure?"

"The water got him," he said.

"Oh, no!" She looked at the river. "He pulled up to let me through." She put both hands on the saddle horn, ducked her head, and cried. Her shoulders shook. "I teased and laughed at him, and he gave me his life."

He rode to her side, put his arm around her, and patted her shoulder.

"Ruben. Now San Tone. I hate this damn country. I hate everything about it … the sand, the never-ending wind, heat beating down on you, and water that comes out of nowhere and kills. We left tree-lined parks and Sunday evening drives. We came here with money, and a happy son, and now what? Oh, Wil, it's so terrible. What am I going to do?" Tears streamed over the dark circles under Sassy's eyes and down her cheeks. Her trembling lips pouted.

For an instant Bones thought she might fall. "Sassy, pull yourself together. We've got a long ride. Wade's waiting."

"Wade," she said the word like it had a bad taste.

Bones watched Potter's men turn and ride away.

CHAPTER TWENTY-ONE

Bones jerked awake. Sassy's shoulder rubbed against his back. Another dream or was it real? The warmth of her, the scent of her hair, all said Sassy. Had he died and gone to heaven? Probably not—the saddle beneath his head smelled of horse. Sassy had moved her blanket next to him without awakening him.

She whispered: "Wil?"

"Yeah, you all right?" The stars placed the time past midnight.

"Woke a while ago and can't go back to sleep. Ruben's on my mind. Tell me about it."

"How much did you see?" he asked. Her voice had brought back the last day's sadness—Ruben, San Tone, and the crew.

"Nothing. I saw him before the shooting started, then two men took me away. I just heard the guns. Did he suffer?"

He took a second. He'd hoped he'd not have to retrace those tracks again. "No, fact is, he was alive when I got there. Told me he didn't hurt. Now you rest easy on that, Sassy," he lied. Ruben had suffered terribly, but he'd work that out with God later. "I buried him and the rest of the boys on a sloping piece of ground over there. I'll take you and Wade to it, soon as I get back from dealing with Potter."

"You're not going after that man. Wil, what I said yesterday about killing him and all. I was mad … out of my mind. I don't want you or anyone going back up there. He likes to kill. Besides, it won't bring Ruben back."

"It's out of your hands, Sassy. I'm going to kill him. Your and Wade's boy was part of me, too. I'm going to kill the son of a bitch. Don't worry about me. I've lived too long anyway. It doesn't matter. San Tone, Ruben, all those brave ones in the war, General Jackson … they're all gone." Bones was glad it was dark so she couldn't see the tears wetting his face.

"Don't say that. It isn't true," Sassy objected. "You've been so wonderful, done so many great things. You always took everyone else's burden and carried it. Why, Wade nearly drove himself crazy during the war, knowing you had taken his place. Word trickled to us of your gallantry in all those battles, earning a commission and all. Your granddaddy didn't think anyone in the world could do things as well as you. Don't you ever let me hear you say you don't matter. Don't you do it, Wil Malone."

Bones sat upright, his blanket dropping from his shoulders. He put his face in his hands and wept. "The war part's a lie, Sassy. I was in a bunch of fighting, and I did good in some, but I run so hard once I near died. A place called Little Round Top. The Yanks came at us with bayonets, and I ran. Lord, how I ran. And, Sassy, I killed Stonewall Jackson … shot him. If he hadn't died, we would have won the war. Lee same as said it, and I caused it."

"I don't believe that. How could you know a thing like that? And if you did, he must have been in the wrong place. I won't hear any more of that."

He took a deep breath. This had gone far enough. "Wade was a little tuckered out, last I saw."

"Was he injured?"

"Just a scratch. Sure he's all right by now. Sassy, did Potter … you know … did he bother you?"

"I'm not the girl you remember, Wil. Things are no good

between Wade and me now. You're not responsible, but when you walked away, there in the barn, I realized I had changed, hadn't loved him in years. Virgil Potter raped me, but truth is he wouldn't have had to force me had he not attacked Ruben."

"You don't mean that."

"I do. He's everything I was looking for, only more ... more cruel. Now I want him dead, but I don't want to lose anyone else to make it happen." She put her head on Bones' chest and in a few minutes slept.

His last thought was of the tenderness he felt for this woman who, as a girl, first woke him to manhood. A short time later, he saddled the stud in the dark, then went to Sassy. He gently picked up her saddle, and she stirred. "Be light in a couple of hours," he said, slapping her rig on Maude. "Want jerky?"

"In about ten years." She yawned.

* * * * *

They rode into headquarters through fading sunlight. Wade rocked on the porch. He rose and met them at the hitch rack. Looking at Sassy, sadness covered his face, then his head dropped. His body shook silently.

Sassy dismounted, dropped Maude's reins, and moved to her husband. She put her arms around him, and they turned and slowly went inside.

Peaches and Angel took two steps to each of Owen's one. They crossed from the bunkhouse to the porch.

"Malone, you take the cake," Owen said. "By God, you did it, didn't you?" He took Maude's reins.

Bones looked at Peaches. "San Tone didn't make it."

"I'm sorry, Wil. I didn't know him well, but I liked him. And I know he kept good company." The little drover's hard face was tender as a schoolboy's. "Come on, you and Angel sit over there in front of the bunkhouse while Owen and I take these horses to the barn."

The sun rested too low in the southwest for the bunkhouse roof to offer shade, but at least the wooden bench didn't move, and it rubbed different places than the saddle had. He loaded his pipe while watching Angel nimbly fashion a cigarette. He lit the cowboy's smoke, then his own pipe. "You drink?" he asked.

"When Sylvia's out of sight and upwind."

Peaches and Owen joined them.

"Peaches, I know for a fact it was a taste for brandy, not preserves, got you that nickname," Bones commented. "You got a bottle?"

A minute later they passed Peaches' red-eye around the circle. Bones gave them the bare details of Sassy's rescue and the full story of San Tone's death. He concluded with his intent to go back to Yellow House Draw. "You boys wanna come?"

"All the way," Owen said.

Peaches nodded.

Angel stared at the bunkhouse. "Don't like guns ... blood makes me sick, but he killed too many that I know. I go."

"I'll spend the night here and head for Sundown City in the morning. Maybe I can pick up some men there. Juan and Jesse still at Hayrick?"

Peaches nodded.

"We can use them. If you think they might want to help, go see 'em. Anybody wants to, meet me in town three days from tomorrow ... noon." Bones motioned his head toward the big house. "What's he been doing the last couple of days?"

"Nothing," Owen said. "Just stays up there to hisself."

Bones stood, then made his way to the house.

Wade greeted him at the door. "What do you want?"

"Wondered if you got anything would oil a man's tonsils. I'll replace it first chance I get." He waited just inside.

Wade made the trip to the liquor cabinet, returned, and handed him a bottle. "Don't bother to replace it. I'm in your debt." A strange look washed across his face. "I owe you this whole damn' place. And, Wil, she told me about San Tone. I'm sorry."

"Wade, come morning, I'm heading for town. Can I find some men, and some way to make it legal, I'm going back to Yellow House Draw and string that bastard up. I'd feel lots better if you and Sassy were out of here till that's taken care of. It ain't safe."

"I'll see Sassy leaves. So long, Wil."

Bones watched Wade stagger slightly as he walked away. He scratched his head. It was strange to see him even a little out of control. He shrugged and walked to the bunkhouse.

After dark he and Angel and two other cowboys played poker by lantern light. The bottle passed freely. Sylvia sent the boy for Angel. Groggy, Bones stood stretching. He checked the sky, then glanced at the balcony of the big house.

Wade's cigar blinked from the deep shadows. A chill went down Bones' back at the thought of him standing up there, probably lonely, hurt, and too damned snooty to come down and join the game. But to hell with it, better save his sympathy for himself. Wade drew the line between the big house and the bunkhouse, deep and straight.

* * * * *

Bones followed the smell of coffee toward Sylvia's kitchen. Walking challenged his body; a drowsy fog draped his mind. He washed at the well, tucked in his shirttail, and then knocked quietly on the kitchen door.

The cook's greeting held a little frost, but she waved him in. "Coffee be ready in a minute."

He bet Angel's morning had started a little rocky, also.

"Mister Malone, would you go light the lamps in the drawing room? She likes them lit when she comes down." Sylvia handed him matches, loosening a bit. "I'll pour you a cup, time you're through."

"Yes, ma'am."

He walked from the kitchen into the dark shadows of the long hallway that led to the huge parlor at the house's front. The doorway framed lighter shadows at the end of the hall. His shoulder bumped something, and he grabbed and caught the teetering hat rack before it fell. A long hall opened to a room from the side of the staircase. A slight movement to his left stopped him. At eye level, a darker shadow caught his attention. He instinctively reached for his pistol. His fingers closed on the grips, then he felt foolish. Only Sylvia's ironing, something she'd hung there. He took two steps, reached, and touched the heel of a boot.

He recoiled, took a step backward, and struck a match on the underside of a small table. Light flared. Wade hung suspended from the balcony. His head twisted grotesquely, a neatly tied hangman's noose taut behind his ear. Bones held the match higher and looked at the bulging eyes, the ashen face, and, most hideous of all, the tongue bulging from the lifeless lips. Pain scorched his fingers, and he dropped the match. He stood in the dark, breathless.

He crossed to a lamp. It lit on the second try. He wheeled and took the stairs two at a time. He crouched and opened his pocket knife with his teeth and one hand while holding the rope with the other hand. My God! He couldn't do it this way without dropping Wade. He had to have help, a ladder. But there was no time. He slashed the rope, and a sickening *thump* came from below as Wade's body dropped to the floor.

Bones bolted part way down the stairs, then vaulted the railing to land on hands and knees beside Wade. The coldness of the lifeless form told all. He heard a door close behind him, then Sassy's scream. From the corner of his eye, he saw her release the railing and rush to the stairs. Halfway down, she stopped and sagged to her knees. He rushed to her.

She pounded the stairs with her fists and cried, deep torturing sounds. "No! No, Wade. Why … why did you do it?"

Sylvia came and knelt by their side. "Let's get her to her room," Bones snapped. The cook crossed her chest, her lips moving before she grasped her mistress.

Sassy's scream had brought the hands from the bunkhouse. They helped move Wade's body to a divan. They stood beside their boss' body, hats in hands, grief and confusion on their faces. Bones motioned them to follow, and walked to the porch. He added his own confused search for tobacco to theirs.

"Knew he was in a bad way, but never thought he'd do something like that," Owen drawled.

"How long you been with him?" Bones asked while lighting his pipe.

"About a year. Helped him buy most of this stock down in South Texas."

"How about you, Angel?"

"Known him four or five years, since Sylvia went to work for Señora Malone in Galveston. I joined the payroll about the same time Owen did."

Bones pulled on the pipe, tasting its flavor, thinking of the old days. "Knowed him twenty-eight years in Mississippi, man and boy. 'Course, our daddies were brothers. We was always different." A strange thought came to him. "I'll miss him. Guess he's been my mirror. Sort of measured myself again' him. Maybe one of you boys would say something when we bury him. Don't seem proper for me to be the one. I'll let you know when Sassy wants to do it."

Owen nodded, then struggled with his words. "Wil, any man I ever rode with, I'd do my best to speak for … you know, after his passing. But, well, there's something I want you to know. Me and him had words. I said some pretty hard things to him … things I wouldn't never say sober, 'less I meant them." Owen scraped the toe of his boot at dried horse manure on the heel of its mate. "It had to do with all them boys we lost up near that damn Cap Rock. Anyway, I wanted you to know."

Bones nodded. "It's all right. I understand. No need to say more. He was an easy man to have hard words with. But one thing I can say for him, he respected folks that did good work. I didn't say he liked them. I said he respected them. I think he and Sassy would be honored, and I know I would, with words from any or all of you." He looked at the three men before him, and knocked ashes from his pipe before continuing. "You know him and me fought nearly ever' time we got together. Not just wrestling and fooling around like me and San Tone did, but honest, knock-down drag outs. San Tone could have whipped us both, but he just sat back and watched." Bones put a hand in each back pocket and squashed an ant on the floor with a boot heel. He moved away and reentered the house. He wanted to deal with Wade's body and make sure there wasn't anything lying around that might upset Sassy.

He knelt beside Wade and buttoned his shirt collar to hide the rope marks. A bruised spot remained exposed above the collar, and he remembered seeing Wade put a scarf in a bureau in his study. He found the neckerchief and walked to Wade's desk. Two envelopes were side by side. One had Sassy's name on it. The other had his and San Tone's names scrawled in Wade's handwriting. He put the neckerchief in his pocket and opened the envelope marked to him and San Tone. Wade must have written it before receiving the news of San Tone's death. It read:

Boys:

I've done you a great wrong, but at the time I didn't know where you were, and thought likely we'd never meet again, even if you lived. There's a paper in the safe explains everything. It's from Granddaddy. Papa had it.

I found it when Papa died. The money he tells about, I took, so half of everything I have belongs to you two. San Tone, I'm glad to have been your cousin. Wil, you go to hell! The safe's open.

Wade

Bones replaced the paper in the envelope and walked to the safe. He guessed Wade had been drunk when he wrote the letter. He was mixing cousins, friends, and probably even facts about money.

The age of their granddaddy's papers made them easy to spot. They were wrapped in a yellow-brown packet and tied with a green silk ribbon. He carried it to Wade's desk and discovered the packet contained, in addition to the paper written by his grandfather, records from a Paris bank. The handwriting of their grandfather's papers was familiar. Bones scanned the page, then reread it:

March 20, 1861

There are things in this old mind that could put good men on the gallows, and I'll take most of them with me, but some you've a right to know. First the money! I made that trip to Paris in '47, not long after my Emile succumbed to the fever. I changed the last of the booty to francs, and it's there in this bank in Paris, today. Boys, it's in your names. It amounted to $67,000, Yankee, when I put it there. I lose track of what they add each year.

Yes, I threw my lot in with Jean Lafitte when I was seventeen, and a truer man never drew a breath. But, getting back to now, Wilbur and San Tone, this money would have gone to just my two boys, Phillip and Maurice, but your daddy's death means his half goes to you two. San Tone, Wilbur, Maurice fathered both of you. You're not only mates, you're brothers. It's the reason he died, and, Wilbur, I always thought it probably caused the broken heart that killed your mother.

San Tone, Azalea's man killed my boy, your daddy, one and the same. It happened two months after Maurice got her in a family way. I hung the colored, but I didn't blame him. If I don't see you no more, you boys live good. Wil, hope you get out of that war, and, if you do, remember it takes the stench of death a while, but comes a time the tides take it away.

Love,

P. F. Malone

Bones carefully placed the papers on the desk and sat, open-mouthed. His mind whirled. He had always thought of his father as an image of saintliness. He thought of Azalea and wiped at a tear with the back of his hand. With the thought of San Tone it had formed. He scolded himself, thinking, in spite of his kindness, his grandfather wouldn't have shown such emotion. He picked up both envelopes and carried them from the room. He carefully tied the neckerchief around Wade's neck and moved on to Sassy's room.

She opened the door after his knock. She looked at him a moment and held her hands open, palms up. "Why did he do this to me?"

"Ain't sure he had you that much in mind, Sassy. Here's a letter to you he left on his desk. Maybe it'll tell you something. They's another we'll talk about later. It's to San Tone and me. It's just business."

Sassy took the letter, and he walked from the house.

He found himself in front of the bunkhouse, got his bedroll, and carried it to his saddle in the barn. Returning, he passed Peaches leaning against the post of the brush arbor, helping Owen shoe a horse.

"You want, we'll shoe that black stud," Owen said.

"Yeah, go ahead," he answered. He moved on back toward the house, his mind working hard. He owned half of the biggest spread in Texas, and Sassy not only owned the other half, she was a widow. Wade was out of the way and half the whiskey in those cabinets belonged to him. Hell, he might just put Charley out of business.

He went to the kitchen, got a water glass, and walked to the liquor cabinet. He poured half a glass and, tilting it up, studied the kitchen ceiling over the bottom rim of the glass. Angel nodded at him as he passed through to where Wade's body lay. Bones could have kicked himself for not having thought of having someone sit with Wade. Likely this was Sylvia's doings. The vaquero sat in a straight-backed chair, examining the brim of his hat. Bones continued to the study. He tipped the glass at his Uncle Phillip's picture hanging over Wade's desk. "Here's to the Malone boys," he said.

"Wil," Sassy called from the stairs, "where are you?"

He walked back toward the parlor. "In here."

Sassy's hand rested on the railing, holding Wade's letter in one hand and a wadded handkerchief in the other. She wiped at her eyes. "He said he wanted me to know he loved me."

"Anything else?"

She came down the stairs. She looked at Angel and whispered: "Said he caused all those deaths and wanted to be with Ruben, be buried by him, and you and I would be free to be buried next to each other." Her eyes flashed anger. "Damn him … even in death he makes me feel guilty."

"Is that what you want … him buried next to Ruben?"

"Yes, it's what he said. Of course."

Bones had the feeling she had saddled him with Wade's part in all this. It was a load he could do without. "Sassy, gather stuff for a few days. We'll take his body in the buckboard and bury him with Ruben and Cecil and them other boys. We'll be halfway to town by then, and I'll feel better knowing you're there till I take care of Potter."

"Leave now, with my husband barely cold? Wil, I need time to collect myself … mourn."

"I'm sorry. It's dangerous here. Waiting is not in the cards."

"His letter said you had some papers I should honor. Do you know what he meant?"

"Uh-huh. I have them, but it can wait. We'll talk later. Do you want Sylvia with you?"

"I guess so. Give us half an hour."

* * * * *

Wade's corpse rode between two trunks in the buckboard. Sylvia sat with Sassy on the seat. They moved past the corrals, with Bones and the others leading the way. Angel's boy rode behind his dad's saddle.

The next morning the dry plains and wilted grass near Welcome received rain. It fell steadily on the small Crooked Letter I group, then ran in small rivulets on the ground to form in puddles along the hillside containing Ruben's grave.

Bones stood, bareheaded, with shovel in hand. The smell of wet dirt from the grave beside him mingled with odors of damp cedar and sage from nearby. His black hair became plastered against his head, and water dripped from the point of his chin.

Owen and Miguel gently picked up Wade's canvas-covered body and lowered him into the muddy grave. Sassy and Sylvia stood with bowed heads, and the boy watched from under a man's slicker. Sylvia's fingers moved from bead to bead on her rosary, her lips forming silent words of prayer.

Owen, with head bowed, spoke. "Lord, take this man in your arms and care for him. Things turned bad here. Save us in heaven. Amen."

They filled the grave quickly. Bones placed an unmarked rock at its west end. They mounted, and he rode to the buckboard where Sassy sat.

"I'll get Maurice to chisel their names on a rock and bring it out here first chance we get."

Sassy nodded.

He took the lead, heading toward Sundown City. Ruben's memory was vivid here, and he knew it would be hard to keep his word about coming back. Maybe Charley would come with him. Estella was on his mind. He wanted to tell her about San Tone and Ruben. There was so much bitterness and venom in Sassy that talking to her was like dropping pebbles in a well. Nothing came back to you but a hollow sound. Maybe that's what he'd get with Estella. If so, he'd see if the bottom of a bottle at Charley's offered better company.

CHAPTER TWENTY-TWO

The river bent around Sundown City. It came down from the north, twisted out around rail's end, then turned east below the tracks. Travelers who wanted to go south to Mexico crossed the river, and, if they headed west, to El Paso, they rode through town and forded the west leg of the bend. The day after Wade's burial, Bones and the remnants of the Crooked Letter I rode into town. The sun rested an hour above dirt across the river, pointing the way to distant El Paso.

He'd learned Maurice owned the town's hogs. Thanks to the poor excuse for a fence the hombre maintained, they owned the town. Today it appeared the old man had reduced the size of the pen's gaps, for the piglets shopped in town without the sow. They rooted and jostled each other down the street toward the water trough.

Bones stepped from his saddle near the hotel. He helped Sassy to the ground, then braced Sylvia as she followed. "How many rooms y'all need?"

"I'll bed down out there at the wagon yard," Owen said.

"One for Angel's family, then me, and one for you," Sassy said.

He got two rooms. He and Angel managed the trunks while

Owen headed toward the livery with the animals. Sassy fussed at him for not getting himself a room. She made him promise to come back and take her to eat, mentioning he'd have time for a bath. He headed for the café.

Bent, Estella was wiping a table, her back to the door. He noticed A. J. and another bone buyer seated nearby. A. J. nodded, but his companion's eyes stayed on Estella. *Wouldn't notice an elephant's entry*, Bones thought. Strange, the way he could dislike a man he'd never met. But A. J. generally hung out with nice folks.

He touched Estella's elbow. "Howdy, ma'am."

She grabbed his hand and squeezed, smiling happily. "Welcome, sir," she mimicked. "Sit down." She brought him coffee. "Look's like you've been riding sort of hard."

"Have, Estella. I want to tell you about it, and I will later, but, right now, let's just say Potter's outfit killed near everybody. San Tone and Ruben … and Wade killed hisself."

She sat in the chair beside him and placed both hands on his. "San Tone and your nephew both dead? Oh, Wil, I'm sorry." Her eyes peered deeply into his.

Returning her look, his face twitched, and he gritted his teeth. "Don't really want to talk about it just now."

"Tonight. We'll talk tonight." She eased from her chair and carried the coffee pot to the bone buyer's table. She glanced back and smiled in his direction as she poured.

Singletree Sadler walked in minutes later. Bones waved him to a chair at his table. At sight of Bones, Singletree's already grim face soured more. If there was ever a case of a job ruining a man, Singletree was it. Next to High Pockets he used to be the most fun-loving man in town. Now he acted like a smile was a sin.

"Sit down. I need legal guiding," Bones said.

"Ain't surprising. Knowing you, you're probably beyond help," the city lawman said, and waved at Erma Lou, standing in the kitchen door. "Who'd you kill?"

"A bunch … but I'm serious." Bones blew on his saucer of coffee. He told Singletree about Potter's kidnapping of Sassy and the murders.

The lawman showed real concern. "I knew he moved from Buffalo Gap up to the Cap Rock country. Got a telegram a couple of weeks ago, then last week a poster came. They've put a reward on Virgil's head."

Bones said: "The thing is I want to make it legal, get some men together, and go after him. Can you deputize me or something?"

"I can't do that, Bones. I got no authority outside of town."

"You mean, I can ride down to Seven Wells with old Charley and rob him, and you can't no nothing about it?"

"That's right. 'Course, Charley would likely shoot you." The thought softened Singletree's scowl.

Bones studied his coffee to hide his grin. "Old friend, I ain't interested in Charley. What I want is to be deputized so I can get up some men and go hang that son of a bitch over there at Yellow House Draw."

"Maybe the judge can help. He'll be in on the train tomorrow." The lawman leaned forward with an air of secrecy and whispered: "Maybe he can give you a writ, or something."

"What do you think? When I get this thing together, will you ride with us?"

Singletree stood, tucked in his shirt, and shifted the pistol at his hip. "Doubt I can get away, Bones, but I'll help you any way I can." He nodded and walked out.

Bones found a tub at the barbershop and paid Arnold a dime for a shave and bath. He changed into a gray pinstriped suit he had stored there. A ruffled shirt, vest, frock coat, and ribbon tie completed his facade of respectability. His other clothes were with the wagon, near Ruben's grave. He was clean as a new whistle and dressed for Sunday when he made his way to the Sea Breeze. His face was scraped raw, his hair oiled slickly under his hat, and the knotted tie only slightly less uncomfortable than the frock coat. The torture of his dress enhanced his need for pleasure.

Charley put both hands flat on the bar and stared when Bones entered. Alice Marie's gaze swung past him. Her face lit with recognition. She smiled. "Ain't you hot?"

He hung his hat on the rack and unbuttoned the coat. Stepping to the bar, he winked at her. "Honey, just want you to be proud of me."

She dealt three cards, face down, to a grinning, freckled-faced cowboy. "I'm proud, Bones."

"Preaching or what?" Charley poured him a drink.

"What," he replied, and downed the shot.

Charley refilled the glass and left the bottle. "How you been?" he asked with a frown, grabbing a rag and wiping the bar vigorously.

Bones caught his friend's eye. "Charley, San Ton's dead ... Ruben, too. That damn outlaw caused it all. Wade hung himself."

Charley brought a glass from under the bar and poured himself a drink. He downed it, poured another, and leaned over the bar, customer-fashion, his ear not far from his friend's face.

The light of day dimmed in the streets outside, and inside the shadows deepened. Bones recounted his story. Charley stopped him to light the lamps, then returned. Moments later, Bones finished the drink, capped off his tale, and replaced the bottle's cork. "I'm going after him, Charley." He made no mention of the letters.

Charley looked at the darkened windows. "When you're ready, I'll tag along."

Bones noted the deepening shadows outside. He wheeled and headed for the door. "Gotta go." An image of his granddaddy acting as host at High Manor's ballroom stopped him. "Charley, suppose a man needed to make two women, one to the other, acquainted with each other. How does he do that?" Charley knew things.

"Present the oldest to the other."

"Suppose he don't know their ages?"

"Then you can ask them." Charley grinned. "Knowing you, I'd advise against prying their mouths open to check teeth."

Alice Marie's face was serious, standing there and shaking her head.

Raising both hands, he waved, then grabbed his hat.

* * * * *

He found Sassy sitting in the lobby of the hotel. Small red spots, high on each of her cheeks, caught his eye. He knew the sign.

"Where have you been?" she asked.

"I was pretty dirty," he said. "You hungry?"

"You're late. They've already closed the kitchen. I guess our only choice is that place your chippy friend operates. Don't look so surprised ... San Tone told me."

He stepped to the boardwalk and put his hat on. "They set a good table."

The jinglebob bell on the café door seemed louder than usual when he pushed it open. Sassy stepped in and stopped.

He stuck his head in the door. "Y'all still open?" He'd never noticed that whining tone in his voice before, and he'd be damned if there wasn't a hint of amusement in Estella's face.

Erma Lou smiled. "You're just in time."

"Sassy," Bones began, "I'd like for you to meet these two friends of mine. This is Estella Emory and Erma Lou Pinella. This here's my cousin's wife ... er ... widow, Missus Wade Malone."

"Pleased to meet y'all," Sassy said.

Erma Lou tilted her head. "Mutual, I'm sure."

Estella's smile was gone. "Missus Malone, I'm very sorry to hear of your husband's and your son's death."

"Thank you. That's nice of you," Sassy retorted.

Erma Lou took their order. Estella's gaze avoided his. He didn't know if he ate steak or sawdust. His hat and coat hung on the rack at the door, but still the collar and tie galled. Sassy frowned when he poured coffee in his saucer. His brain turned barren and drifted like loose sand. What could he talk about?

When they were done eating, Estella cleared the table and brought more coffee.

"Have a cup with us, Miss Emory. I've heard so much about you, I feel I know you. I would like to take this chance to visit." Sassy's voice dripped of Mississippi sugar cane, but her eyes sparked.

Estella looked at Bones with a hurt expression. He wanted to tell her he hadn't talked of her to anyone, much less Sassy. These two had him treading barefoot and wearing knickers in a field of rattlesnakes. Estella got a cup and sat.

Bones squirmed. "Sure is hot, ain't it?"

Sassy shot him a sideward glance, then looked at Estella. "Tell me, Miss Emory, are you enjoying your new life?"

"My new life?" Estella looked cautious.

"Yes, I understand you were an entertainer. Do you like restaurant work better?"

Estella stood with fists doubled, one on each hip. She started to speak, but closed her mouth. Her color drained, and she wheeled and rushed to the kitchen.

Bones looked at Sassy. The red spots were back.

He stood. "I'll take care of this bill later!" he called through the kitchen door.

A few steps toward the hotel, Sassy stopped. "Oh, Wil, what are you thinking? You have grace and refinement. You can do so much better than that woman. Don't lower yourself. You ..."

"Sassy, that's enough. Whatever may or may not happen between me and that woman, as you call her, is between us. You got nothing to do with it." He turned to walk away, then stepped and looked at his cousin's widow. "Sassy, I'm sorry about what's happened to your life, but I ain't the one to fix it."

Sassy threw both hands to her face and her body shook. She ran for the hotel.

Bones returned to the café. The front door was locked. He knocked. Erma Lou came to the door and opened it a few inches.

"Is she in there?"

Erma Lou nodded.

"Can I come in?"

"Bones, she said she didn't want to talk to you." She looked over her shoulder at the kitchen.

"I got to talk to her."

She held the door open, turned, and said in a voice loud enough to reach Estella: "Bones Malone, don't you push your way in here."

He hurried in, not stopping until he got to the kitchen door. Estella stood at a pan of dirty dishes. She wiped the back of her wrist over her eyes.

"Hon, I ..." A large wet rag, thrown with perfect accuracy, hit him in the face, and behind it came a cyclone of wrath beyond belief.

CHAPTER TWENTY-THREE

"You got a big mouth, cowboy!" Estella cried. Water dripped from Bones' chin down to the ruffles of his town shirt. "'Meet my friend!' The very idea of you telling that woman about us!" She stomped his toe, making him miss when he grabbed at her. She stepped back and pushed damp hair out of her face. Somehow, in the short time he'd spent outside, she'd worked herself into a real lather.

"I ain't said nothing to her about us … not a word. Maybe San Tone did. She's got a way of digging, then digging some more. He told me she rode with him a little ways one day. I was back here." He took a much needed breath. "There was a day I cared for that girl, but it's gone. You're what puts stars in my head now."

Estella sank to the floor and sat, cross-legged, like a child. "Cared for her? *I* put stars in your head? Where the hell does that come from?" Her slow smile warmed its way across her face. "You big galoot, can you say the word love?"

"I don't know if I can say it, but I caught it. Caught it from you."

She rose and threw her arms around him. They kissed—a long, warm, loving kiss of promise, of giving and taking. Erma Lou peeked around the kitchen door and smiled. They broke apart, and Estella searched his eyes.

"It ain't an illness. You don't catch it." She laughed.

Her hand felt at home in his. He gave Erma Lou a schoolboy wink.

She nodded, and said: "Go, you kids, get out of here. I'll clean this place up and close it down. Go on, get!"

In the street Bones slapped his hand against his shoulder. "My coat, where's my coat?"

"It's on the rack in there. You hung it up when you came in. Where're we going?"

"How about the wagon yard?"

She gave him a mischievous look, then nodded agreement. Passing the livery, he took his blanket from behind his saddle. Later, they rested on a pallet high on a hay-filled wagon and watched dark close about them. The scent of newly cut grass rose to sweeten the cooling air.

He repeated the story he had told Charley earlier. Again, he left out the part about the letters. She wiped at her eyes when he told her about San Tone. "You know," he said, "we seem pretty poor, sitting here, hid out on this old wagon, but I think I may be one of the richest men in Texas."

"Wil, that's wonderful. In spite of all that's happened, you see beyond the bad. We *are* lucky. We have life, and each other ... a lot to be thankful for."

"No, that ain't what I mean. I think I'm rich in money. Well, not money anymore, but in land and cattle. You see, my granddaddy was a pirate, and I think he and his partner got a lot of the gold and silver the Spaniards took out of Mexico." He told her about the letters in Wade's office.

She was silent for a long time. "Does that mean you'd be partners with Sassy?"

"Ain't sure how that's gonna work, but I don't think she's much interested in hanging around this part of Texas."

"Don't bet on it."

"If she wants to stay, I'll just sell my part."

She lay on her back, with her head resting on her arm. "San Tone never knew what your granddaddy wrote about you and him being half brothers?"

"Don't think so." He propped on an elbow, looking down at her.

She smiled up at him. "I've got some news. My father and his wife are coming in a couple of weeks."

"That's quick," he said. "You happy about it?"

"I'm so excited, I don't know what I'm doing half the time. Imagine after all these years of dreaming about him, actually being able to know ... hopefully love him. Yes, I'm happy about it."

He tickled the corner of her lip with a straw. "Oh, you two will love each other." There, he'd said it. "Love ... love," he added, laughing.

She grinned, then laughed back at him.

Suddenly he turned serious. "Estella, I'm old, and I've been through some things, don't know much, but, knowing you and Ruben the last few days, it learned me some. I feel things I ain't felt in a long time. These days, seems to me, all that matters is what you think about my doings." He paused. "I reckon I do."

"Do what?"

"Do ... love you."

She reached, put both arms around his neck, and pulled him to her.

He'd found the Promised Land, crossed the desert, parted the oceans—all things were possible. This woman gorged his senses: smell, taste, touch, passion, all of them. Unraveling her mystery would be his life's mission.

A few minutes later, he lay on his back, exhausted. Above, the stars grazed the heavens like cattle on a lush, dark prairie. The Milky Way spanned the vastness, and for a rare moment he had his loop around it all. He heard a rustling sound by the side of the wagon and something soft and round, but big enough to be dangerous, fell from the sky. He shoved it away and reached for his six-gun. From below he heard a voice.

"Hey, is somebody up there?"

The voice was Owen's, and Bones was reasonably sure the panther that sprang on him was the cowpuncher's bedroll.

"Find another wagon, cowboy, this one's took," Bones said.

"Bones, is that you? It's Owen. I'm coming up. Uh … you alone?"

"I may be … I may not be. I said find another one." He picked up the rolled blanket and flung it in the direction of the voice.

Owen's grumbling faded away, and in a moment his silhouette appeared against the sky as he crawled over the side of a nearby wagon.

"You weren't very friendly," Estella said. "He sounded like he knew you."

"He does, but two's company."

"And three's a crowd?" she finished.

"Hon, there's something I ain't told you yet, and I want it off my chest."

"What?"

"The night I found Ruben … dying … his arm nearly off. Well, seeing that, a strange thing come over me. I ain't told you, but part of the war was missing out of my head. Seeing Ruben like that … it came back." He raised up and sat quietly, struggling for words.

She sat beside him.

He stroked her shoulders, dropped his arms, then grasped the back of his own neck and leaned his head back. "You ever hear the name Stonewall Jackson?"

He barely heard her whisper: "Of course."

"Well, on a night darker than this, I think I was the one who shot him and caused his death … All these years, it's worked on me. Sometimes I didn't even know for sure what I'd done … just that it was terrible bad. You see, he was the best we had, a true fighting man, smart, with honor and religion, and the bravest man you ever saw."

"You said you think. How'd it happen?" Her tone was earnest.

"It was in Virginia. We gave the Yanks hell all day. That night, I was checking the pickets when we heard this noise out to our front. They were close, maybe twenty-five yards. None of our folks was supposed to be there. They were some North Carolina men over to our left, but nobody in front. Like I say, we heard noise, and I wheeled and fired. Just a second later, the picket got a shot off. There was a commotion … people thrashing in the brush … and then them North Carolina boys fired a volley. About that time the ones out front started hollering … they were Rebs and we found out what we'd done."

"You can't be sure you hit him, are you?"

"Those days I didn't often miss, even with a handgun."

"You were firing a pistol?"

"Told you they was close."

"Oh, Wil, I'm so sorry. And you've tormented yourself all these years, trying to forget, afraid to remember."

He looked at her. "How do you know all that?"

"All of men's evil isn't tied to war."

Down by the river, a coyote yelped, and he heard the pigs grunting under the wagon. "You want to talk about it?"

"Not now. Tonight, I want to enjoy you and think about my father coming."

"Why don't we go get me a drink, and you can play us a tune?"

"We can do that."

* * * * *

Charley looked up when they entered, then came to meet them. He took Estella's hand and nodded at Bones. "See moving to the other side of the street ain't improved your taste in men none."

Estella laughed. "Charley, there isn't but one side of the street in this town."

"Give it time," he replied.

Estella stopped and talked to Alice Marie, while Bones and Charley sauntered on to the bar. The place had gathered only three other customers. One nursed a bottle with his foot on the rail. The other two played poker at one of the tables.

Bones said: "You getting slovenly in your old age? This place needs airing out."

"Dropped a keg in the back room this morning. Didn't know you had such a refined nose."

"Oh, there's lots you don't know about me. I'm still learning myself. For instance, being an old Gulf sailor like you are, you probably heard of my granddaddy's partner."

"Who'd that be?"

"An old Frenchman named Jean Lafitte."

"He was before my time, but I heard of him. Your grandpa sailed with him, huh?"

"Sure did. I found a paper at Wade's from Granddaddy. Told all about it."

"I'll swear," Charley said.

Estella moved to the piano. She ran her fingers across the keys, tentatively at first, then warming to the mood. She was not unlike a good bronco peeler, soothing the nerves of a wild-eyed green one before climbing aboard. She gained control, and the instrument responded, sending its magic to all corners of the saloon and beyond to the streets.

The doors leading to the boardwalk swung inward, slammed. A battered and blood drenched figure staggered in. It was the young woman Bones knew vaguely as Trina. She fell to the floor, raised to her elbows, then collapsed.

Alice Marie was first to her side. Estella joined her. The men were slower to react. Trina was young, maybe twenty-five, and it had been her boy that had brought Allen's horse to Rosco's stable. She added color to the drab interior of the River Cantina.

Charley brought a pan of water and some cloth to the ladies. Estella washed the woman's bloody face.

A man stepped through the doors. He glared at Trina. Slender and blond, his shirt was blood-splattered. His eyes sat close on either side of his long nose, and a brace of Colts rested on his hips.

Trina's gaze rested on the stranger. Her body jerked. She struggled, trying to rise.

The two-gun man hesitated, then turned and backed out through the door. Hoof beats replaced the sound of his steps, then thundered westward out of town.

"Did he do this?" Alice Marie asked. The battered woman nodded. They helped her to her feet, then to a chair. The men returned to the bar, and Charley broke out a new bottle.

After only a couple of minutes, Estella motioned the men back to the table. As they approached, she looked at Bones. "Y'all better hear this."

Trina looked at Charley. There were tears streaming down her face. "Mister Lonzo, I'm sorry. I knew he was a pig, but he spent easy."

"Who is he?" Charley asked.

"His name ees Ira Millett, and he rides weeth more bad ones near the Cap Rock. He drinks too much, last night 'specially. He asked eef there were fabrics or pretties from thee stores that would please me. Meester Lonzo, they're coming to town. They're going to … how you say? … make a raid. Said Lawrence, Kansas was notheeng. 'Wait,' he said, 'see what we do here.'"

"When?" Charley asked.

"The day following tomorrow. He ees hungover today. He slapped my boy. I don't stand for that."

"Did you hear the names of any he rode with?" Charley asked, looking at Bones.

"I did … but I do not remember," Trina said.

"Virgil Potter?" Bones asked.

Her eyes brightened. "*Sí*, that ees one. He said that name."

Bones turned, senses alert, and walked out to the street. He looked both ways, listened, and returned to the saloon. Some way he had to counter the moves of the outlaws.

CHAPTER TWENTY-FOUR

Bones crawled from beneath his blanket in the early light of first dawn. He sat a moment on the edge of the wagon, smoking and reviewing the night's events. Trina had said Ira Millet mentioned Lawrence, Kansas. Stories of the butchery Quantrill's bunch had inflicted there were common. Potter could do as much here, just on a smaller scale.

Owen stood in a wagon a few feet away. He stretched and rubbed his eyes. "Bones, didn't mean to bother you last night,"

"Aw, it was all right. That old bedroll just sort of took me by surprise. Thought for a minute one of them old yeller panthers had moseyed up from the river. Did Charley get in touch with you?"

"No."

Bones told him of Potter's threat to attack. "When do you expect Peaches and Juan to get here?"

"Maybe this evening. If not ... tomorrow," Owen said.

"Hope they make it. We need their guns."

"If they ain't whittled up too bad to fight, after fencing with that barbed wire." Owen grinned.

"Wire! Wire, that's it!" Bones hollered. He jumped to the ground and rushed to Owen's wagon. The words of the fencing crew came back to him. The wire broke and ... what had they said? 'Whipsawed like a blue prairie racer trying to coil.' There was still a boxcar of wire down there at the track. Maybe they could fence in the outlaws, or out.

"Owen, you ever fenced any?" Bones asked.

"A week once ... over east of Abilene. Ain't something I cared for."

"They tell me, if you ever turn loose of her while she's new, the darn stuff wants to coil up. Is that so?"

"It is for a fact. Acts like it's got a mind of its own."

"What if we take a wagon and drive along, reeling that stuff out as we go ... given enough slack, would it kink up in coils and make a barricade around this old town?"

Interest and understanding spread across Owen's face. "Pardner, it would for a fact and an ugly one at that."

"Would she stand high enough to turn a man on a hard-ridden horse?"

"If we put a single wire through her and maybe a stake every so often to hold it up, she would. A crew of men could roll it out near fast as a team could walk. No time a-tall we can put up enough of an obstacle to hold back Custer's Seventh."

"We don't have to hold 'em," Bones advised. "Just slow 'em enough to put a little lead in their gullet. Maybe keep 'em from rushing us."

"Bones, you're wasting your time plucking them old skeletons. Colonel MacKenzie could have used you in chasing red devils around here a few years ago."

"Matter of fact I scouted for him once. A good man, but I've rid with better," Bones said. "Wade owned a carload of wire down at that depot. What say we spend the day seeing if we can build a proper fence to welcome old Virgil Potter with? C'mon."

* * * * *

Townspeople gathered early near the town's hand water pump. Most of the men wore side arms and carried rifles or shotguns. Women talked in hushed tones with children lurking close, gazing wide-eyed and white-faced near their skirts. Constable Singletree Sadler and a half dozen men gathered in front of the hotel. Smaller groups huddled along the front of buildings. Charley crossed the street toward them.

Singletree called out: "Here comes Charley … and yonder's Bones! Y'all gather up, and let's get our heads together. Charley, was it tomorrow or today Trina said they're coming?"

"There she is. Ask her yourself," Charley answered, pointing to Trina who stood at the edge of the crowd with Maurice's family.

The constable looked at the young woman. "How about it? Which did he say?"

Trina wore a shawl over her head, covering most of her face. She nodded as she spoke. "He say tomorrow. They weell come tomorrow."

"Reckon that'll hold true," Charley put in, "but we got to be ready in case it's sooner. After that gun hand gets back to them, they may change their minds."

A small man jumped up and down at the back of the crowd, raising his hand like a schoolboy.

"What is it, Eugene?" Singletree asked, impatience only partly hidden in his voice.

"The telegraph is dead," Eugene said.

People stared at one another a moment, allowing the meaning of being without outside contact to sink home.

Arnold, the barber, raised his voice: "Where we gonna put the women and kids? They ain't none of these buildings safe from bullets. The darned old train isn't due until day after tomorrow. Was it earlier, I'd send my family back to Abilene. My woman tried to get me not to come west of Fort Worth. What do y'all think?"

A throng of voices mingled in nervous babble. Others shouted to be heard. Reason quickly gave way to frenzy.

Bones took Charley's elbow, pulling him to the side a short distance from the crowd. He rapidly laid out his thoughts and the plan that continued to grow in his mind. Charley nodded in agreement, then grasped Bones by the arm and moved toward Singletree.

A metal bar forming a triangle swung near the pump. On a good day, it served as a dinner bell—on a bad one, a signal of alarm. Charley rang it loudly with the attached rod. "Quiet!" he ordered. The *clanging* quieted the crowd. "Folks, Singletree, y'all listen. We got to be organized. We got to get to work, and we got to do it now. Bones Malone, here, has some ideas, and I think we ought to give them a try. Y'all know him as honest, a little peevish, but straight. He fought with good men in the war and he's been up the trail more times than a lead steer. I think we need to hear him out." He turned to Bones, saying: "Tell them."

"I'm going to give you folks my thoughts, along with directions to go with them," Bones began. "If you are in agreement, best follow the directions. If not, step up here and give us a better idea." Bones paused and studied the crowd. They stood silently. "When I'm through talking, form three squads of men, one with Singletree." He pointed. "Another over there with Charley, and the last with Arnold. I'll try and help where I'm needed. Now, I ain't got to tell you your lives and the lives of your families are at stake here, so they ain't time to talk about this no more. When we break up, here, them three men are gonna pick a spot down the street. Every one of you over fourteen years report to one of them. They'll give directions. If too many of you are in one bunch, shift to another.

"We're gonna protect our people by reinforcing that partly finished rock depot down there. We'll use the crossties and bridge timbers piled down by the tracks as needed. Them rock walls would stop a cannon. Be sure and put in a supply of water for two or three days."

Nods of approval could be seen throughout the crowd.

"Some of you are gonna be spreading barbed wire. We're gonna circle this town with it. It'll only take a jiffy, or so. We'll leave an opening on the east end of town, with sentries, and that's it. The bluffs on the banks of that river will stop riders from the west and south. The Crooked Letter I has a boxcar full of wire down at the tracks. It'll work as well for our purpose, in loose and kinky coils, as it would in a proper fence. Besides, there's no time for putting up posts, just a barrier. We're gonna make it about waist high. A man afoot might work his way through or over, but it's riders we wanna stop. If they can't rush us a horseback, we'll cut 'em down before they get at the heart of the town.

"We'll stretch and hang more strands above the streets, from roof to roof. At the right time, if it comes to it, men posted on the roof will cut it if those butchers make it down the street. That wire'll come popping around, this way and that, a-curling and cutting everything it touches. Since these men like to play with barbed wire, we'll give them a taste … a little payback for Ruben and the boys of the Crooked Letter I." Bones gritted his teeth and swallowed at the boy's name.

"Keep your guns ready. I mean ready … I don't mean fifty feet away." He looked around, asking in general: "What did I forget?"

"I want men in the bank at all times," Milton Quinley said.

Bones nodded. "What else?"

"You don't think they're smart enough to see that overhead wire and be scared away?" Quinley asked.

"That's a chance we'll have to take unless someone can come up with a way to hide it," Bones answered, and pushed on. "Do your part, everybody. Whatever chore you're assigned, stay with it, and, when we're through, this country is gonna be a lot safer. Now I need a minute with these three men before you take your place with them."

"What do you want me to do, Bones?" Arnold asked, after walking over.

"Have your people get teams and wagons and get them crossties. You're gonna fortify the town and the depot, too. Drop off some of those ties for protection for the guards along that wire barricade.

Put out more at the opening east of town for the men there.

"Owen, you go with Singletree. Y'all take charge of wire on the edge of town. Leave a gap, there, to the east. Soon as men are available, get that overhead wire strung downtown. It may be our best bet. You ready?" Bones waved and pointed as he spoke, then finished with that group by saying: "OK, do it!" He turned. "Charley, take your bunch and gather up all the weapons in town that aren't being carried. Decide how to best use 'em. You're in charge of fighting. Post sentries with backup around the clock. Have the men guarding the wire perimeter build shelters to fight from. Make sure everyone knows where they're assigned."

* * * * *

Bones was inspecting the defenses. Arnold's men had done a good job at the depot. They had even constructed blockhouses of crossties from which the defenders could fire. Workers had three wires strung above the streets. Alice Marie had suggested hanging painted advertisements celebrating the Fourth of July on bed sheets over the high wire to hide its true intention.

On the outskirts of town, Owen's group worked east to west. With his group, Singletree worked north to south. Both had almost completed their work. Three strands were loosely coiled, almost overlapping. A jack rabbit would grow old trying to get through the tangled maze. There was no way a horse could cross without becoming entangled.

Near the north edge of town, Charley rode toward Bones.

"Where are your outposts for pickets?" Bones asked.

The bartender pointed to locations on the north and the east sides. "There're more south and west, across the river. We're going to have to put some of these rolls of wire in a couple of draws down the bluff of that river. There's two trails a horse could take."

"Glad you found them, and not Potter."

Bones found himself at the plowed furrow leading north to Welcome. When Charley first told him of the farmer's plowing the marker, he thought it wasted effort. Yet now, worn wheel ruts were fast cutting a road beside the upturned sod. He scanned the horizon, stopped, and turned back the mustang, searching for a distant movement. He looked away, and, blinking, looked back. Yes, something was moving, and a second object behind it. He worked his pipe, waiting for whoever approached to grow to recognizable size.

He relaxed at sight of a single rider and a buggy. Yet he remained wary, remembering that the first time he had seen Potter, he had been riding in a buggy. It seemed unlikely he would find him in one today. Still, there was something familiar about the crooked shape on that rig.

Recognition came as Lester and family, from Welcome, rode nearer. And the big jasper behind them wasn't horseback, he was muleback. He rode Barney. Bones' throat tightened, and his stomach flopped. *For God's sake! It can't be, but it is. San Tone!*

CHAPTER TWENTY-FIVE

The black stud moved restlessly under Bones. A slackening of the reins released an explosion of energy. In jubilation, he touched spurs to the animal. It shot forward. "Hallelujah!" he shouted. He swung his new hat in a circle above his head, then sailed it into the air. "San Tone ... San Tone ... San Tone! I thought you'd be wartin' Saint Peter 'bout now. *Aie-eee-ha!*" He pulled back the stud and it sat down in a butt-scrapping slide. They jolted into Barney, almost knocking him down. Bones reached and pummeled San Tone's shoulders.

"Yuh gone loco?" The big man's grin faded, and he grabbed Bone's shirt front. "Here, that's enough!"

"You old catfish, how'd you do it?"

"I think the good Lord had a hand. First thing I knew, that current threw me up in one of them side cricks with water risin' up all around, and I just climbed out. That old river sure broke her shackles. Never saw such a free-for-all flood in my days."

Bones turned to Lester. "How y'all?"

"OK, Mister Malone, but Granny's hurt some," Lester said.

"What's the matter?"

Granny leaned in front of her grandson. "Mississippi, it's good to see you," she said. "I'm all right, don't you worry. Just chopped off a titsy bit of a finger. These kids thought there might be a doctor over this way ... least a bottle from that saloon to wash the dirt and straw off."

Bones fought the stud into stillness and reached from the saddle to the crown of his grounded hat. "How'd you go and do that?"

"John Lloyd addled that old rooster with a rock, and I put it on the chopping block. Just trimmed my fingernail a mite too close."

He noted San Tone indicating an inch measurement with his left thumb and forefinger. Bones dipped his hat toward the buggy. "You take it easy, ma'am. There's a good barber who fancies himself a doctor of sorts in Sundown. We'll see that he fixes you right up."

Riding along the north barricade around town, Bones briefed Lester and San Tone on the danger the town faced.

San Tone touched his pistol. "I better get some new shells. 'Bout half of these don't shoot due to that river water."

Farther along, Bones told of Wade's death.

San Tone shook his head. "Wade's folks kept him shinin' as a boy. Never saw a man so clean or serious in my life. But that Ruben ..." He clasped his hands around his saddle horn with laced fingers and a tremor shook his huge body. Passing the men putting the finishing touches to the waist-high coils of wire offered a chance to switch subjects. "Darned ole stuff sure do make a ugly blockade, don't it? Who come up with that idee? And how we gonna get into town?"

Bones pointed at himself, answering with a wry smile. "That would be me. Even blind hogs find an acorn sometime. We got a gap a hundred yards ahead."

San Tone shifted in his saddle, seemingly impatient with the pace of the mule. Obviously more important matters than death or gun play gripped him. "I've got a hankering to see Beula. When I was stumbling around them badlands, I couldn't get that gal off

my mind. Think I'll just take time and drop by that big house."
He turned his horse in the direction of the Quinley house.

"OK, but, San Tone, soon as you're ready, come on to town.
I found the letter from Granddaddy he told you about. Wade
left another'n just as interesting. Anything happens before we get
together, they're in my saddlebags."

Alone after San Tone's departure, concern for Estella's safety kept
pestering Bones' mind. He had confidence in the town's defenses
but, thinking of her, made him realize this battle threatened a life
more precious than his own. After a search of the town, he found
her passing out sandwiches at the train depot. He stole a moment
to glory in the grace of her movements.

Seeing him, she held up two sandwiches and set the basket
aside. "Hungry?" she called.

Bones nodded, dismounted, and, leading the stud with one
hand and holding Estella's elbow with the other, assisted her a few
steps to a boxcar parked on a siding. He tied the black to the car and
pointed upward. "Let's eat up there. It'll make a good lookout while
I catch you up on some good news amidst all this ugly."

"Will we be safe up there?" she said.

He placed the wrapped sandwiches inside his shirt, then locked
his fingers, stirrup fashion, and bent to assist her up to the first rung
of the ladder. "When they come, they'll be in a hurry, trying to
surprise us. They won't be giving themselves away by shooting, 'less
it's to get rid of someone blocking their way."

The height of the car gave him a good view of the buildings
making up the town and the men at the barricade on its outskirts.
Satisfied they were safe for the moment, he told her of San Tone's
return. He concluded with: "He brought in an old Arkansas lady
from Welcome to see Arnold. Her finger's messed up. She's a smart
ol' fox … sort of partial to handsome young fellers like me." He
searched the horizon again, then handed her a sandwich before
eating his own.

Estella ignored his attempt at humor. "Have you told him?"

"You mean about me and San Tone being the same blood and all?"

She nodded.

"Going to soon as he comes on in. He couldn't wait to see Beula."

Estella finished her sandwich and her eyes searched the distance. "Do you think they'll hit us tomorrow?"

"Dunno. Potter'll likely send in a scout. The wire on the outskirts, there, may delay him a little. But, set on blood and booty, he'll not be swayed for long. Don't you worry, he bit off more than he can chew this time."

"I hope so. Thanks to you, I believe he has. This town is pretty high on Bones Malone at the moment. Makes me proud."

Her eyes measured him—held a soft promise in their depths that turned him awkward as a foal in its first hour. Potter, Sundown City, the whole of this plains country—all were unimportant compared to this woman. San Tone wasn't the only one running in circles. He made an effort to bring himself back to earth. His eyes drifted to the lettered signs hanging from the overhead wire. He pointed. "Baiting that high wire with signs may be the best idea yet. No way Potter's gonna see through that decoy. You want to hide a full house, you show two pair."

Estella looked puzzled for a moment, then smiled her agreement.

Later, back on the street, he excused himself and walked to Rosco's corral to wait for San Tone. He rubbed the back of his neck and fidgeted with his feelings of prebattle uneasiness. With civilians around, things often had a way of getting out of control. Bullets sometimes found the wrong target. The old doubts gnawed his insides.

He watched San Tone ride up, marveling in awe at the fact of their brotherhood. He'd always longed for a brother. He couldn't think of a better one. He held Barney while the big man stepped down. Bones handed him the two letters and nervously fumbled with his pipe, waiting for him to read the one written by Wade.

Wrinkles grew in San Tone's forehead the more he read. Bones handed him their granddad's letter. San Tone opened, then labored over it. Bones pulled on his dead pipe, watching his brother's mouth open.

San Tone looked at him without expression. He took his finger and traced slowly beneath each word. He slid to the ground, his back to the fence.

Bones squatted beside him. "Ain't that the most mortifying thing you ever heard of?"

San Tone shook his head, then diverted his attention to the pigs fighting for position near the trough.

Bones could stand it no longer. He grabbed both of San Tone's shoulders and shook him. "Hey, Brother, how does it feel, owning a big part of Texas and all?"

San Tone smiled, then laughed, and shoved Bones backward. "Feels a lot better than being your brother." As they stood and dusted themselves, San Tone added: "What do Sassy think about this?"

"She doesn't know about it yet. Damn! I ain't told her you're alive, neither. C'mon."

San Tone walked beside him to the hotel, then followed Bones up the stairs to Sassy's room. Bones knocked on her door.

"Who's there?" Sassy called.

"Sassy, it's me," Bones answered. "We need to talk."

"I don't think we do," she said, her face peering through the partially opened door.

"San Tone's alive," he said, and stepped aside.

Sassy grabbed her mouth and burst into tears. She flung herself at the black man.

"Oh, thank God!" she cried. She looked at Bones half crying, half laughing. She reached out and tousled his hair. She looked back to San Tone. "Oh, I love you," she said.

San Tone hugged her till she gasped for air, then released her.

Bones backed away a couple of steps and waited as the two

childhood friends shared the excitement of San Tone's return. Sassy took a deep breath, clapped her hands together, then took both men by the hand and led them to chairs on the hotel balcony. Bones watched the preparations in the street below while San Tone explained the events of his survival.

San Tone finished his story with: "I wandered around a day out on that prairie till I caught that old ridin' mule of Wil's. I spent a little time with a family of dirt farmers out there at Welcome. Rode into town with them this mornin'. The granny of the clan taken a shine to Wil some time back. Thinks he's handy as a pocket on a shirt."

Sassy gave Bones a smile. He was relieved to find no malice showing on her face.

San Tone folded his hands and leaned his chair back against the wall, signaling the end of his story.

Now was his chance to tell Sassy about the letters, Bones thought. Instead, he heard himself giving instructions. "Sassy, you know Potter's coming. When you get the word, go to the depot till it's over. You hear me?"

Sassy said: "Wil, when its over, and, if that train makes it in this week, I'm leaving for New Orleans. You and the rest of Texas can take care of Potter."

Bones thought he caught a hint of color return to her face. Maybe he'd given one order too many. He stood and held the letters out to her. "Wade left these. What do you make of 'em? Me an' old San Tone are about flabbergasted." She took the letters. "They were on the desk by the safe," he stated.

She read her husband's letter, wiped at a tear, and opened the other. A moment later, she lowered it, and looked from one to the other.

Bones sat forward, watching her features for a clue to her feelings. San Tone did likewise. She raised the letter and read more. Dropping it in her lap, she clasped her hands and wagged her head. "Can you believe?" She scalded them with another look. "No wonder you Malones are so onerous. It's in the blood." She grinned.

He took comfort in the grin widening on his brother's face. "How is this with yuh, Sassy?" San Tone asked.

"Looks like I'm going to leave my half of a mighty big ranch in good hands. I'll send you my address when I get to New Orleans. Just send me a report and my half of the profit once a year." She smiled at San Tone and reached for his hand. "I'm glad you're my boy's cousin."

San Tone swallowed. "I shore did like him."

Bones struggled to his feet.

"Wil," Sassy began, "I know, now, there was so much I held back from Wade because of you. Don't feel badly toward him. He did the best he could, and I didn't help."

Damn that lump, Bones thought before he said: "I know, Sassy. Seems we never see a thing till the fight's over and the smoke clears."

"I'll see you later, before I go." She stood and moved to the door with them.

Outside, they met Lester as they stepped from the hotel. The nester moved toward them rapidly. "I went to the barbershop, but I didn't find barber, doctor, or nuthin'," he said.

Bones looked toward the shop and saw Arnold crossing toward it. "C'mon. I'll take you to him," he said. "Where's Granny?"

Lester waved at John Lloyd who was across the street with her. They joined them, and then the group approached the barber.

Bones made the introductions. "Arnold, this is Lester and his granny, from over Welcome way. The boy goes by John Lloyd. Granny needs your doctoring services, if you can take the time."

Arnold moved to the old woman. "What's wrong with you, ma'am?"

"It's my finger. An ax bit it."

"Have a seat in that chair," Arnold instructed Granny. "I'll get a razor and needle and thread. Y'all, been keeping plenty of whiskey on it? Lester, you got money?"

"Whiskey ..." Granny answered, "don't keep it on the place. My only husband was too partial to the stuff. Money, the same ... don't seem to keep it about, either. We brung you half a dozen fryers, though. Will that work?"

"Better than nothing," Arnold said, and headed to the back room from which, a few minutes later, he emerged with soap and water and a bottle of whiskey. He found a razor near the chair and thread in a drawer. "We're gonna fix you right up," he reassured the old woman.

At sight of Granny's bloody finger, Bones headed for the door.

Her words followed him out. "Oh, it ain't nothing. Say, Mississippi, while I'm to town, I want to meet that new girl of your'n. Let me tell you, Doc, she's favored with luck if she catches that boy. Can't tell a book by ..."

Arnold chuckled.

CHAPTER TWENTY-SIX

The next day proved uneventful—a contrast to the one prior. Yesterday's actions and preparations had left little time for nerves. Today, empty streets played hosts to dust devils and lazy cloud shadows that proved fertile ground for raw nerves. Around them the town stood ready at their posts. Bones knew that Potter must realize he had lost the edge of surprise. But he would come. His kind always did. Morning turned to noon, then evening to darkness. A worse night followed the grinding day. But, still, no raiders showed.

Bones slept fitfully and at first light mounted the black stud. The deserted streets echoed no brassy sound of bugle, no drum roll, and no thundering hoof beats of frantic messenger's delivering last-minute dispatches. Still, the eerie quiet foretold battle.

He expected action any moment. By midafternoon, tension beat hotter than the weather. In the east, smoke rolled skyward. At least the train from Abilene was making it in before Potter hit. Its few more guns would help.

Minutes later, he held the mustang, watching the engine roll in, whistle blasting. It seemed the engineer was growing bolder at the throttle. He brought her in fast. Suddenly a cold chill ran down Bones' back. Something wasn't right.

He shouted: "San Tone, the train, do you see anything wrong?"

The train could be their weakness. They should have barricaded the track, stopped it for inspection. Damn his hide, it was too late. With room for a lot of men, four cars were in their wall of wire. He saw a Stetson inside the engine's cab, and knew Potter had played a hole card of his own.

"They're on the train!" he hollered, pulling his pistol and firing three shots into the air. He holstered the revolver. Locked brakes *screeched*. Bones leaped on the black and headed the stud toward the bank. People burst into the streets. Women ran with struggling children, heading for the depot. He caught a glimpse of Estella, running hard, with a child. Men bolted to their positions—rooftops, doorways, wherever they were assigned.

San Tone rode by Bones' side. Owen, Peaches, and Angel, lashing their horses, close behind.

Doors from boxcars slid open while the train still moved. Horses leaped from within, knees bent and eyes rolling. In that instant, Bones knew they were up against raiders that would look death in the eye and challenge for more. As long as they lived, nothing would stop them.

Many of the horses slipped, stumbled, and went to their knees. Some rose, others stayed down, but most only faltered before gaining footing and charging in the direction of the bank.

Pulling his rifle from its scabbard, Bones heard the first shots and sensed with pride that they came from the townspeople, not the gunmen. A few outlaws veered down the track toward the depot. The townsmen were well positioned, and, with repeating rifles and double-barrel shotguns, they would make a deadly force.

The shooting became a roar as the train stopped. Bones twisted and fired at the nearest rider. Owen's pistol blasted. Two defenders on the bank's roof fired at the oncoming outlaws. Bones pulled the mustang to a sliding halt. He ran for the bank and shinned up a ladder onto its roof in time to see the first outlaw ride around the corner. Owen, with a rifle now in hand, approached from the opposite direction. The rider's pistol swung toward the cowboy, but Owen's rifle roared, unhorsing the rider and dumping him in a heap on the ground.

Bones brought his sights to a fast-moving rider. The octagonal barrel of his rifle bucked with the shot. His ears rang, and the man somersaulted backward. He switched his view toward the depot to see fast-moving raiders repelled and turned up the street toward the Sea Breeze. Eight to ten feet above, wire formed an unsuspected web of death.

At the signal the men positioned and protected behind false-fronted store roofs cut the overhead wire. No spider web ever trapped a fly better than the falling, slashing ribbons of steel. The dangling strands grabbed while falling, hit the ground, then curled and twisted, snaring again with a bloody bite. Horses squealed. Men screamed as horses thrashed, hopelessly entangled. Seeing the threat, some of the outlaws turned, only to become entrapped by wire.

From windows, doors, and rooftops defenders fired almost pointblank into the unprotected raiders. Another group of renegades ran their animals west, in front of the bank. They fired as they rode. Now Bones hollered to the man with cutters beside him. The man squeezed the cutters and the henchmen below met the same fate as had those near the saloon.

The courage and recklessness these men showed in riding into a reinforced, armed camp, in the middle of the day, was not unlike that of men he had ridden with all his life.

Then, as suddenly as it started, the shooting stopped. This—all the blood—was Potter's doing. Bones thought of Ruben. Then it dawned on him: *Potter. Where was Virgil Potter?*

Charley stepped from the saloon and, with two other men, took command of what looked like the last three prisoners. Singletree held another two in front of Arnold's. A horse struggled in the street nearby. It was the outlaw leader's buckskin entangled in wire between the lawman and the hotel.

Bones reloaded his pistol and climbed from the rooftop. He carefully made his way through barbed wire to the center of the street.

"Singletree, you need any help?" he asked.

"Thanks, I got them. Bones, by God, we did it, didn't we, boy?"

It sounded to Bones as though the constable thought his reelection was in the bag. Bones raised his voice to be heard over the groans of injured men, cut horses, and the squeal of the red sow, trapped in wire. "How many of ours did we lose? Anybody know?"

"Arnold's hit, but not bad. Don't know about around the corner." Singletree herded his prisoners the other direction. "It worked, Bones!" he cried triumphantly.

Movement in the alley, between the hotel and mercantile store, caught Bones' eye. Virgil Potter stepped into the street, a Colt in each hand. Bones struggled, dragging frantically at his holstered pistol. Potter swung both revolvers toward him. Bones thumbed his hammer and a single blast roared as he and the outlaw fired as one.

Something slammed against the side of his head. He saw Potter drop one gun, grab his side, and fall. Bones staggered, tripping over wire. His pistol slipped from his hand, and he went to the ground.

An evil grin crossed Potter's face. The outlaw squatted and raised his second six-gun. Slowly he took careful aim. A shot sounded above the street din. Potter jerked, looking surprised, and dropped to his knees. The pistol fell from his hand, and he rocked back and forth. The front of his shirt showed a large gaping hole, near his belt. Blood stained the cloth's opening.

Above, on the balcony, Sassy stared down, holding a smoking rifle. The red sow squealed and fought against the jagged wire. A few feet away, the other end of the wire twisted around a dead horse.

Bones kicked free of the wire, retrieved his six-shooter, and held it steadily at the outlaw. The bead of his front sight rested between Potter's eyebrows.

The outlaw struggled, picked up his pistol with both hands, and looked at Bones. Seeing he was covered, he smiled crookedly and pointed the handgun at the swine. "Damn hawgs," he gurgled. His pistol roared and the sow flopped, shot between the eyes. A grin crossed Virgil Potter's face before he pitched forward into the dirt. His last breath blew a puff of dust from about his nose.

Bones wiped at blood coming from his head where Potter's bullet had clipped his hairline. He looked back to the balcony. Sassy was gone. He owed his life to her—little, spunky Sassy.

* * * * *

Charley's bar hosted a crowd. Most of the town was either inside the Sea Breeze or on the street, rehashing the day's battle. Inside, Singletree held the group's attention. He held up a shot glass. "A. J. has a bullet in a leg. Arnold and two others are hurt a little. Put that up against seventeen dead outlaws and six prisoners. Wait till the world hears of how we take care of law and order here on the Colorado River?"

"Think it'll be a while before anyone tries y'all again," the badly shaken train engineer said. The man's forehead boasted a large, ugly knot.

Bones walked outside. His eyes searched the crowd for her. The sound of battle and excitement had waned. Now his heart held an empty void fed by a vision—a vision of a smiling face and eyes that welcomed. Tired, worn, and used up, he'd fought his last battle. But he couldn't rest until he told her, held her again. Facing Potter's gun and staring into the bitter cup of death had washed a lot of fog away. It was the thought of her that made life precious. He had things to say.

Estella stood on the sidewalk, her back to Lester's granny. Her head turned slowly as she, too, searched the crowd. Her eyes locked with his as he approached.

She pointed. "She's over there ... at the hotel." Her voice quivered slightly.

"Who?" Bones asked.

"Sassy. I saw it, Wil. I was coming to find you, and I saw her save your life. Go to her. It's what you've always wanted. It's OK. You're alive ... that's enough for me."

"She ain't the one on my mind, lady."

Granny stepped in front of Estella. "Excuse me, ma'am, but it's you, isn't it? You're the one put him into new duds. I can tell by the way he looks at you. What's your name?"

Estella's gaze, looking over Granny's head, remained fixed on Bones. She gave no sign of hearing the old woman. Her face was pale—her lips firm and set in a straight line.

Granny had a story to tell, and she did. "Don't you let him get away. Men like Mississippi are hard to find. It must be the schoolmarm in me, but I'm partial to his kind ... men that take off their hats indoors, squat, propped against a wall on a porch rather than dirty a good woman's fresh-scrubbed floor."

Bones grabbed Estella by the arms. "That trains going back to Abilene tomorrow. Can you be ready?"

"Ready for what?" she asked.

"Take a ride to Abilene to see if we can find a preacher to marry us."

"Marry who?"

"You and me."

"You don't think we need to talk about this some?" Estella asked, a smile working at her lips. She moved closer.

"I told you I loved you, and you grabbed me. What's there to talk about?" Bones opened his arms, nodding at the old lady as he did so. "By the way, this is Granny."

Estella came into his arms eagerly. His lips met hers. They were warm, inviting. The crowd swayed into oblivion behind her, and he lost track of time.

Estella broke free and murmured: "Yes, I'll be ready. I wouldn't miss it." She turned and put a hand on Granny's shoulder. "Thank you. How am I doing?"

The old lady smiled, nodded, and briskly walked away.

THE END

ABOUT THE AUTHOR

Mackey Murdock grew up on a stock farm sandwiched between four of Texas' larger ranches. In tune to the rhythm of horses, livestock, and the people who nurse them, his writing echoes that early beat. Later, he served in the Korean War, taught school, and spent thirty-three years in industrial management. Although Murdock crosses the line between fiction and nonfiction, the Southwest typically provides the setting for his work. *Last of the Old-Time Texans* and *Texas Veterans Remember Korea* are his two nonfiction works. His first novel was *Chute #3*. Murdock is a member of the Dallas Fort Worth Writers' Workshop and an active member of the Western Writers of America. He writes full-time and lives with his wife Joanne in Garland, Texas. His first Western was *Blood for Brother*. He is currently working on his next book.